"Who Dares to Seek the Wizard Onym?"

The great bronze doors swung slowly inward. Beyond lay an enormous room. Against a far wall was a dais topped by a great stone throne, flanked by braziers of iron. On the throne sat a man wearing robes of pale blue satin. His eyes were the same shade of blue and affixed the visitors with a penetrating, inhuman stare.

"O great and mighty mage," the prince began, "we come from afar seeking your assistance. I am Prince Abderian of Euthymia. This is Lady Maja of the line of Thalion. Long have I sought you regarding a matter of grave concern both to myself and the Kingdom of Euthymia. I most humbly beg you to hear my petition." Abderian bowed his head before the mage and awaited a reply.

"Meow," said the wizard.

"I beg your pardon?" Abderian said.

KARA DALKEY

THE CURSE OF SAGAMORE

ACE FANTASY BOOKS
NEW YORK

To my father, for introducing me to science fiction;
To my mother, for introducing me to fantasy;
To Nate, for convincing me I could write;
To the rest of the Scribblies for believing him;
And to Curtis, for his support, love and use of his
    word processor (not necessarily in that order).

ONE

"CAN'T I BE left alone?" cried young Prince Abderian as the rock slammed into his desk. It was not the fact that the rock broke the stained-glass tower window that bothered the prince. Nor that it stained his silken sleeve, or spilled ducksblood ink on his fine desk. It was that he had been interrupted in his favorite activity: writing suicide notes. He didn't actually intend to kill himself, he merely enjoyed writing the notes. It made him feel better.

Abderian picked up the rock and tore off the piece of parchment that was tied onto it. On the parchment was a note that read:

> Beware, ye House of Sagamore
> Your downfall is at hand.
> Whose heart is dark shall darkness spread,
> Like stains upon the land.

"Not another one," the prince groaned.

He examined his blotted sleeve, uncomfortable with the coincidence; stains mentioned in the note and the stain upon his arm. Abderian was not the sort to look for omens in everything, but he did take sorcery seriously. And something about the shape of the stain disturbed him. Rolling the sleeve back, Abderian's fears were confirmed; the stain was very similar in size and shape to a mark he bore on his right forearm. *It's too close*, he thought with a shudder. *Somebody knows*.

The note was like many others the prince had seen recently. It was clear that his family was not well-loved. The Kingdom of Euthymia had been in decline for the past century and many blamed it on the change in royal line. Four generations ago, King Thalion, called the Wise, feeling that none of his kin were fit to rule, gave his crown to his jester, Sagamore. The jester became King Sagamore the Shrewd, who begat King Vespin the Sneaky, who begat King Valgus the Brutal, Abderian's father.

Since Sagamore's reign there had come strange, unpredictable weather, rebellions, and riots. Misshapen offspring were born to man and animal alike, and strange plagues mysteriously came and went. One such plague had taken Abderian's eldest brother, Paralian, a year ago. And Euthymia was currently in the grip of the worst drought it had seen in decades.

So the rock and the note were no surprise to the prince. But the target was. *Why am I taking the blame now?* he thought. Being thought the ultimate source of evil seemed a bit unfair to the fifteen-year-old princeling.

Abderian ran to the window and saw, far below, a raggedy longbeard brandishing a prophet's staff and shaking his fist at the prince. Abderian threw the rock back at the prophet. He missed, but at least had the satisfaction of sending the man running off.

I wonder if this is one of Cyprian's jests, the prince thought, returning to his desk. *It's his kind of cruelty. But he doesn't know about the mark. At least, I hope he doesn't.* Abderian lifted his sleeve to look at the mark again. It was cinnamon-colored, and from a distance seemed vaguely liver-shaped. But seen up close one could discern intricate, intersecting lines weaving throughout, like the web of a drunken spider. It was a magical mark, he knew. He had read of such things. But its power and purpose he did not know. The only thing of which he was certain was that his life depended on keeping the mark hidden.

The prince looked at his desk, littered with pieces of parchment on which were inscribed various attempts at parting words. He sat down and tried to calm himself by thinking of more. Mopping absentmindedly at the spilled ink with a kerchief, he tried to compose in his mind the perfect phrasing.

Suddenly, in the distance, knells rang from the belltower. "Evening meal already?" This second interruption annoyed him further. He stood and gathered the notes in his hands. Then, in frustration, he crumpled them and threw them against the wall. As far as the prince was concerned, this day had not been at all worthwhile.

Abderian headed for the stairs leading down from his tower chamber and stopped just before the first step. His hands sought a thread hidden in a mortar crack in the rough-hewn stone wall. Finding it, he pulled slowly, and a mirror hanging on the wall farther down the stairwell caught a sunbeam and illuminated the usually dark stairs. In the mirror Abderian could make out an odd shape lying just behind the curvature of the inner wall.

Now what? Living in a castle of many towers made stairways tempting places for pranks. Two days before, Abderian had nearly slipped on a fruit rind someone had placed on the stairs. His youngest sister's guilt was easy to determine when she couldn't keep a straight face through dinner.

Unable to determine the extent of the trap that lay in wait for him, Abderian chose to take a different way out. He went to his bed and pulled a long twig out from under the feather mattress. Then he went to a stone slab in the middle of the chamber floor, found fingerholds, and lifted. Beneath, a smooth chute angled away into darkness. Abderian carefully poked the stick down into the chute. In a moment he felt weight on the twig, and he pulled it back into the light. Dangling from the end was a large, hairy black spider. With a start Abderian tossed the stick down the chute and slammed the trapdoor shut. He hadn't expected his brother to actually carry out his threat. *Cyprian finally filled the chute with spiders!* Supposedly there would be scorpions and snakes as well, but Abderian had no wish to find out.

It was difficult, Abderian reflected for the umpteenth time, to be of a royal family descended not from great heroes or gods, but a court jester. It sometimes seemed the royal succession was not determined by who was wisest, best in battle, or firstborn, but by who was the wittiest, sneakiest, and trickiest. It made for rather bothersome family relations.

Abderian decided next to try leaving via the south window, which had not yet been broken by note-bearing rocks. He unlatched the stained-glass pane and opened it, then pulled himself over the window frame. Turning to face the wall, he lowered himself until his toetips touched the stone buttress that connected his tower with the main portion of the castle. Slowly the prince turned until his back was against the cool stone of his tower, and he faced out over Castle Mamelon.

The castle had been designed by Sagamore himself, who was no architect, but knew what he liked. He liked stairways that led nowhere, doors many feet above the floor, windows onto stone walls, and archways that supported nothing. And towers . . . lots of towers: some straight, some twisted, some inaccessible to all but levitating wizards. Abderian would have been enthralled by the view before him had he not been afraid of heights.

The prince took several deep breaths and tried to amass the courage to walk across the slim buttress ahead of him. He wondered if he stood there long enough whether he would turn to stone and be mistaken for one of the many gargoyles that decorated the castle. *Nothing for it,* he thought. He inched forward, holding his arms out for balance and trying not to look down. Then his steps became more confident. It wasn't until he was halfway across that he saw the glistening of the stone beneath his feet.

"Someone put oil on the . . . waaaaah!" His feet slid out from under him and he fell. He tried to grab the side of the buttress, but his hands slipped too, and he fell down, down, splat into a pile of hay and manure, causing an explosion of startled chickens.

Gasping and gagging, he dragged himself out of the pile while groundskeepers, maids, and nobles stared in amusement and disgust. A familiar voice rang out;

> By Sagamore's bell-cap and Tingalut's tongs!
> Abderian's fallen right where he belongs!

That rat! He got me after all, thought Abderian, recognizing his brother's shrill tenor.

"How the mighty has fallen!" the fair-haired Cyprian continued, winning more laughter from the crowd.

Abderian faced his older brother defiantly and said, "Despite my new coating, I still smell sweeter than you, Cyprian." But his retort was lost amid the howls of derision from the growing gaggle of gawkers. Abderian felt his face grow hot, and he clenched his fists. He tried not to scream. He tried not to cry. He tried not to breathe through his nose. Instead, he leaped at Cyprian, his hands reaching for the culprit's throat.

The elder prince took a few quick steps backward, saying,

"Now, now, dear brother, you know they say that fratricide is cheating."

"Actually 'dear brother,' I don't care." Like a hound after a rabbit, Abderian chased after Cyprian, itching for vengeance. The crowd cheered as the princes tore past the stables and the sheep pens. They ran around the west side of the castle, finally dashing into a storage shed cluttered with straw bales and rusting tools.

Cyprian stopped in the center of the shed and turned to make faces at Abderian. Abderian stopped and flung out a fist. It might have connected with Cyprian's nose had Abderian not slipped and fallen on the straw. Cyprian pointed and laughed, "You clumsy idiot! Who taught you how to fight? Amusia?"

Abderian did not care for the comparison between himself and his six-year-old sister. He grabbed a handful of the muck he wore and threw it at Cyprian, who ducked the muddy missile easily.

"Ha! Looks like no one taught you how to throw either. Or perhaps that stuff would rather stick to you."

Propping himself up on his elbows, Abderian snarled, "If Paralian were here, he'd mash your face into the mud so fast you couldn't breathe first! He'd—"

"Paralian, Paralian! You hopeless lump of sheep's dung, you're nothing without your precious Paralian to protect you, are you?"

Abderian felt his anger turn cold and hard. Slowly he got up, brushing himself off. "What do you mean, 'your precious Paralian'? He was your brother too."

Cyprian's grin faded just a little. "Was he? He didn't act like it much."

"Because he always took my side against you? Because he was better at jests than you?"

Cyprian's mouth fell into a tight line and his eyes grew wary. "Perhaps. What of it? It doesn't matter. He's dead now."

"You seem pretty certain, considering no one has claimed to see him die, or even sicken. And his body wasn't displayed at the funeral."

"They didn't want to risk the spread of plague, as I heard it." Cyprian's eyes narrowed. "What are you getting at?"

"Well, I've been wondering lately if maybe one of your jests didn't go a little too far."

Suddenly Abderian was slammed up against the shed wall, with Cyprian's hands clenched around his neck and Cyprian's face contorted in rage before him. "Are you trying to say I killed him? How *dare* you! You piece of goat's bowels! You runt of a rat's litter! I should sweep the stables with you! I should throw you off the High Tower! I should—"

The sound of heavy footsteps approaching caused Cyprian to pause. He removed his hands from Abderian's neck and Abderian slid to the floor with a thump. Cyprian ducked behind a rack of groundskeeping tools as a large figure filled the doorway.

It was Queen Pleonexia—a matronly woman wearing a stiff, white wimple and a copper-colored gown. She frowned at the prince in dark disapproval.

"Mother!"

"Cyprian! Have you been wenching in the stables again?"

"No, I'm Abderian, Mother."

"Oh, it's you. Taking after your brother now, are you? For shame. Now stop cowering on the floor and tell me why you're covered with that . . . that . . ."

"One of Cyprian's jests." He glanced toward the rack, but Cyprian remained hidden.

"Tsk. I wish you boys wouldn't play your jests so close to mealtime. Well, you'd best go wash up and change your clothes before too many see you like that. I swear, it's a good thing the kingdom doesn't depend upon such as you, else we'd be in more trouble than we are already. Now, hurry along. I've had a . . . premonition that something wonderful is going to happen this evening, and I don't want you to spoil it." The queen rustled away.

Abderian shook his head. His mother's dabblings in mysticism rarely seemed to have any relation to the real world. He stood and Cyprian came out from behind the rack. "Well?" said Abderian.

"Well what?"

"Did you kill him?"

"No, you foul-minded little dungball! I didn't see him die either. And just to give your morbid mind something more to think about, at the funeral I peeked into his casket. There was nothing in it." With a final cuff to Abderian's shoulder, Cyprian stormed out of the shed.

Abderian stared at the doorway. *Paralian's coffin was empty?*

He wondered if this was another one of Cyprian's artless lies. Abderian was fairly certain Cyprian didn't kill Paralian. But somehow he couldn't accept that the plague did.

Trying to be as inconspicuous as possible, Abderian ducked out of the shed and headed back to his tower. His route took him past the guardhouse, where two women guards were relaxing and singing:

Now Davy a very fine sword's been bequeathed,
The maids love to watch when he wears it unsheathed.
It's long and it's strong and more quick than the eye,
And when he thrusts with it, the ladies all sigh.

Abderian hurried on, glad that because of his mud bath they could not see him blushing.

Though he had managed to get Cyprian upset, it wasn't enough. It wasn't a proper revenge, to Abderian's mind. *There has to be something more I can do . . . something,* he thought as he passed the stables. Something his mother had said gave him an idea. *Ah, there's a possibility.* Off in a corner of the stables, a servant girl was sweeping fresh hay into a stall.

"Kiss me, my sweet!" Abderian shouted, running at her, arms flung wide.

"What? Who are you? Ugh! Keep away!" she vainly tried to send him off with her broom.

"Dost thou not recognize me, my beauty? 'Tis I, charming Cyprian. Come, let us make better use of this hay."

"Cyprian! Your Highness, please forebear! Stay away from me! Ugh!" She managed to wriggle past him and run out of the stable, puncturing the air with shrieks of disgust.

Abderian was still laughing when he reached his tower. He hoped the girl liked to gossip—the sooner this addition to Cyprian's reputation made the castle rounds, the better. *It will serve him right for that story about Paralian's funeral.*

Ascending the tower stairs, Abderian could not get the vision of an empty sarcophagus out of his mind. *What if it's true? What if it's true? What if—* Suddenly Abderian fell forward, hard, onto his elbows, his feet flying out from under him. Behind him, something skittered down the stairs.

"By the bloody red eyes of the Lizard Goddess!" he growled through gritted teeth. He mentally whipped, hung, and quartered himself for his forgetfulness. Getting up, he searched the stairs for the object he had tripped on. He finally came across a toy pull-dragon that belonged to Amusia, his youngest sister. He let out a low whistle. *Only six years old, and already she's deadly at jesting,* he thought.

Resolving to devise better safeguards for his tower, Abderian dashed up to his room. He flung off his soiled clothes and sponged himself, then checked his wardrobe for a change of clothing. In a drawer containing garments he rarely wore, he found a long-sleeved tunic of green velvet. It was too heavy and warm for the season, but it would have to do. He quickly threw it on, and a new set of hose and boots, and dashed out of the tower.

He set off across the courtyard, hoping he could make it to dinner before too many noticed his absence. A hot, dry gust of wind from behind him sent swirling columns of dust through the nearly deserted courtyard. Abderian squinted, trying to keep sand out of his eyes. Halfway across, the prince saw two figures, robes flapping in the wind, approaching him from the west end of the courtyard. One of them seemed to be pointing at him. As the dust settled, Abderian got a clear look at the figures, and stopped in shock. The person pointing was the old prophet who had thrown the rock through the prince's window. The other was Tingalut, High Priest of the Temple of the Lizard Goddess.

Abderian went cold. Tingalut was feared in Castle Mamelon, and was said to be a powerful sorcerer. The rites of the temple were mysterious, and rumors abounded of horrible things that happened there. Abderian thought that Tingalut, with his narrow face and small, dark eyes, resembled the very lizards the priest worshipped. And it was this same priest who now nodded and smiled at Abderian from across the courtyard. The prince nodded in return, then hurried on. *Either Tingalut will tell the prophet his declamations are foolish,* he thought, *or I'm in very big trouble.*

TWO

ABDERIAN SLIPPED THROUGH the dining hall door and immediately tried to blend in with the wall. The seated lords and ladies were engaged in lively conversation and seemed not to notice him. *So far so good,* the prince thought.

Abderian glanced up at the mannikins on the ceiling. King Sagamore had had nailed to the ceiling an exact duplicate of the table and chairs on the floor below. Plates and glassware were often affixed to the upper table and "diners" set on the chairs in realistic poses. This had the effect, if one had imbibed too much of the dinner mead, of giving one the impression of being seated on the ceiling, looking down, rather than on the floor looking up. Apparently Sagamore found vertigo amusing.

In recent years, however, the servants had made a game of dressing the mannikin diners on the ceiling in a fashion that reflected the mood of the king or the court. They would be dressed in bright holiday garb for festivals. Abderian remembered well the day the mannikins were all dressed in black— it was the day Paralian's death was announced. This evening, however, they wore ordinary dress.

So much for Mother's premonition, he thought. Returning his gaze to the floor on which he stood, Abderian looked for an open seat. The great table was U-shaped, with seating around the outside. King Valgus, a beefy, brown-haired man, sat at the bottom center of the U. Beside him, at his left, sat Queen Pleonexia. Cyprian sat next to her. A comely earl's daughter sat holding Cyprian's left arm. Next to her were the Princesses Amusia and Alexia. Amusia was fidgeting in her seat, and Alexia, who was twelve, was looking anxiously around the

9

hall. The rest of the left side was filled with lesser nobles, leaving no seat available.

The right side of the table seemed also full from Abderian's vantage point. Beginning to worry, he slinked along the wall until he at last saw an empty seat. It was at the left of Lady Chevaline. That was fine by Abderian—Lady Chevaline was the grande dame of the court at eighty years old, but nonetheless spirited and savvy. Abderian would have looked forward to enjoying her company—except that her adjoining seat was one away from the king's right hand. Slipping in unseen would be nearly impossible. But it was the only seat left.

Oh, well, nothing for it. Here goes—

"Well, Abderian," boomed the king, "deigning to join us at last? And what all-important task has forced you to keep us all waiting?"

"Uh . . ." Abderian looked at the queen, but she offered no sympathy or assistance.

"Yes, Abderian," chimed Cyprian. "I'm sure we'd all like to know."

"Uh . . ."

"By the Goddess, son! It's bad enough that you keep us waiting, but you could at least come up with a good explanation. Or a clever one."

For once Abderian was not grateful that he lived in a family where sassing one's parents was considered a proper thing to do. "Uh . . ."

"His Highness was with me, Your Majesty," Abderian heard Tingalut say behind him. The prince started a little, but did not turn around.

The king rubbed his bearded chin and studied the priest. "Indeed?" His eyes flicked back to Abderian.

"That is so, Your Majesty," Tingalut's smooth voice continued. "I had detained His Highness to ask him if he would do me the honor of visiting me at the temple later this evening. There are some things I wish to discuss with him. His Highness most graciously agreed. Did you not, Abderian?"

The prince was stuck. Tingalut was handing him a perfect excuse, yet not one Abderian welcomed. He decided he would rather face Tingalut's strangeness than his father's wrath. "Yes, of course."

The king's eyes narrowed even farther, but he said nothing. "Well, Tingalut," piped up Lady Chevaline, "we haven't seen you for quite some time. Will you be joining us for dinner tonight?"

"Alas, My Lady, such would give me great pleasure, but ... my duties..." Tingalut shrugged and smiled ruefully.

"Ah, yes, your duties. Petitioning the Lizard Goddess for answers to the country's problems. She's taking Her sweet time in responding, isn't She? One would almost think you worshipped a snail instead of a snake."

Stifled chuckles erupted around her as Tingalut's brows furrowed and nostrils flared. "Time is Her plaything, My Lady," he replied softly, "as are we." He turned to Abderian and said, "Until later, then, Your Highness." With a rustle of his lizard-skin robes the priest glided out of the hall.

Abderian sighed as if a massive weight had been taken off his shoulders. He sat down, willing his hands to stop shaking. Lady Chevaline rewarded him with a half-sad, half-amused smile.

King Valgus, however, still regarded the prince suspiciously. "So. And what does Tingalut intend to discuss with you?"

"I honestly don't know." Here, at least, he could tell the truth.

The king gave a dissatisfied grunt, and turned to face the room at large. "Dinner is to be served!" he shouted.

Relaxed conversation resumed as servants entered bearing plates and covered dishes. An appetizing aroma of fresh-baked bread and spiced meat filled the room. Though there seemed to be food in abundance, Abderian wondered if there weren't fewer dishes of less variety than had been served in previous years. *Is memory playing tricks on me or is the drought now affecting Castle Mamelon?*

As the dishes passed by, Abderian began to feel hungry. He was disappointed, therefore, that after everyone else was served, no dish arrived for him. It was only after several agonizing, mouth-watering, stomach-grumbling minutes of watching others eat, that finally a servant appeared at his elbow and placed a covered dish before the prince.

Abderian was about to remove the lid when he noticed, across the room, Princess Amusia staring at him in rapturous anticipation. Princess Alexia was trying very hard not to look at him at all. The whole room seemed to become quieter. And Abderian became instantly suspicious.

Pulling his hand back from the cover, the prince said, "Er,

perhaps the princesses would like to have this dish more than I. Please take it to them, as I am not feeling hungry just now."

"Nonsense," said Queen Pleonexia, "the girls have already been given enough, and you've not eaten since morning. You should at least have some of it."

"Aye," said the king, "you need fuel for your wits, son, especially if you're to speak to Tingalut. And Cook has made a delicious meat pie for us tonight. You must try some."

Coming from the king, that was an order. Abderian slowly, reluctantly, lifted the cover off the plate. Beneath it lay what appeared to be a perfectly normal meat pie. Abderian took his knife and pried open the crust—

Suddenly a dragonlet jumped, squealing, out of the pie. It scrambled up the surprised prince's arm and bit him on the nose. His chair nearly fell over backward as the reptile bounded off his chest onto the floor and skittered away on its hind legs.

Peals of laughter resounded through the dining hall. Many of the nobles began to applaud, and there were scattered shouts of "Huzzah!" and "Author!" Blushing coyly, Alexia stood up and gave a dainty curtsy. "Brava!" came the cries, and "Pretty trick!"

King Valgus murmured to the queen, "Sometimes I think I owe my popularity to the fact that I have such an entertaining family."

Abderian checked his nose to be sure it wasn't broken or bleeding, then noticed everyone was staring at him. He gulped and looked down at his trampled pie, trying to think of something to say. With regret he recalled that his chair was not one of those with a trapdoor conveniently located beneath it.

Suddenly in horror he noticed that the lizard's claws had torn his sleeve wide open, exposing the mark on his arm. He gasped and covered the mark with his left hand and started to move his arm to beneath the table when a hand reached out and clamped hard onto his left wrist.

"Hold!" cried King Valgus, who had stretched across the lady at his right to grab Abderian's arm. "What is that upon your arm, boy? Let me see." The king pulled the prince's hand away from the mark. Valgus stared and hissed, "So, this is where it went! How did you get this?"

"It . . . it's only a stain! I got it this afternoon when—"

"Do you think me an idiot, boy? That is the Mark of Sagamore! I bore it upon my own arm for twenty-two years. Your brother Paralian assumed it at his birth. Cyprian should have gotten it upon Paralian's death. Why do *you* have it?"

"I—I don't know. It just appeared there. . . ."

"When? A year ago, wasn't it?"

Abderian, having no ready lie, only nodded. Behind him, he heard Lady Chevaline chuckle.

"All this time, My Lord, you have been sending my grandson Burdalane in search of Paralian's fictitious bastard child, when the mark has been right here all along."

"This is not a matter for jesting, Lady Chevaline." The king roughly released Abderian's arm and stood. "So, now we know why Tingalut wishes to speak with you, eh?"

Queen Pleonexia, who had been staring at Abderian in shock, suddenly said, "No! My Lord, you must not let him speak to Tingalut! He must not go near that temple! You remember how Paralian—"

"Memory has not failed me, Pleonexia. I remember." King Valgus shoved past her and paced back and forth, glaring at Abderian. The prince sat perfectly still, not daring to move.

The king strode over to Cyprian and paused. Ferociously he grabbed Cyprian's right arm and tore back his sleeve. Seeing no marks of interest there, the king dropped Cyprian's arm back onto the table. "So, what does this mean, Cyprian? Are you no flesh of mine, that the mark goes to your brother and not to you?"

"I—I don't know anything about it!"

King Valgus turned back to the queen. "What say you, My Lady? Have you betrayed me? Is Cyprian not of my seed?"

"My Lord! I have ever been faithful to you! Cyprian is as much yours as Abderian!"

"My Lord, this is not seemly!" said Lady Chevaline. "If you must make such accusations, choose another time and place than this!"

The king stared daggers at the elderly Lady Chevaline, then returned his gaze to Abderian. "Very well. Have your little chat with Tingalut. But you will come and speak to me directly afterward."

"But, My Lord—" the queen protested.

"Since you have such concern for our son, you may arrange an escort of our strongest guards to accompany him to and from the temple."

"Yes, My Lord," the queen whispered.

Valgus spun on his heel and addressed the room. "Go on! Enjoy yourselves. I've no further interest in eating." As he turned to leave he stopped at Cyprian's chair. "And you, Cyprian, come see me as soon as you finish."

With a final glare at Abderian the king strode from the room. What most struck Abderian about the king's expression before he left was that it contained as much fear as anger. And, to Abderian's surprise, sorrow.

He looked around. Cyprian regarded him with open resentment. Many of the nobles whispered excitedly among themselves, giving Abderian sidelong glances. The woman at his left, who had sat silently through the entire scene, coughed into her napkin and stood up.

"Excuse me, Your Highness," she said, "but I fear I am also no longer hungry." She bowed and left.

The prince turned to the queen. "Something wonderful, eh, Mother?"

Ignoring the taunt, the queen said, "Abderian, why didn't you tell me about this mark when it appeared?"

"I couldn't, Mother."

"But there are people I know who could help you, could protect you."

"Protect me from what?"

Rising shakily from her chair, the queen said, "I—I must arrange for your escort now. But please, Abderian, you mustn't tell Tingalut anything about the mark."

"That won't be difficult. I don't know anything about it."

"Good."

"The priest will learn of it soon enough, the way the gossip's flying," Lady Chevaline commented.

"By that time I might be able to arrange help."

"Couldn't either of you tell me something?"

Chevaline put her hand on his arm. "Abderian, it's—"

"No, Chevaline!" said the queen, "Not now."

"But Pleo, the boy ought to know—"

"Not here!" the queen whispered huskily. "We can tell him later. I need you to come with me now."

Lady Chevaline squeezed Abderian's arm and gave him a regretful smile. As she stood up she moved her plate toward him. "Here, take my dinner. I've hardly touched it. At least it hasn't been trampled by a lizard. I'll talk to you when I can." Then she followed the queen out of the hall.

Taking Chevaline's plate, he picked up a piece of bread, but his hand was shaking so much he had to put it down again. Also, he found that his appetite had left him. Abderian stared at his hands and wondered if he should have told the truth. Though it happened a year ago, he remembered clearly the night he had gotten the mark.

Abderian had been lying in bed in his tower, trying to sleep. Paralian had slipped into his room and sat down on the bed beside him.

"Who? What? Oh. Paralian, you scared me."

"I'm sorry, little brother. I did not intend to frighten you."

"Well, what are you doing here."

"I'm afraid I must lay a heavy burden upon you."

"Huh? What?"

"Shhh. Hold still." Paralian moistened a finger and drew an intricate design on Abderian's forehead.

"What are you doing?"

"Hush! When you awaken, you will find something on your arm. It won't hurt you, but you must never show it to anyone. No one, understand? If others find out, you could be in great danger. It's just our secret, all right?"

Abderian nodded as Paralian finished and turned to go.

"Good-bye, little brother."

"Are you going away?"

"Yes." Paralian's voice was so filled with sadness, it was as if he meant forever. Perhaps he did, since two days later Abderian heard Paralian was dead.

Abderian was jolted out of his reverie by the sound of something dropping in his lap. Looking down, he saw a folded piece of parchment. He unfolded it and read:

To the true and future King, Abderian,
Greetings. Beware. Your life is in danger.
There are those who do not wish you well.
I have 30 horses, 25 bowmen, and 117 foot troops.
When you choose to take that which is rightfully yours,
These shall be yours to command.
Success and long life to you.
With hopes that you shall remember my name kindly,

It was signed by an obscure nobleman from the southern reaches of the kingdom.

Abderian looked up, hoping to catch the eye of whoever dropped him the note. Though other faces stared back at him, none gave any knowing nods or winks. He looked back at the note, bewildered. Abderian had never been involved in court intrigue beyond the jests he played upon his siblings. *Why does the mark make me a candidate for intrigue now? Is this why Paralian told me never to let it be seen?* With growing dread Abderian wondered which of the faces around him belonged to those who wished him ill.

"Your Highness."

Abderian was startled for a moment, then saw the two burly guards standing by his chair. Sighing, he tucked the note into the top of his boot and stood. "Very well, let's go."

At the dining hall doorway, the queen said, "Be careful, Abderian." Her face was pale, and creased with concern.

The prince glanced once more at the "diners" on the ceiling. He wondered if they would be wearing black before the night was out.

THREE

THE CRUNCHING OF their bootheels on the courtyard flagstones was loud in Abderian's ears as he and the guards approached the Temple of the Lizard Goddess. The prince for once longed to hear the usual rough banter of the guardsmen, but they were grimly silent. Abderian felt alone with his fears.

The prince shuddered as they drew near the temple. Torchlight flickered against the low, mud-colored domes, illuminating stone images of the Lizard Goddess. Abderian wished the priests could have afforded better sculptors . . . or was She supposed to look that repulsive?

"You have a quarter-hour to speak to the priest, Your Highness," said one of the guards. "If you have not come out after that time, we will come in and get you."

"What's the matter?" Abderian laughed nervously. "Don't you expect me to come out again?"

"We have our orders, Your Highness."

"Oh. Of course." Abderian sighed and turned to knock at the temple door. But it was already open and an acolyte in a lizard-skin robe stood waiting.

The acolyte bowed and stepped aside. Resisting the urge to look back at the guards for reassurance, Abderian entered. The acolyte silently closed the door behind the prince and led him down a low, torchlit hall. The air smelled faintly of ashes and incense. Along the walls were small niches containing bronze carvings and the burned remains of what may have been small reptiles. Abderian did not look closely.

The hall turned to the right and Abderian was shown into a small room. Tingalut sat behind a bare wooden table and motioned, smiling, for Abderian to take a chair opposite him. The prince did so, watching the priest warily.

"I thank you, Your Highness, for agreeing to see me," Tingalut began. "I trust we will find this discussion to be mutually beneficial."

"Uh, well, I hope you're right." Abderian noticed, to his dismay, that his voice came out pitched higher than he had intended.

Tingalut studied the prince a moment. "I realize that many at court consider me intimidating. It is often a useful image for a priest to cultivate. However, there is no reason for you to fear me. It is my intention that we should be friends. That we should help each other, for the good of the kingdom."

"Oh. How can I help you?"

"We can begin by discussing the mark of power you bear."

Abderian shut his eyes and felt his stomach grow tense. How could he avoid telling Tingalut what he already knew?

"Do not look so surprised, Your Highness. You saw yourself the moment when I learned of it. The old prophet in the court-yard informed me this afternoon."

"How did he know about it?"

"He told me some story about seeing a vision in which he was to set the kingdom on the 'true path' to peace and happiness by exposing the mark on your arm. I was not certain I should believe him, but from the events in the dinning hall, at least part of his vision was confirmed. You do bear the Mark of Sagamore."

Abderian let out a deep sigh. "Very well, it appears I do. But why is everyone making such a fuss over it? What does it mean?"

Tingalut leaned forward over the table. "It is an avenue to great power, Abderian. Power for good or evil. We both know of the kingdom's ills. I have reason to believe they will continue to worsen. But if you allow me to guide you in the use of that power, then together we can reverse the decline of Euthymia and make it a prosperous kingdom once more."

And make you the most powerful sorcerer in Euthymia as well? thought the prince. "But I don't understand. Father said he wore the mark for twenty-two years, and it didn't seem to help the kingdom any. And Paralian had it for nineteen years after that—"

"Your father had no understanding of sorcery, Your Highness. He had no concept of how to use the mark, and would not listen to my suggestions. Paralian was beginning to understand the mark before he . . . passed away."

Abderian felt a warning in the back of his mind. "Did you make this same offer to Paralian before he died?"

Tingalut looked suddenly wary. "Yes, as a matter of fact. Why do you ask?"

The prince shrugged. "It might not be important. I had heard a rumor that his casket at the funeral was empty. And I've heard sorcery is a dangerous subject of study. One can't help but wonder. . . ." He shrugged again.

Tingalut sighed and managed a half-smile. "Of course. I know you loved him well. But I can assure you nothing arcane was done with his remains. He was not made a sacrifice to the Goddess, as some might have told you. His body was burned to prevent the spread of plague, that is all. I can show you his ashes if you wish."

"Uh, no, thank you. But . . . couldn't your sorcery have saved him from the plague?"

Tingalut coughed. "Your Highness, we are not all-powerful here. It is said 'The Lizard Goddess steps sideways as She walks.' Things do not always occur as we mortals would like. I admit we may have made some mistakes in our approach to Paralian's training. I assure you we will not make the same mistakes with you."

Abderian did not feel reassured. He fidgeted in his seat and wondered how to get out of the interview gracefully.

"What I would like," Tingalut went on, "is for you to agree to come live at the temple and allow me to teach you. In that way we can draw upon the power of the Mark of Sagamore together, to solve the problems of Euthymia.

"Shouldn't I ask my father about this first? As king, he should—"

"No, Abderian. Your father would only . . . misunderstand. He fears the power of the mark. And I believe he fears me as well. It would be best if we just tell him we discussed the possibility of your joining the priesthood. It is close enough to the truth."

Abderian felt tension between his shoulder blades, reflecting an inner discomfort. It seemed as though everyone expected him to become a traitor to his father. *First the note on my lap, now this. Why didn't Paralian tell me?* Unfortunately the idea of learning sorcery was tantalizing to the prince, so he could not reject the offer out of hand. He did wish, however, that it had not been Tingalut who had made the offer.

A knock came at the door and the acolyte poked his head in. "Brother, two guards outside request that His Highness be released into their custody."

Tingalut looked at Abderian with concern. "It seems your father may have harsh plans for you. If you wish, you may claim asylum here."

"It's not like that. Father ordered them to let me speak to you for only a quarter-hour. If I didn't come out by then, the guards were to come in and find me."

Abderian stood to leave.

"So His Majesty truly does not trust me. But stay a moment, Your Highness. I have not yet heard you agree to study with me."

"I, uh, I'd like to think about it."

Tingalut's eyes narrowed. "You do not have much time to consider, Your Highness. Here you will find protection and strength. Elsewhere, danger will seek you out like vultures seek the dying. The Mark of Sagamore can be a curse to those who do not understand it. Who knows, even the plague that took Paralian may come again."

FOUR

THE GUARDS LEFT Abderian outside one of the small chambers in the king's quarters. From behind the heavy oak door Abderian could hear his father shouting and Cyprian responding. His brother's tone seemed to be alternately angry and pleading, but Abderian could make out no specific words from either speaker.

Sitting on a low stone bench, Abderian tried to prepare what he was going to say. *Should I tell him about Tingalut's plan?* Abderian knew if he had any thought of taking up the priest's offer, that was not at all wise. But he doubted the story about joining the temple priesthood would mollify his father.

The longer Abderian sat, the more he wanted to flee. He needed time to think about things. He needed to talk to someone, preferably someone who could tell him more about the mark. But along with responsibilities, royalty seemed to confer a curious lack of companionship.

Lady Chevaline seemed to know something, but if Mother is with her, she'll send me back here, he thought. *Who else could there be? Wait . . . perhaps now I should finally see Dolus.*

Dolus was officially the court wizard, though he had not been seen outside his quarters for some time. The gossip was that he was deep in his sorcerous studies and no longer cared for worldly matters. Abderian suspected the real reason was that Tingalut had unofficially usurped Dolus's position. As a child the prince had been friends with the wizard. And when the mark appeared on his arm, Abderian immediately had wanted to ask Dolus about it. But his brother's warning was "show it to no one." Paralian, to Abderian's envy, had studied a little

21

with Dolus. If he had thought it safe to show the wizard, surely he would have said so.

Well, thought Abderian, *There's no need to hide it now. The whole castle knows I have it.* The prince looked around. No one was in the corridor, not even guards. *Apparently Father doesn't want his conversations overheard tonight.* Feeling deliciously truant, Abderian slipped away, down the east end of the corridor.

He went east because the west end of the corridor ended abruptly in a sheer drop to the story below. Abderian had once heard a tale from an elderly servant regarding that drop. It was said that young King Valgus was once asked by a visiting dignitary the directions to the castle water closet. Either because he did not like the dignitary, or because he was living up to his name, King Valgus directed the dignitary to the west end of the hall. It was said Valgus's laughter was nearly as loud as the scream from the dignitary on his way down.

At the east end of the corridor the wall was painted with a scene of the corridor stretching off into infinity, its wall lined with beautiful women. Marring the effect was a dent in the center of the painting, caused by the nose of a drunken lord who had tried to continue into the imaginary portion of the corridor.

Abderian, knowing the perils of this hallway, turned right just before the painting, entering a scroll room used by the castle scribes. It was unoccupied at the moment. Though it had been over a year since he'd been in the room, Abderian went with certainty to a particular place and found a scroll that seemed permanently affixed to its shelf. Turning the end-knob of the scroll, the prince heard a faint click in the wall behind it. He pushed aside the shelves, revealing one of Sagamore's beloved secret passages behind them. Abderian ducked inside, then slid the shelves back into place.

Abderian turned and began to descend a damp stone staircase that was dimly lit with fluttering torches. Down and down the stairs wound, flight after flight. The prince's light footsteps echoed against the walls. Down and down, stair after stair, step after step Abderian trudged, endlessly it seemed, until at last he shouted, "Stop it, Dolus!"

Abruptly the stairs ended at a rotting wooden door. Its hinges wailed like banshees as the prince pushed the door open. Before him he saw a dusty, musty, cavernous room, cluttered with pots and potions that only a wizard could identify.

"I thought you'd stopped using that Endless Staircase Spell," Abderian said as he stepped inside.

"I like to see who my visitors are before they arrive," said a stooped figure shuffling out of the darkness. He wore a smudged purple robe with fraying silver embroidery, and a drooping pointed cap with tattered tassels. Poking out from the sleeves were gnarled, knobby hands, and beneath the hat was a face that seemed centuries old.

"And you're still playing with disguises?"

With a sigh the bent figure straightened, the fingers relaxed, and the face took on a younger appearance. "There's no pleasing children. Was a time when you enjoyed my disguises."

"I'm sorry. I guess I'm not in a mood for games tonight. And I'm not a child anymore."

"That's true. You've grown since I saw you . . . when, a year ago? We've become like strangers, lad. A pity you couldn't have found time to visit. It's been rather lonely down here since Paralian died."

Abderian felt a pang of guilt and shrugged. "Sorry. I've been . . . busy."

"Hmm. Anyway, this guise is no mere game. I dress this way to satisfy the expectations of important visitors. Specifically the members of the Grand Council. That *is* why you are here, isn't it?"

"What?"

"To inform me that the council is about to begin—that's why you've come to see me."

"No, Dolus, the council was last week. Didn't they tell you?"

"Last—" The wizard's mouth dropped open. Then he squeezed his eyes shut and clenched his hands. Dolus turned and slammed the heel of his hand into a tabletop, making the little vials jump and wobble. In a ragged voice he said, "Of course. I should have expected . . ."

Abderian didn't know what to say. "I'm sorry" was all that came out.

The wizard waved away the apology and sighed. "I only hoped that . . . well, never mind."

"Father doesn't consult you anymore, does he?"

"I said never mind! Now, to what *do* I owe the honor of your presence? Need a sleeping potion?"

"No, it's—"

"Good. Those who come to depend upon potions to sleep lose their dreams to the Fish Folk of the Crystal Sea."

The prince paused. "They do?"

"No, but it sounds nice, doesn't it?"

"Oh, Dolus."

"I see it's no use trying to be cheerful for your sake if you can't be cheerful for mine. Come, then, what's on your mind?"

"Dolus . . . I'm in trouble."

The wizard chuckled gently and shook his head. "My boy, if you are due a thrashing for some misbehavior, I cannot—"

"No, it's not that. It's, well, look at this." Abderian pulled back his torn sleeve to display the mark.

"Well, what have we here? A cursemark, I see."

"A *cursemark?* Father called it the Mark of Sagamore. He said nothing about it being a curse!"

"The Mark of Sagamore, hmm?"

"Yes. Do you know what that is?"

"No, what?"

"You mean you *don't* know? But you're the castle wizard!"

"The position does not confer wisdom, Abderian. Some days I think I am here more to be kept ignorant than to dispense knowledge. I can tell you it's a cursemark, due to its reddish color. Other magic marks tend to be black or brown, or, on rare occasions, blue. Marks that are black and blue, of course, are something else altogether."

Abderian made a face.

"Very well, why don't you tell me what *you* know about it."

"It is supposed to be a mark of great power. Father wore it for twenty-two years and then Paralian had it and gave it to me just before he . . . died."

"Gave it to you?"

Abderian described what Paralian did the last night he saw him.

"Hmm." Dolus paced the room a little, rubbing his chin. "Now I understand those very odd questions Paralian asked me. So you've had the cursemark a year, then. Why haven't you shown it to me sooner?"

"Paralian told me not to show it to anyone. I assumed he meant not you either."

Dolus frowned. "And now because of this mark you are 'in trouble'?"

Abderian described the events at dinner when the mark was exposed, and the talk with Tingalut afterward.

"So, Tingalut is interested in this too, eh?" Dolus shook his head. "You may have made your troubles worse by coming here. Shouldn't you have asked your father about the mark? It would seem he knows more than I."

"He wasn't too pleased that I have it. I don't think he'd tell me much."

"Naturally he'd have expected Cyprian to bear it, since magical marks tend to transfer to the next oldest sibling."

"And he's not pleased that I spoke to Tingalut. I don't know why Father's so suspicious. I don't even *like* the priest."

Dolus smirked. "You ought to at least respect him, lad. Tingalut carries a lot of weight in Castle Mamelon these days."

"You mean Father listens to him more than to you, eh?"

Dolus winced. "As you say."

"How can you let him replace you like this?"

With a shrug Dolus said, "Cults come and cults go. Before this one was the Cult of the Star Goddess, who was said to have been a great sorceress. Before that was the Cult of the Moon God, whose members accomplished little except making the cult's founder a very wealthy man. The Temple of the Lizard Goddess shall pass like the others. I expect, when it does, the king will be pleased enough to have me back.

"Now, to return to your curse. It would seem that Paralian has caused you to be in the midst of a power struggle. One that he himself, perhaps, was hoping to avoid. Yes . . . that mark clearly connotes power of some sort; the intricacy of the lines implies that."

"Please, isn't there something more you can tell me? Don't you have a spell or magical object that could tell me more?"

Dolus looked thoughtful for a moment. "I may have something. Though I cannot guarantee how helpful it may be." The wizard went to a set of shelves and removed an ornately carved box. Putting it down on the table, he opened it, revealing strips of cloth. Dolus selected one and put the box away. He immersed the strip in a clear liquid that smelled faintly of vinegar and ginger. After a moment the wizard pulled out the cloth and snapped it twice. When he brought it over to the prince, it was dry.

"Now," said Dolus, "hold out your arm and let's see what this will make of it."

Abderian did so, and the wizard draped the cloth lightly over the cursemark. Then he pulled the cloth from left to right. Golden-red symbols formed of light appeared over the mark, changing as Dolus moved the strip.

"What does it say?" the prince asked eagerly.

Dolus frowned and shook his head. "I'm afraid this method of divining was meant for simpler spells. With something as complex as your mark, it merely reduces its meaning to absurdity."

"But what does it say?"

Dolus sighed. "It reads, 'Smile and the world smiles with you.'"

"What does that have to do with anything?"

"You see what I mean?"

A bat above the door shrieked.

"What was that?"

"Oh, dear. I forgot to reset the Endless Staircase. That was my doorbell. Are you expecting anyone?"

Abderian shook his head and looked worriedly at the door. A muffled voice came through the thick wood. "Is Abderian in there?"

Dolus asked the prince softly, "Do you want anyone to know?"

Abderian shook his head again.

"Allow me to suggest that dark corner over there to hide in, then."

The prince heeded the wizard's advice and slipped behind a large urn.

"Open up, Dolus!" came the voice again. "I've got to find Abderian. Is he in there?"

"Who wishes to know?" the wizard croaked, again acting the ancient mage.

"I'm his brother! Now, let me in!"

Dolus waved his hand and the door flew open, allowing Cyprian to stumble in, coughing, through clouds of dust.

"Many thanks. Where is he? Have you seen him?"

"Any particular reason why I should tell you?"

"Because he's in danger, you fool! I've come to warn him."

"Now what?" said Abderian, emerging from his hiding place.

"Ah-ha! There you are!" Cyprian rushed over to Abderian

and grabbed his collar, lifting him off the ground. "You little idiot! Have you any idea how much trouble you've gotten yourself into! The trouble you've gotten *me* into?"

"Hold!" cried Dolus, and Abderian felt as if a giant spring suddenly appeared between him and his brother. The princes were violently pushed apart, setting both on their rumps on the floor. "I'll not tolerate violence in my home," said the wizard. "Too many dangerous things could be broken."

Abderian saw there were faint red welts on Cyprian's face. "What happened? What did Father say to you?"

"He kept asking me how you got that mark. I told him I didn't know, but he didn't believe me." Cyprian rubbed the welts on his cheek. "After Paralian died, I was supposed to get the mark, I guess. When it didn't show up on my arm, Father had figured that Paralian had some bastard kid somewhere who got it. But now that it showed up on you, and Tingalut is so interested, Father figures something else."

"Does he still think you're not his son?"

"I don't know. But he seems to think you've turned traitor. And"—Cyprian got up and advanced on Abderian—"you know what happens to traitors, don't you?"

"Father wouldn't actually . . . execute me, would he?"

"Wouldn't he? Listen, little brother, just before coming here, I looked at the mannikins in the dining hall."

Abderian gulped. "Are they dressed in black?"

"No," Cyprian said softly, "but some of them are missing heads."

FIVE

ABDERIAN'S MOUTH DROPPED open. "Why?"

"Father says whoever wears the Mark of Sagamore is destined to be the next king of Euthymia."

"Tingalut didn't tell me that."

"That's another thing. Father thinks Tingalut is helping set you up to overthrow him. The priest was, by all accounts, the last person to see Paralian before his death. Kind of suspicious, don't you think?"

"Yes, to be sure, but I don't want to be king!"

"Well, someone wants you to be. A guard found a note in your tower offering you money and men for when you want to 'take what is rightfully yours.'"

Abderian frowned and reached into the top of his boot. He pulled out the note he was given at dinner, surprised it was still there.

"What's this?" said Cyprian, snatching the note from his brother's grasp. "Ha! Don't want to be king, huh?"

"That was dropped in my lap at dinner! I don't know who gave it to me! I really don't want to be king!"

"I think you ought to believe your brother, Cyprian," Dolus put in.

"You do, eh? Well, when Father hears Abderian's been down here, he'll think him a traitor for certain."

Abderian turned to Dolus. "Why is that?"

The wizard grimaced. "I have . . . inconvenient relatives. And it's best I say no more about that. What do you suggest as a course of action, Cyprian?"

"If I were you, Abderian, I would move my little behind

28

so fast out of this castle, I wouldn't leave footprints."

"But where will I go? What will I do?"

"Frankly, little brother, I don't give a gnat's ass, just go."

"How? According to you, there'll be guards all over."

"Just a moment," said Dolus, "I think I may have something." The wizard walked to an arched doorway and paused. "I'd appreciate it if you wouldn't kill each other while I'm out of the room. I have enough trouble with housekeeping as it is." With that, he went into the dark chamber beyond.

The princes glared at each other for a moment. Then Cyprian looked around the room. "I knew you'd come here. You and Paralian seemed to love this place, Goddess knows why. Huh. What's this?" Cyprian walked to a shelf containing a crystal globe.

"That's a sphere of seeing. Dolus told me about it once."

"Hmm. That's odd. I can see things in it. I see a crown turning over and over. And a wedding procession."

"Let me look." Abderian went over and gazed into the sphere. "That's not what I see." The younger prince saw, in rapid succession, a pile of bones, a demonic face with fangs, and a black and white kitten.

Dolus returned, grunting and dragging a huge chest behind him. "If it isn't in here, it isn't anywhere," he muttered.

"Dolus, come look at this," said Abderian.

"Eh? Look at what?" Dolus went over to the princes. "The seeing sphere?"

"Cyprian sees one set of things and I see another."

"Well, that's to be expec—" Dolus stopped, and his face became a shade paler.

"What is it? What's wrong?"

"I see a hand coming out of a starry night sky. The hand now fills the sky and grows larger until it covers everything."

"What does it mean?"

"There is a sorcerer at work here. Someone is using wizardry to gain control of . . . events."

"Tingalut?" whispered Abderian.

"It could be . . . although I—"

The bat above the door shrieked again.

"I seem to be popular tonight," said Dolus. "Or someone is." He looked at Abderian.

Abderian looked at Cyprian. "Think it's the guards?"

"How should I know?"

"Perhaps you two ought to make yourselves scarce," said Dolus.

Abderian looked back at the sphere, which had gone blank.

"C'mon," growled Cyprian, pulling his brother along to the urn in the corner. They managed to squeeze behind it just as a heavy knock fell on the door.

"Open up in there!"

"Just a moment." The wizard again took on his antique persona.

The door banged open, nearly falling off its hinges. In strode a tall, powerfully built man dressed in leather armor, followed by two others wearing the uniform of the guards. "Where is the boy?" he demanded.

"Boy? What boy? Surely you don't need me to find play-things for you, Captain Maduro."

"Cease the act, conjurer. Where is Prince Abderian? We suspect he's here."

"Well, yes, he was here, but I magically transported him back to his tower a while ago."

"Liar. We've searched his tower. Besides, you couldn't 'magically transport' a flea from one dog to another."

"What a pity for you," muttered the wizard.

"How's *that?*"

"Nothing, nothing."

The captain stamped into the center of the chamber and sniffed the dusty air. "Cyprian's been here. I can smell his cologne." He wrinkled his nose in distaste.

"Yes, he was here too," Dolus said. "He came to pick up a love philtre I was making for him. Apparently he has a tryst tonight."

"I wish," muttered Cyprian.

"Shush!" said Abderian.

"It's a very good philtre," Dolus continued, taking a little blue bottle off a shelf. "It not only excites one's beloved, but it also cures pox at the same time. Here, perhaps you ought to try some, Captain."

"You insulting old fool!" shouted the captain, swatting the bottle out of the wizard's hands. It shattered on the stone floor, emitting a foul odor from the shards. Maduro coughed. "So! Trying to drive me away, are you? You two, search this room!"

"As you wish," Dolus said, making a vague gesture.

As the guards began poking around the chamber, the atmosphere seemed to grow darker and more malevolent. Strange shadows shifted on the walls, and eerie lights flickered in the gloom. As one guard neared the urn behind which the princes were hidden, the shadows formed into a monstrous shape looming out of the corner.

The guard gulped and hastily backed away. "Nothing over here, Captain."

"Nor here," said the other guard, retreating from the opposite corner.

"I ask for men and they give me sheep," growled the captain.

"I won't say a word," cackled Dolus.

"Shut up, wizard! We'll continue our search elsewhere. But if we don't find him, we'll be back."

"I'll be waiting with bells on."

"Feh." The captain spat on the floor. "You're as crazy as the rest of them." He strode out the door, the other guards following closely behind.

Dolus bolted the door behind them as the princes came out from hiding. "This time I am definitely replacing the Endless Staircase," The wizard murmured. He traced a pattern on the door with one finger, then slapped the wood. The door seemed to fade and blend into the stone until there was only a bare wall in front of the wizard. "That's better."

"You see?" Cyprian snarled at Abderian. "There are guards searching for you. Now will you leave?"

"How can I leave with guards all over looking for me?"

"This place is full of secret passages. Just pick one."

"*Within* the castle, yes," Dolus put in, "but very few leading out. The castle would be impossible to defend otherwise."

"Say, could you 'magically transport' me, like you said to the captain?"

"No." Dolus chuckled. "I couldn't transport a dust mote. However, I do know of another possibility. Er, Cyprian, for your own safety I'd suggest that you leave us. What you don't know can't hurt us. Say as little to the guards as possible about Abderian's whereabouts, and I'll take care of the rest."

Cyprian looked uncertain for a moment, then said, "All right."

"If you need to, tell the guards I've transported Abderian to the top of the High Tower—the one without stairs. That should keep them busy for a while."

Cyprian looked from wizard to prince, then nodded and

went to where the door used to be. "How do I get out?"

"It's still there," said Dolus. The wizard opened a section of the wall as if it were a door.

"Oh." Cyprian turned and glanced at Abderian. "Good luck," he said, and bounded up the stairs.

Dolus closed the door/wall once more and slapped it as if a fly had landed there.

"You know," Abderian said softly, "I think he actually cares about me."

"What's that? Oh, undoubtedly. Now come look at this." Dolus opened the chest and rummaged through its contents. "Ah! Here we are!" The wizard took out a parchment scroll and unrolled it on the floor. The prince peeked over Dolus's shoulder. Before them was a detailed map of a castle interior—but no castle that Abderian had ever seen before.

"Where is that?"

"Directly beneath us, lad."

"I didn't know there was a floor beneath this one."

"Very few people do. Even fewer have seen it in the past century. I've been there only twice myself."

"According to the map that floor is called 'Castle Doom'?"

"Yes," Dolus said distastefully. "You see, this area was another manifestation—or should that be infestation?—of old King Sagamore's warped sense of humor. Before Mamelon was built, he and his court wizard created 'Castle Doom' as a sort of recreation area for the romantically deranged. It was designed to look like a ruined castle sunken into a swamp. Sagamore had it filled with improbable, disgusting creatures, some of which are actually dangerous."

"He deliberately built a ruined castle?"

"It's not so surprising. Many people create their own ruins. It was said that Sagamore liked to take evening strolls through it, particularly late in his life. At any rate, after the king's death, the entrances were blocked and the new court wizard set guardians to keep Sagamore's nightmares from escaping into the rest of the castle. In order to place these guardians, however, one entrance to the area had to remain accessible. And that is fortunate for us, dear boy, because that is precisely how we are to escape."

"Through a dangerous magical ruin and swamp?"

"You'll admit we're not likely to be followed that way."

"Yes, but I'm wondering if surrendering to the guards wouldn't be safer."

The bat above the door screamed again, and the rhythmic thump of marching feet came pounding down the stairwell.

"You haven't much time to decide, lad. Cyprian must not have been as convincing as I'd hoped."

"I'll take the swamp."

"Good lad. Roll up the map." Dolus returned to the trunk and pulled out a few more items. "You'll need some supplies other than the clothes on your back. Here's a bag of coins . . . it's not much, but it might buy you a hiding place. Here's a traveling cloak—might be a bit large for you. And here's a dagger." He handed the items to the prince.

Abderian looked nervously toward the enchanted door, from behind which descending footsteps continued to pound, accompanied by muffled curses. With renewed urgency the prince examined the things Dolus gave him. "Are they magical?"

"Don't be silly. Of course not."

"But wouldn't they be more use to me if they were?"

"Not at all. We haven't the time to train you in the use of magic items."

Abderian sighed, disappointed. "This dagger is rusty," he grumbled.

"Fine. You can poison your enemy as you stab him."

"And this cloak is stained and torn."

"It will make you look less like the prince they'll be seeking. Stop complaining and follow me."

Captain Maduro's voice boomed through the wall. "Blast you wizard! Make your door appear or, by the Goddess, I'll tear this stairwell apart until I find it!" There came a pounding on the wall and stone splinters flew across the room.

"Come on, lad!" Dolus grabbed an ornately carved staff out of the chest and slammed the lid shut. Running to a faded wall hanging, he tapped the wall behind it with the staff and a door appeared in the stone. The wizard pushed it open and leaped inside, pulling the prince with him. Just as the opposite wall burst open, Dolus slammed the stone door shut and it melted back into the wall.

He heaved a great sigh of relief. "This is one door I believe they can't crack. Still, we'd better put distance on our side as well." He scraped the tip of his staff against the wall, and a yellow flame appeared on it, illuminating a narrow corridor ahead of them. "Let's go."

As they walked, Abderian asked, "Dolus, won't the fact that you're helping me escape make you a traitor in my father's eyes too?"

"Yes, I imagine it will, lad."

"And yet you're still willing to help me?"

The wizard stopped. "Abderian, if I understand your brother's words correctly, I am a traitor for even letting you into my quarters. What matter that I'm also letting you out?"

"Well, I—I just wanted to thank you for taking this risk for me."

Dolus put his hand on the prince's shoulder. "My Liege, it is the greatest honor that I may fling my soul across the vault of Heaven, so that you may have a bridge beneath your feet."

Abderian gasped at the wizard, "Dolus, that's . . . beautiful! What does it mean?"

"Absolutely nothing, but it sounded appropriate, didn't it?"

The prince exhaled noisily between his lips. "I should have guessed."

A rumble of sundering stone behind them sent the wizard and the prince scurrying farther down the corridor. Presently they came to a wrought iron gate whose bars were twisted and coiled in bizarre shapes.

"More of King Sagamore's 'artistry,'" Dolus said. "Now, remember, Sagamore's imagination was as twisted as the iron on this gate. Beyond this point, anything might happen. Do you understand?"

Abderian nodded. He shrugged the cloak over his shoulders and held the rusty dagger at ready. Despite this, he did not feel ready at all.

Dolus touched his staff to five places on the gate, muttering strange words. Slowly the gate swung open. Beyond it, leading down into darkness, stone stairs glistened wetly. A dank smell drifted up from below.

The two proceeded down the stairs, hands on the damp walls for balance. After several steps Dolus said, "Careful, here is a landing, and the stairs turn." But on the step above the landing Dolus stopped abruptly, flinging his arm to the side to stop the prince.

"Whaa—?"

"Shhh! Listen." A rustling sound came from around the corner. And a noise like a parrot cawing to itself. "The guardians," Dolus whispered. "I'd forgotten about them." The wizard stepped cautiously onto the landing, Abderian right behind him.

The rustling grew louder and a hideous, twisted face appeared below. It smiled a grin full of fangs, and great leathery wings stretched out behind it. With a shriek it rushed at the pair, claws extended, eyes ablaze, charging with the fury of a cyclone. Abderian hid behind Dolus, sure he was going to die.

And the creature stopped an inch from the wizard's face. "'Evening, Master!" It laughed.

"I wish you wouldn't do that, Frakas," said Dolus.

"Scared ye, didn't I? Huh? Didn't I? Huh? Huh?"

"Actually I was perturbed by your foul breath."

"You feed on toads and bats for years and see what it does to you!"

"Is there something you want, or are you just feeling friendly?"

"Well, Master, since ye ask, me an' some of the others were wondering if you could let us have a holiday sometime. We've been guarding this place for years now an' nobody or nothin' comes through here. We're nearly mad with boredom. Have some pity, Master."

"Hmm." Dolus thought a moment. "Very well—"

"Huzzzah!"

"On one condition."

"Whazzat?"

"There are guards in my quarters seeking us. If you could see that they are, um, distracted a bit, we'd appreciate it."

"Not to worry, Master! We'd love to, wouldn't we?" There came a chorus of assenting cackles and giggles from the darkness behind him.

"Excellent. In that case, I hereby release you. Good night and enjoy yourselves."

Continuous thunder rumbled up from below as demon after demon rushed past Dolus and the prince, shoving them flat against the wall. Each creature wore the gleeful expression of a child whose studies had just ended. Finally the last one went by with a loud whoop, slamming the iron gate shut behind him.

Abderian poked his head out from under the wizard's cloak.

"Those are guardians? I'd hate to see what it is they're guarding."

"Fear not. You will. Onward." Dolus moved on down the stairs, Abderian tiptoeing after.

The stairway twisted and turned again, at last ending beneath a tall pointed arch. Abderian looked through it and gasped. Beyond the arch lay a vast chamber lit by a faint greenish glow. Its floor was a carpet of bubbling mud, out of which poked ornate columns, archways, stairs, and alcoves, tilted at crazy angles. Will-o'-the-wisps played around the columns and unseen bats squeaked and fluttered in the high, vaulted ceiling. The soft chirruping of frogs and crickets could be heard in the distance.

"It's wonderful!" sighed Abderian.

"You are indeed Sagamore's kin," Dolus said wryly.

"I wish I'd known about this place before. I'd love to explore it."

"No doubt. But fortunately, we are in a hurry—"

"Couldn't I just hide out here for a while?"

"And live on toads and bats like the demons?"

"Hmm. I guess you're right."

"Now that you have attained wisdom, stand aside while I make a path for us." The wizard raised his arms and chanted:

> Slime a-creep and muck a-crawling,
> Your master's kin does come a-calling,
>   Make a path for us to tread,
>   And lead us from this place of dread.

Then Dolus struck the mud with his staff. A brilliant flash lit up the room, and green fire snaked across the vast space. The mud seemed to boil, and mounds raised themselves and blended into a smooth pathway stretching away from the stairs. The swamp subsided, and silence fell upon the chamber.

"I'm impressed!"

"Much as I enjoy your praise, we'd best move on quietly, lest other creatures wish to examine my artistry close up." Dolus gingerly stepped out upon the path and set off at a swift pace. Abderian hurried after.

At the first bend in the path, on the far side of a large, fluted column, was a statue of a woman. She had sunk up to her hips in the mud, and her arms and nose had broken off. As Abderian passed the statue, not only did her eyes seem to follow him, but her lips mouthed the word *welcome* and smiled lasciviously. The prince stumbled backward into the wizard.

"Watch where you're going, lad."

"Sorry." Looking this way and that at the askew architecture, the prince mused aloud, "I wonder how this place has held up at all."

"Rivets. Rivets," said a deep voice somewhere off to their left.

Abderian jumped a little. "Dolus, that was just a frog, wasn't it?"

"In this place, lad, you can never be sure."

Farther along, Abderian saw some yards away a portion of stone wall that seemed to be perpetually sinking into the mire, but never disappearing below the surface. "I wonder how deep this swamp is?" he said softly.

"Knee-deep. Knee-deep," came the voice again, closer than before.

Abderian looked wildly around but could not find the source of the voice.

"Hush! Hurry, lad, there's the exit!" Dolus pointed at a doorway several yards ahead.

"Wait up! Wait up!" said the deep voice right behind them.

Abderian spun around and saw sitting in the path a large, warty amphibian about a hand's-width tall. Its yellow eyes gleamed malevolently in the gloom. Abderian laughed nervously. "Look, Dolus, I was right. It's just a frog."

The wizard turned. "That's no ordinary frog. It is the Bullfrog of Castle Doom."

"Is it one of those creatures that is dangerous? Or is it merely disgusting?"

"In this place it could be either, or both, depending upon your grandfather's warped imagination."

"Bigot," burped the bullfrog.

"Let us assume it's the dangerous kind and make haste for the doorway. Go on ahead, lad, I'll chase off our visitor here." Dolus waved his staff at the frog. "Shoo! Go away! Beat it!"

"Beat it?" growled the bullfrog angrily. It leaped for the wizard's throat.

"Fly, fool, fly!" Dolus cried, trying to pry the angry amphibian off his neck.

"Fly? Dolus, I can't—"

"Run, idiot, run!"

The prince dashed for the doorway and turned in time to see the wizard and the bullfrog fall off the path into the muck. "Dolus!" Abderian tried to run back to help, but as Dolus sank beneath the surface, the path subsided to become swamp once more. The prince was stranded on the doorstep.

Abderian stood staring for a minute, then heard angry voices echoing in the distance. One of them sounded like Captain Maduro. The prince hesitated. Then, deciding there was nothing he could do for the wizard, Abderian ran through the doorway and up the stairs beyond it.

Panting and gasping, three flights later, the prince came to an opening that led into fresh, cool night air and dry ground. He staggered out and leaned against the outside of the castle wall, trying to catch his breath. After a minute he saw the opening he came through disappear and become part of the wall. The prince felt only slightly relieved.

Shaking from fear and exhaustion, Abderian stared at the starry sky and murmured, "Now what do I do?"

Too late, he heard the rustling of the bushes next to him. Before he could move, something reeking of herbs and alcohol was slapped over his face. He heard a gravelly voice growl, "Got 'im!" just before the world went black.

SIX

THE DARKNESS WAS filled with stars. Among them floated a gigantic pale spider, who drew nearer and nearer to the prince. Abderian struggled, but his hands and feet were bound tightly to her invisible web. Soon She was upon him, Her claws sticking into him. As She opened her jaws to devour the prince, Her breath smelled incongruously like fresh-cut grass. Abderian tried once more to shake himself free, crying out for help

With a jolt he awoke. His hands were tightly bound behind him, and his ankles were tied as well. He was covered over with hay, and he itched where it poked him. From the rumbling of wagon wheels below him, Abderian deduced he was in a haycart. The prince tried to cry out, but his mouth was gagged with a foul-tasting rag.

From somewhere ahead of him he heard a gruff voice say, "Sounds like the boy be awake, Bismer."

And another say, "Aye, Gnoff. I still tell ye we should'a sold 'im back to the King. Then we'd be done wit' 'im quick-like."

"An' I still be tellin' ye the king would sooner see 'im die than part wit' any of 'is gold for 'im. An' we'd be found and 'ung right after— 'Is Majesty ain't called 'The Brutal' for nothin', ye know. Not t'mention what the wizard would do to us for crossin' 'im."

"We might be caught anyways."

"The wizard knows 'is business, Bismer. 'E told us 'zactly where to find the lad, didn't 'e? Maylike 'e put a wardin' spell on us so's we won't come to 'arm while doin' 'is business.

39

Besides, I say a thousand ruyecks an' a spell apiece is plenty worth the trouble for me."

Wizard? thought Abderian. *I wonder who they mean. Can't be Dolus. Why would he do this to me? Tingalut? It's possible the priest knew of that exit . . . but wouldn't my captors call him 'the priest'? Who else could it be?* The prince sighed. Euthymia was full of wizards of varying skill, most of whom Abderian had never heard of. Some rebellious group could easily have hired a wizard to arrange this. It might have nothing to do with the cursemark. Somehow, the prince could not believe that.

"'Ey, Bismer, what kinda spell ye gonna ask for when we get there?"

"I dunno. Mayhap somethin' to cure me backaches."

"No, no, no, ye're not thinkin' big enough. Wouldn't ye like to be rich, or 'ave bootiful wenches crawlin' all over ye, or—watch out for the rut!"

"Wha—?"

With a wood-rendering crunch the cart jolted to a stop, sending the purloined prince and the hay sliding into a forward corner of the cart.

"Aww, now look what ye done!"

"T'weren't me fault! Ye should'a told me sooner. T'weren't no way I could turn ol' Dirdum quick enough."

"I only saw it just when I told ye! Tch, by the blood o' the Dung Beetle, looky that. The 'ole wheel an' axle are broke."

"T'ain't me fault, I tell ye. 'Sides, these carts is made so cheaplike these days, they'll break for anywhy."

"Sure. Ye just be makin' excuses now."

"Nay, they don't make 'em like they used to. It's them accursed cartwrights. Ever since they put together that big guild o' theirs, they be makin' these cheap carts. An' they's fixed it so's nobody else can make 'em anymore."

"So ye say. Next ye be sayin' they got wizards who curse each cart to break down at a certain time."

"Wouldn't surprise me. 'Oo knows what they been doin' up in that big estate o' theirs—ey . . . we got comp'ny comin'."

Abderian heard hoofbeats approaching. *More than one horse. Maybe more than two.* He wondered if he should hope or dread that he might be rescued.

"Whadda we do now, Gnoff?"

"Act casuallike. Don't give nothin' away."

"Right."

The hoofbeats came very close, and stopped. "Ho there!" called a firm, commanding voice. "You are blocking the road!"

"Sorry, Yer Lordship, sir. Ye see, our cart broke its wheel an' we're stuck. Mayhap if Yer Lordship would be so kind as to 'elp us out . . ."

Abderian, deciding to hope for rescue, began thrashing wildly about. He yelled as loud as he could through the gag.

"What is this?" said another voice. "It would seem, good fellows, that your hay is alive."

"Well, er, it only seems that way, in a manner o' speakin', sir."

"How do you mean that?"

"Well, ye see, Yer Lordship, sir, this is a load o' . . . uh, Beksikam jumpin' 'ay. Heh-heh. Aye, that's it. 'Tis a special kind o' grass, sir."

"Aye, uh, we be takin' it to Pokelocken for the 'arvest festivals."

"But harvest is still months away, I believe."

"Oh. Aye, but, well, the mayor, sir, he, uh, likes to plan these things early, ye see, sir."

"I have traveled far and wide through many lands," said the commanding voice that was sounding more and more familiar to Abderian. "But I've never heard of Beksikam jumping hay. Are you certain there isn't someone in there?"

Burdalane! thought the prince joyfully. *It's Burdalane!* Lady Chevaline's grandson and Abderian's boyhood hero, Burdalane was the best person the prince could wish to rescue him. He shouted with all his might, "Help! Burdalane, help!"

"What is that noise?"

"It's the 'ay, sir. Good Beksikam jumpin' 'ay always shrieks when it's fresh."

Abderian struggled to his knees and tried to stand up. But the cart was tilted at such a severe angle that as the prince poked his head out of the hay, he lost his balance and fell out of the cart onto the road.

"Here, now. What's this?" said Burdalane, dismounting.

Despite his discomfort, Abderian felt a surge of joy. His handsome, tawny-haired cousin, wearing a gleaming breastplate, came striding toward him. Two other soldiers remained on horseback, watching the shabby peasants cowering by the cart.

"Are you all right, lad?"

"Burdalane!" the prince exclaimed when his gag was removed.

"Your Highness!" said the commander in surprise.

"Run for it!" said the peasants in terror.

"Arrest them!" shouted Burdalane, and the other soldiers took off after the kidnappers.

"Am I glad to see you!" said Abderian with relief.

"I thought it might be you," said Burdalane. "Lady Chevaline sent word that you were missing and asked me to look out for you." The commander untied the prince's bonds and helped him to stand. "Are you otherwise unharmed?"

"I seem to be," Abderian said, rubbing his wrists and ankles. "Who are those two?"

"I don't know. Gruff and Dismal, I think their names were. They said they were working for some wizard, but they didn't say who."

"Ah," sighed Burdalane. "Then it was Dolus who took you away."

"No, it wasn't like that. He was helping me escape."

"Escape? From your own home?"

"It's . . . Burdalane, I'm in trouble. Everyone at court is acting very strange. Tingalut wants to control me. Father wants to execute me for a traitor. Cyprian is furious with me. And Dolus is probably dead—"

"What have you done, Abderian?"

"It's . . . it's a long story. Please don't take me back to Castle Mamelon. At least not right away. They'll kill me! Take me somewhere safe, and I'll tell you all about it."

"Kill you? I find that hard to believe. Still, if it upsets you so, we can return to my camp and talk there. We can think up some excuses for your father later. And," Burdalane added with a chuckle, "hope he will not wish my head as well."

It was late afternoon when they reached Burdalane's camp, a small cluster of tents nestled at the foot of a range of low brown hills, somewhat obscured by blowing dust from the dry plains. Castle Mamelon was several miles to the south, and the distance eased Abderian's mind.

As they entered the encampment two officers came out of a tent and Burdalane dismounted to speak to them. One of the officers took charge of Gnoff and Bismer, while another helped Abderian dismount.

"Welcome, Your Highness. We were not expecting a royal inspection of the troops, so I apologize for our unpreparedness. Still, we'll provide you with what comfort we can." The officer grinned and made a short bow.

Abderian grinned back. "That's all right. This isn't an official visit."

"So I understand, Your Highness. Follow me, please."

They threaded their way through the tents, Abderian scarcely getting a glance in his old, hay-specked cloak. *Dolus was right. This does make a decent disguise.*

As they passed a colorful tent Abderian heard a woman singing:

> Now Tam has a sword that's too small and too thin,
> His foes hardly notice when Tam sticks it in
> Compared to most others, he's smaller by half,
> And when he displays it, the ladies all laugh!

The officer shrugged apologetically.

"Popular song," said the prince.

"Unfortunately," said the officer.

Presently they came to a large blue and gold tent near the center of the camp. The officer pulled aside the door flap and Abderian entered the cool but stuffy tent.

"The commander will rejoin you shortly, Your Highness," said the officer. Abderian heard the soldier's bootheels crunch away.

The prince wandered around the spacious tent, trying to forget his troubles for a time. He stared, fascinated, at each of the strange and exotic weapons hanging from the tent supports, wondering where each came from and how it was used, and the horrible effect it might have upon its victim.

The tent flaps slapped open and Burdalane strode in. He was followed by an aide-de-camp who brought in a small table laden with sausages, hardbread, and mugs of ale. After saluting Burdalane and bowing to the prince, the aide left without a word.

"Thank the Lizardess that's over," said the commander. He flopped heavily onto large velvet pillows, grabbing a handful of sausage and bread on the way down.

"A hero's work is never done, eh?" Abderian grinned.

"You could say that."

"Do you have time to talk now?"

"Well," said Burdalane after swallowing a mouthful, "all the dragons I know are dormant, no maidens I know of need rescuing—if, indeed, any remain in the kingdom—and what evil remains to be undone can wait until tomorrow. I am, as the enchanted chamberpot said, at your disposal."

"Good. First off, what does that do?" Abderian pointed to a long iron object with two prongs at one end and a wicked spiral point at the other.

"That? I take it on long campaigns. One can roast meat with one end and open wine bottles with the other."

"Oh."

"Now, cousin, what of this trouble at court?"

Abderian paused, then said softly, "I know that your true mission here is to search for a child who bears the Mark of Sagamore."

Burdalane took another swallow of ale. "And if it is?"

"Then you need look no further." The prince held out his arm for the commander to examine.

After a moment Burdalane sighed and sank back against the pillows. "Well. And how long have you had this?"

"Since Paralian died. One year."

Burdalane's eyes grew wide and he struck the pillow beside him. "You mean to say I've been raiding villages to look at bare babes for a Goddess-loving year for nothing!"

Abderian cringed. "I'm sorry! Paralian told me to tell no one about it when he gave it to me."

"You should have heeded his advice. One moment—he gave it to you?"

With a sigh Abderian described how he got the cursemark, and explained the events of the previous day.

"Hmm. Now I see why His Majesty considered the mark important enough to search for."

"But is it important enough to kill me for?"

Burdalane considered a moment. "If your father feels he cannot control you, yes. A throne is no seat of security, cousin. Your family is still seen as usurper from the House of Thalion. And there is always some legend or other about a 'return of the true king.' It's not surprising your father fears for his crown."

"But what can I do? I don't want to be a traitor! I didn't want this cursemark! I'd give it up in an instant if I had the chance."

"Then perhaps that is what you should do."

"What?"

"Return home and offer the mark to Cyprian if he is the rightful owner. If the mark could be 'given' to you, perhaps it can be 'given' to Cyprian."

Abderian thought a moment. The idea of sticking his brother with the troublesome mark seemed a delicious revenge to the part of him that still harbored resentment. And yet, if the mark was, as Tingalut said, an avenue of power, what might Cyprian do with it? And the part of Abderian that cared for Cyprian thought it was far too cruel to wish the mark on him. "I don't know," Abderian said finally. "Father might prefer to transfer the mark by lopping my head off. And since Dolus may be dead, only Tingalut could do a magical transfer, and I know Father wouldn't care for *that*. I don't know."

"Well, you may stay with me a day or two while you consider. But soon your father's guards will seek you here, and I know not if I can hide you."

"But I don't know where else to go! No other noble house will take me in if my name is tainted with treason. Or, worse, that's why they'll want to take me in."

"Aye. Thy father's reputation for ruthlessness . . . But you should be safe here until tomorrow. By then I may have thought of somewhere else to send you. And perhaps your intended kidnappers will have offered up some information by then."

"Let's hope." Abderian sat silently for a while, still troubled. *If only I knew more about this cursemark!*

"Burdalane, do you have a wizard working for you?"

The commander laughed. "Do you think your father would trust any wizard with the knowledge of the bearer of the mark? Of course not."

"Oh. I see. I was only hoping to speak to someone else who understood magic. You have nothing to do with magic, do you?"

"A wise commander learns to keep wizards off the battlefield, Abderian. They only make a mess of things. But I would not say I have 'nothing' to do with magic."

"Oh?"

A sly grin twitched at Burdalane's lips. "One item. But if I tell you about it, you must swear not to reveal it to anyone else."

Abderian grinned and covered the mark with his left hand. "I swear by the Mark of Sagamore!"

"Careful, cousin. It is not wise to swear by that whose power is unknown. But come. I will show you something."

Burdalane led the prince into a curtained-off portion of the tent. There he took from a wooden chest a long object wrapped in black silk. He placed it reverently on top of the chest. "I have never shown this to anyone," he said softly. "Behold."

Burdalane unwrapped the black silk to reveal a gleaming sword. Its elegant hilt was polished obsidian, inlaid with silver tracings, and the blade bore symbols resembling stars.

Abderian could swear the sword seemed to be humming and, when he did not look at it directly, it seemed surrounded by a faint glow. "It's beautiful," whispered the prince, and he reached out his hand to stroke the blade.

"Touch it not!" Burdalane grabbed Abderian's wrist. "It is a powerful weapon, and could well destroy you even in a mere touch."

"Sorry," the prince said as the commander let go of his arm. "But where did you get it?"

"I would prefer not to say."

"I see." On impulse, Abderian suddenly reached out and rubbed the blade with the tip of his finger. The sword hummed loudly and green fire raced around its edges.

"Touch it not, I say! Are you deaf?"

"I'm sorry! I—I couldn't help it. I just wanted to touch it so much. It's so beautiful."

"So, it calls to you also," murmured Burdalane. "Then I'd best save you from further temptation and put it away." He quickly rewrapped the sword and stowed it away in the chest.

"What do you mean, 'it calls to you'?"

"When I first found it," said the commander, leading the prince back into the main section of the tent, "I believed that it called to me also. And still, at times, I feel her—its call, and I ache to wear the sword."

"Why don't you, then?"

Burdalane looked away. "I . . . cannot. It is not for me. To grasp it only brings me pain. I cannot wield it."

"Then why do you keep it?"

Shrugging, the commander said, "I wouldn't trust anyone else with it. I know not whom I would give it to."

"Is that it? Not some other reason?"

Burdalane regarded Abderian with a rueful smile and sighed. "You know me too well, cousin. Sit and let us finish our meal and I'll tell you."

Between bites of sausage Burdalane explained how, after touching the sword, he'd had dreams of a beautiful pale woman. The dreams were so vivid, and he was so taken with her, that he kept the sword in her memory. "Somehow, so long as I have the sword near me, I feel closer to her."

"I see. But I don't understand. You're the closest thing to a hero Euthymia's ever had. Why wouldn't the sword allow you to carry it?"

Burdalane shook his head and looked on the prince with patient pity. "You misjudge the nature of magic swords and myself. Not all magic swords wish heroes to wield them, and not all who wish to wield them are heroes."

"I still don't understand."

"Clearly. Abderian, even if the sword seeks a hero, it would decline my attention. For I do not have the heart of a hero."

"What? How can you say that? As long as I've known you you've—"

"Aye, since I was your age I have been a fighting man. Even though, before your age, 'twas the last thing I would have wanted. Gentler pursuits were my first calling."

"But . . . if that's true, why did you become a soldier?"

Burdalane paused a moment, then replied softly, "To impress the fair sex."

Abderian almost burst out laughing. "Indeed? Well, you must have succeeded in that!"

"No," the commander said, staring at his ale mug. "A warrior's life is a lonely one. Few women wish to marry a man only to watch him leave her for war. And my heart would ache for any woman I would have to leave thus. So, I have not married."

"But . . . but you could have, um . . . brief encounters, couldn't you?"

Burdalane's face grew heavy with distant sorrow. "When a man seeks a mate to cherish a lifetime, half an hour doesn't do."

"Oh."

There was an uncomfortable pause during which Abderian noticed the tent seemed darker than before. The sun was setting, he realized. Feeling a need for something to do, the prince took a tinderbox from his tunic and got up to light a small oil lamp that hung from a tent support. As pale yellow light filled the tent, a voice came from the entrance.

"My Lord Commander, I would speak with you."

"Enter," said Burdalane.

A tall, slender but muscular woman walked in, wearing only a brief leather chestband, loincloth, and sword. Her hair was black and held back with a red headband. Her tanned skin was covered with scars large and small. On her inner right thigh was a tattooed star. She bowed to the prince and saluted Burdalane.

"You have a request, Hirci?" said the commander.

"Aye, sir. The others have returned from the outlying villages with no success, as usual. We wish to know what areas we will be searching next. And, I confess, sir, some of the troops are complaining that the search is a waste of time."

"Well, Hirci, the troops may be pleased to learn that we have had word from royal authority"—the commander nodded at Abderian—"that the search is to be ended. There is no need to continue."

Hirci's eyes widened. "Indeed?" She looked at the prince. "Yes, they will be pleased. Pray tell me, Your Highness, where was the mark found?"

"Uh."

"I will explain the matter to the troops myself," said Burdalane. "Assemble them in midcamp and I will come explain. By the way, have you heard anything to indicate that our prisoners have been convinced to speak their minds?"

"No, sir, not yet." Hirci still stared intently at Abderian.

"Ah, well. Call the assembly, then, and I shall be there presently."

"Thank you, sir." The woman warrior strode gracefully out of the tent.

Abderian was impressed. Hirci was nothing like the female guards the prince saw around the castle. Those were heavily armored and built like bricks. But Hirci seemed beautiful and dangerous at the same time.

Burdalane got up, grunting, from the pillows. "Well, cousin, we shall have to continue our discussion later. I must invent a believable story to tell my troops concerning the finding of the mark. Fear not, cousin. I shall see no one learns the truth until you are gone from here."

Abderian nodded. "Say, Burdalane, if you want a woman who can be near you, have you thought of choosing someone like Hirci?"

Burdalane's eyes grew large, and he suddenly burst into laughter. He winked at the prince. "But cousin, don't you remember that women warriors give themselves only to men who can best them in battle? Hirci was recommended to me by Her Majesty as one of the best swordfighters in the kingdom. Hirci could probably slice me to ribbons in seconds. No, thank you, I'd prefer a less deadly wife. You may stay here. I shall return ere long." With that, the commander left.

Abderian sat among the pillows and hugged his knees. He wondered if he was safe here with Burdalane, and for how long. And he worried about where he might go if he could not return home.

He found his mind turning to Burdalane's magic sword. He wanted to look at it again. *If I'm careful, I won't have to touch it. If I just look at it for a little while, I can resist the temptation to touch it for that long.*

Abderian waited until he heard Burdalane speaking to the troops, then he tiptoed to the adjoining room. In the dimness he groped toward the chest. He raised the lid carefully and felt inside for the sword. His hands closed on a bundle of soft material that contained something hard. Abderian lifted it out of the chest and set it on the ground in front of him. He could almost see the sword glowing through the material. The prince peeled back the silk and gazed on the sword in wonder. It seemed even more beautiful now than when he first saw it.

Again he stroked the blade with one finger. The sword hummed in response and green flames licked out of the blade. A thrill of excitement raced down Abderian's spine. *To be so close to something so powerful.* All other thoughts fled his mind.

Slowly his hands reached for the hilt, his breath coming out in shallow gasps. The ebon haft felt warm between his hands, and a satisfying surge of power flooded his arms. Not thinking of the danger, Abderian tightened his grip and slowly lifted the sword.

The humming from within the sword grew louder, and Ab-

derian could feel the vibrations deep in his bones. The green
fire spread from the blade to the hilt, enveloping his hands.
As he raised the sword, sparks of energy, like small bolts of
lightning, shot out from the sword, striking the prince. At first
they only tingled, then they became painful. Soon, white-hot
fire was seething through the prince's arms, up into his chest
and neck. His mind began to spin. He wanted to drop the sword,
but his hands ignored his will. Darkness flowed out of the tip
of the blade, pooling and spreading before him. Abderian thought
he could dimly see glowing points, like stars, through the
blackness. Then the pain became too much and he screamed.

Rough hands grabbed the prince and spun him aside, tearing
the sword from his grasp. There was a dull clang as the sword
was flung to the floor, and Abderian felt Burdalane's great arms
enfold him and hold him as the prince sobbed in pain.

"'Twill pass, little cousin, 'twill pass."

In time, Abderian began to breathe deeper and he felt the
pain ebb away. His arms felt heavy and numb, as if they were
false limbs someone had stuck on his body. Burdalane guided
the prince back into the main portion of the tent and set him
down on the pillows. Then the commander went to put the
sword away.

Abderian felt acutely ashamed. But when Burdalane returned, there were no told-you-so's. He only said, "You should
rest. Sleep will help. This tent shall be yours for the night. I
shall use another." He paused to stroke Abderian's brow, concern lining his face. Then he quietly left the tent.

Abderian sank back on the pillows, weary and frightened.
Presently darkness surrounded him once more, but this time it
was only gentle sleep.

SEVEN

HE FLEW OUT of the darkness into a world of starlit wonder. Below him lay a dark green sea, stretching away endlessly to the horizon. The waters were tossed by a warm breeze that gently buffeted the prince's face. Above him was a velvet black sky filled with stars so bright it hurt to look at them. He was flying, floating, being pulled to an unknown destination.

In time he saw beneath him a small boat without sails rising and falling on the sea swells. A shining figure stood at its bow. Abderian felt himself drawn to it, and he slowly spiraled down, like a sea gull seeking fish. Soon he alighted gently on the deck.

The figure turned, and the prince saw it was a beautiful pale woman . . . the same as Burdalane had described. She was tall and had star-white hair beneath a silvery hooded robe. In her eyes burned a light as bright as the stars overhead. She looked at the prince in gentle surprise and said, "I bid you welcome, Prince Abderian. I have been looking for you."

Abderian felt his voice stick in his throat and could only bow.

"I am pleased that you have come to speak to me."

"If you are pleased, Lady, then why did your sword hurt me?"

"The power of the Nightsword is meant for another, not you."

Nightsword, thought the prince. *So it has a name.*

"This is not the avenue I would have chosen for our meeting—" She took his right arm in her hand and gently stroked the cursemark. It ached beneath her touch, and Abderian wanted to pull his arm away, but could not. She gave him an odd smile and continued. "But the magic in these times

51

runs strangely, and this is the way you have chosen."

Abderian did not understand this at all, and hesitated before asking, "Can you help me?"

Her laughter was sharp and brittle, like shards of colored glass. "But you are going to help *me*." She paused and gazed at the prince searchingly. "In so doing, you may gain what you seek but lose what you do not value."

Riddles, thought Abderian. *I hate riddles.*

"For now, at least, I shall ease your pain." She guided him to the bow of the craft and said, "Look upon the sea."

Abderian did so, and felt the movement of the waves draining the heaviness of his arms. The warm wind soothed him, caressed him, sang to him. The tang of the salt sea air refreshed him. In joy he closed his eyes, wanting to stand there forever.

All too soon the pale lady touched the prince's shoulder and whispered, "You must go now." Abderian closed his eyes and willed himself to stay. But she shook him gently and again said, "You must go now."

He felt himself fall away from the world of the sea and the stars into a dim, sticky grayness. And still he felt her hand on his shoulder, and her voice saying, "Your Highness, you must go now. Wake up!"

Wake up? Abderian stirred on the pillows and moaned.

"You are in great danger, Your Highness. You must wake up!"

The prince slowly opened his heavy eyelids and saw the worried face of Hirci hovering over him.

"Your Highness, are you awake at last?"

"Yes, I'm awake. Why? What is it?"

"His Majesty's men have come into the camp seeking you. You must leave."

Abderian became more alert. "What? Where's Burdalane?"

"He delays your father's men to give you time to escape. He has ordered me to guide you to a safe place."

The prince still felt as if stuck between two worlds, but he managed to stand up on unsteady legs. "All right . . . let me get—"

"There's no time! Quick, this way." She grabbed his arm and pulled him toward the back of the tent, surprising the prince with her strength. She lifted the bottom of the rear panel and crawled under, dragging Abderian with her. Outside, she looked around anxiously, then took off running, still grasping Abderian's sleeve. The prince staggered along as best he could, keeping low to the ground and using the tents as cover.

As they paused briefly behind a pile of crates, Abderian asked, "Where are we going?"

"Shhh! I must not tell you, lest we be overheard."

"Oh. Of course."

In a moment they were off again, running up into the low hills at the edge of camp. Here they had to clamber with hands and feet over steep, pebbly slopes. Abderian found he was hard pressed to keep up with the warrior woman. Their only illumination was starlight, forcing the prince to follow the sound of her footfalls and suffer an occasional pebble in the face as a result. They pushed on through brush and bramble until they reached a hollow surrounded by large boulders. Hirci indicated this was a place to rest.

Abderian sagged against a rock and sat, gasping raggedly. He tried to catch his breath, which he imagined as a dim form making faces and playing hide-and-seek among the shadows swimming before his eyes.

Hirci paced the area grumbling, "Why aren't they here yet?"

"They?"

"We were to meet others here with horses and supplies."

"Horses? Supplies? Just how far are we going?"

"Three days travel, perhaps four."

"To where?"

"You shall know in good time, Your Highness."

Abderian felt a shudder that was not only from the cold wind blowing among the rocks. "I would like to know *now*. I don't think Burdalane would mind."

Hirci turned and looked at the prince. "This has nothing to do with Commander Burdalane."

Abderian felt his neck and shoulders become tense. "I thought so. There are no castle guards looking for me back at the camp, are there?"

"They will be coming for you soon enough. You could say the only lie was my haste in getting you out. Believe me, Your Highness, you will be far safer where I am taking you."

"Wherever it is." Abderian sighed, deciding to try a stab in the dark. "Very well. Tell me, how much is Tingalut paying you?" As he watched Hirci the prince began to get the impression he had said the wrong thing. Perhaps it was her gaze on his face, her hand on his arm, her knife at his throat . . .

"Were you not so precious to my Mistress, little princeling, I would slay you now for that insult," Hirci hissed, apparently quite willing to do a little stabbing in the dark herself. "Tingalut is our enemy, and I would take nothing from him but his life."

"I'm sorry! I mean, I don't like Tingalut either! But he wanted me to join his temple against my father's will, so I only thought maybe—"

"I see." Hirci lowered her dagger. "You need not worry, Your Highness. The Mistress I serve is no friend to the king or to Tingalut. You will be safe in Her care."

Great, thought the prince, *another conspirator. Perhaps that's what this curse does—draws would-be rebels to me like flies to old meat.* "This Mistress of yours . . . is She a wizard?"

Hirci frowned. "Why do you ask?"

"The peasants who kidnapped me said they worked for a wizard. I wondered if it was your Mistress they spoke of."

"Hah. Their wizard is a fool. You needn't worry about them. I slit their throats before we left."

"Oh." The prince felt his stomach sinking into the stone beneath him. Whoever this Mistress was, Her ways were apparently as ruthless as his father's or Tingalut's. Joining forces with Her could not be an improvement in his situation "And if I choose not to go with you?"

"That would be foolish."

"But what would you do?"

"I would carry you senseless," Hirci said, raising her dagger.

"You there! Cease!" called an eerie voice from across the campfire.

"Who is there?" cried Hirci, looking wildly about.

"I am." At the edge of the clearing appeared a thin pale figure, covered with dried mud, holding a dim lantern. He looked like a wraith fresh risen from the grave. Pointing accusingly at Hirci, the wraith intoned, "Do you not know, woman, the ancient Code of Warriors? 'Strike thou not an unarmed opponent, for it shameth thee. Seek thou not revenge, lest thou forge a never-ending chain of blood. Obey thy commander unto death and even after, that thou mayest shine in his glory. For thy skill and thy strength are a sacred trust, not to be wasted or ill used. Live thy life such that Death may not take thee in aught but a fair and honest fight. Thus when thy spirit at last is sundered from thy body, thou shalt be raised to the Hall of Heroes, where thy sword shall be golden, thy shield shall be silver and thy name shall be praised in song by the gods of war forever!'"

Hirci's eyes widened, awe-struck, and she knelt before the wraith. "Wise spirit, did my Mistress send you to chastise me? Indeed, I have not heard such glorious words before."

"No doubt because I just made them up. Now, kindly leave the boy alone.

"Dolus," Abderian whispered.

Hirci sat a moment in shock, then snarled, "Who are you?"

"Perhaps I will tell you when you explain what a minion of the Star Goddess cult wants with this boy. I thought you people normally recruited girls."

Star Goddess? thought the prince. He pictured the pale lady in his dream and wondered.

"How did you—"

"Oh, come now. If you don't want people to know, then you shouldn't display that tattoo in such a provocative place."

Hirci sat, pulling her legs beneath her. "Who I am and what I do are no concern of yours, whatever you are. Leave us and return to the netherworld you came from."

"I'm afraid I cannot do that," the wraith replied amiably, "until I know the boy is safe."

Abderian could not decide if the wizard was alive, or this was Dolus's ghost that spoke to them. The night had been so strange already, he could easily believe in ghosts.

"Then, interfering spirit, I shall have to see if you can be destroyed," Hirci said. Instantly, she lunged with her dagger.

Dolus dropped the lantern and there came a puff of black smoke that enveloped both of them.

"Now, Abderian, *run!*" yelled Dolus.

"But what about you?" cried the prince.

"I'll catch up to you later! I can't hold her long. Run!"

Wobbling to his feet, the prince scrambled out of the clearing. His leg muscles screamed at him as he stumbled blindly, trying to put the shouts from the clearing far behind him. It took so much concentration just to keep himself going, Abderian could pay little attention to where he was going. Before long he found himself lost in a landscape of dark, whispering trees and bright stars. Exhausted, he slid down a hillside and fell against a tree. He curled up among its roots, too tired to even stand. With a sigh he resolved to find his way in the morning.

EIGHT

STIFF AND ACHING, Abderian awoke under a large oak tree. A dim sun floated above the horizon. Slowly the prince sat up, unsure of where he was or how he got there. He felt damp, and, though the air was not cold, he shivered.

Whoever said sleeping outdoors is invigorating must have had rocks in his head, he thought. *I've got rocks in my shoes, burrs in my hose, twigs in my tunic, and leaves in my hair. I'm a walking crazynut bush.*

Suddenly there came a loud screeching and trilling from the branches overhead. "Shut up," grumbled Abderian.

"That's rather uncivil of you."

"What? Who's there?"

"I am," said a tiny brown bird with bright black eyes who sat on a bough above the prince. "You're sitting in my territory. I thought you might like to know that."

"Your territory? But—wait a moment . . . you can talk!"

"Of course I can talk. What kind of dummy do you take me for?"

"Well, I've never met a bird who could talk, that's all."

"Hmp. How many birds have you met?"

"I've seen many, but never one that could speak. So far as I know, you're the only talking bird in the kingdom."

"Is that so? Hmp. And I just thought all the other birds were snubbing me. You know, you look familiar somehow." The little bird regarded him this way and that, then hung upside down under the branch for a different perspective. "Are you sure we haven't met before?"

"Quite sure. I'd remember you if I had." Suddenly the prince had a chilling thought. "You . . . weren't by any chance sent by someone to find me, were you?"

"Nope. Came here on my very own."

Abderian sighed with relief and sagged back against the tree.

"Say, you look a little ragged there. What's wrong?"

"Well, for one thing, I'm lost."

"No, you're not! I just told you where you were. Listen:

> This tree is *my* tree,
> This place is *my* place,
> From the dismal Forest,
> To the lonely Highplace,
> From the dry brown hillsides,
> To the cold creek waters,
> This land is my territoreeeee!

"I'm afraid that's not very helpful," grumbled the prince, pulling his knees to his chest and resting his chin on them. Off to his left was a range of brown hills that he guessed were the same as those near Burdalane's camp. But as to which direction it might be, he had no idea. And the thought of wandering through those hills, risking another encounter with Hirci, was not at all appealing. A few yards to his right lay a path running roughly east/west. The east end seemed to go up into the hills. The west end led to the edge of a forest. Over the tops of the forest trees could be seen the jagged peaks of the mountains known as The Edge of the World, which marked the northern and eastern borders of the kingdom.

"My, you are a grump this morning. Anything else wrong?"

"I'm hungry."

"Hungry! How can you be hungry? There's plenty of food all around! Seeds, grubs, flies . . . and worms if you're early enough. A feast before your eyes!"

Abderian made a face. "You don't understand. I don't eat that sort of thing. I need meat, vegetables, fruit. A little ale might be nice."

"Meat?" The little bird's eyes widened and it backed up on the branch.

"Don't worry. I wouldn't eat you. You're too small for a meal, and besides, I couldn't catch you." Though he could have learned tracking and trapping from the castle huntsmen,

Abderian had never had much interest in the subject. He began to realize just how dependent he was on others. "I'll have to find some people who can give me food."

"Someone to give you food? Just a fledgling, are you?"

"Uh, you could say that."

"Did you just fall out of your nest?"

"In a way."

"Ah. That explains a lot. Though I'm sorry to hear it. Fledglings who fall out of their nests tend not to live long."

"Oh. Thanks."

The bird paced on the branch a moment. "Can you eat berries?"

"Yes, some kinds."

"Well, there's a berry bush over there by the stream. Maybe you can feed on that."

The prince got up, muscles stiff and protesting, and hobbled in the direction the bird indicated. Just a few yards from the tree he found a small creek with a redberry bush growing on its bank. Abderian greedily plucked berries off the bush and stuffed them into his mouth, wincing occasionally as a branch or thorn scratched his hand. After eating all the berries he could find, he lay down on the stream bank and slurped handfuls of clear cold water. Pausing, he noticed the little bird sitting in the berry bush, watching him.

"You certainly are a messy eater. But then, fledglings usually are."

Abderian grunted. His table manners had often been the brunt of jests at home. Even Paralian would pester him about it. With a pang he realized he missed even his brother's teasing.

The prince turned back to drink from the stream when he saw something shiny come bouncing and rolling down the stream bed. As it came level with him the prince reached in and pulled the object out. On a slender silver chain hung a pendant made of twisted silver wire. The wire mesh was oval-shaped, with glittering green stones caught within it.

"What is it?" said the little bird.

"I'm not sure. Looks like a piece of lady's jewelry." Abderian held it up so that the stones sparkled in the sunlight. "It's certainly pretty. Might be valuable."

"What's 'valuable'?"

"You know, worth a lot of money."

"What's money?"

"Oh, never mind." The prince slipped the chain over his head and tucked the pendant inside his tunic. "Perhaps I can trade it for some food somewhere."

"I know that some birds like to fill their nests with shiny things like that."

"Some people do too. Particularly wealthy ones. Speaking of people, could you tell me where I might find the nearest farm or village? I don't think those berries will hold me long."

"The nearest humans I know of, besides yourself, are Horaphthia and Maja. They live on the other side of that forest over there. Just follow this path and you'll find them."

"Horaphthia and Maja, eh? Well, many thanks, little bird. I guess I'll be on my way." Abderian stood and headed for the forest.

"Wait!" said the bird, hopping from bush to bush along the side of the path. "I ought to warn you about the forest. Something . . . unpleasant happens when you get inside."

"Oh? What is that?"

"Um . . . I forget. But be prepared for it. It's a nasty surprise."

Abderian couldn't help laughing. "How can I be prepared for it if I don't know what 'it' is?"

"Don't worry. You will find out soon enough."

The prince shook his head and sighed. "Very well. Goodbye, then. And good luck with your territory and all."

"Good luck to you, fledgling." The bird flew back to its oak tree and Abderian walked on.

After several twists and turns of the path, the prince came to the edge of the forest. It looked quiet, cool, and inviting, and not in the least bit dangerous. Knowing that looks could be deceiving, however, he stepped inside cautiously.

As the prince strode along the path he watched the trees and shadows warily, ready for any attack. But no attack came. In fact, the forest seemed extraordinarily peaceful.

Hmm, this isn't as bad as the little . . . the little . . . hmmm, whatever it was that warned me about this place said it was.

The prince walked on a ways, and the forest around him grew thick and dark, but still seemed benign. *I hope this, uh, place isn't too large. I'd like to find . . . to find . . .* He realized he couldn't remember who or what it was he was looking for.

*Drat, now, that's a bother. How am I going to get some . . .
some stuff to stop the growling coming from my . . . my, well,
that thing in my middle.* Abderian frowned and continued on,
trying to pull more out of his slumbering memory.

With a sudden shock that brought him to a standstill, the
prince realized he no longer knew who he was, or where he
was, or why he was here. He stood alone surrounded by the
dark unknown. There came a pounding in his chest and he
began to shake as fear surged through his blood. Something
caught in his throat and wetness ran from his eyes. He began
to run. Dark things slapped at him and tripped him and scratched
him. He flailed his arms ahead of him, not knowing what he
was doing or why, only knowing he was in the midst of something horrible that he must escape. Strange sounds came from
his throat, and his body could not stop moving, as if possessed
by a demon whose essence was fear.

He knew not how long he ran. But in time the dark grew
lighter and he found himself pounding against something hard
and vertical. It moved, and he was guided into a smoky darkness, where something soft and warm was thrown over him.
He curled up tightly and whimpered, and waited for the fear
to go away.

Some time later Abderian lay on a cot, staring up at a section
of ceiling where a board had broken and thatch was poking in.
"Roof," said the prince, enjoying the feel of the word on his
tongue, delighting in the knowledge that the word belonged to
the object he saw overhead—that he, therefore, knew what he
was looking at. He stretched luxuriously and enjoyed the word
some more. "Roof. Roof roof roof."

"What's wrong with him, Apu?" said a young female voice.
"Does he think he's a dog?"

"Hush, child," said an elderly female voice. "He's come
out of the Forest of Forgetfulness. Ye know how it does strange
things to one. Now, be off with ye to yer chores. I'll see after
our guest."

Feeling satisfied with the ceiling, Abderian expanded his
horizons to include the rest of the room. "Table," he said,
noting the rickety wooden trestle nearby. "Bench," he said,
upon seeing one. "Curtain," he sang, seeing a rotting fabric

that covered a doorway. "Hearth," he cried, seeing the cheery fireplace across the room. "Witch!" he said, seeing the old woman who approached him with a bowl in her hands.

The woman started and dropped the bowl with a clatter, spilling meaty broth all over the stone floor. She stared at the prince for a moment with wide dark eyes. "'Ere, now, I didn't bring ye in just to 'ear meself insulted."

"I'm sorry. I was just spouting words. I meant no insult." Although Abderian had to admit to himself that she certainly looked like a witch, he had no way of knowing if she was one. "Are you Horaphthia?"

She frowned, puckering her bushy eyebrows. "Who told ye t'call me by that name?" She ignored the cat that came out of a corner to lick up the spilled broth.

"A little bird told me."

"Tsk-kha!" She rolled her eyes and threw up her hands. "A wisemouth!"

"No, really—"

"Listen, laddie, I be kind to my guests, but I'll be taking no truck from a wise mouth, be ye noble or no."

"How do you know I'm a nobleman?"

"Tsch, by the cut o' yer clothes, boy," she said, stooping to pick up the bowl. "Lest ye be a foolish thief who's chosen to play the dandy. An' yer speech be too good for that." She shuffled back to the hearth and refilled the bowl from a pot hanging above the fire, crooning a song that either had a highly exotic melody or was dreadfully out of key. The firelight on her face made her craggy features seem like a sandstone carving by some maniacal sculptor.

If she isn't a witch, thought the prince, *she should be some artist's model for one.*

The old woman returned with the fresh serving of soup and placed it on the table. "Now, hereabouts they call me Apu. An' since we be gettin' acquainted, what might yer name be?"

Abderian opened his mouth to reply, but stopped, realizing he had no idea if "Apu" was trustworthy in any way. It occurred to the prince that it might not be wise to announce his identity to every stranger he met.

"Havin' trouble rememberin', are ye?"

Abderian nodded.

"Ah, well, that's to be expected. The forest can leave its

workings with ye for a while after ye leave it."

Grateful for the excuse to remain anonymous, Abderian asked, "Is the forest magical?"

"Magical? Of course it's magical. How d'ye think it got that way. Science?"

The prince thought back on his experience in the forest and suppressed a shudder. He wondered if all encounters with magic were so intense and terrifying. The Nightsword, the bullfrog of Castle Doom, and the events surrounding his cursemark certainly were. *Perhaps it's just as well I was never apprenticed to Dolus.*

"Aye, the forest's been around since Sagamore's reign," Apu was saying, "though it's grown bigger these few years past."

"Do you know a lot about magic, Apu?"

"No, an' I don't care to, thank ye. The forest's enough of a nuisance; I don't need more such things about. Now, ye should eat up and get yer rest. Ye been through rough places from the look o' ye. Yer memory should be returnin' soon, an' we can chat more then." She hobbled out the door and slammed it shut behind her, causing the hovel to shake like a temple dancer. Thatch rained down from the roof and wattle flaked off the walls.

"If I didn't know better, I'd say this place was held up by magic," the prince murmured. He got off the cot and went to the table. He began to dip into the thick broth when he felt something strange and itchy on his chest. Reaching into his tunic, the prince found the pendant he had discovered that morning, and he pulled it out. The gems in it seemed to emit a glow that was rapidly fading—or was it just the firelight? Abderian turned the pendant this way and that, but could see nothing else different about the object. He sighed and shook his head. *Now I'm imagining magic everywhere.* He tucked the pendant back into his tunic and hungrily tackled the rest of the broth.

 *NINE*

AN HOUR OR SO later Abderian sat before the fire, trying to decide what to do next. Could he somehow get back to Burdalane's camp? Would Dolus be able to find him here? The prince rested his head in his hands and stared at the dancing flames in the fireplace, letting his mind wander. He felt his head and eyelids grow heavier, yet disconnected, as if floating on the warm smoky air.

The bright orange flames grew more indistinct, then resolved into a barren landscape. Some part of the prince's mind realized he was seeing Euthymia as a wasted desert, its farmlands and hills parched and empty of life. He was floating over the dry land, seated upon a throne of brilliant gold. He sensed something heavy upon his head. Reaching up, the prince removed what he found to be an iron crown, whose tines were twisted like the gate to Castle Doom. Abderian placed the crown back on his head and looked around. Dark shapes writhed on the ground below him. After a moment the prince realized they were people, emaciated and burned by the sun, clothed in rags. They held up bowls to him, their sunken eyes pleading for food or water. Abderian felt swelling within him a horrible, twisted joy at the scene before him, and to his disgust and shock he heard himself laugh.

Then one of the people below him stood and looked at him, but the prince could not make out the person's face clearly. "Who are you?" this person said. "What is your name?"

The questions struck Abderian like a slap in the face. He felt challenged, betrayed, condemned. He opened his mouth to roar a retort, but what emerged was a wail of anguish and

63

fear. The prince wished with all his soul to be somewhere else. With a shudder he woke up.

"Didn't mean to startle you," someone said to his right.

"What? Oh, it's all right, I was just napping." Abderian rubbed his eyes. His skin felt hot, which disturbed him until he realized it was just from being near the fire. He looked to see who had spoken to him, and wondered if he was still dreaming.

Beside him stood a young girl, perhaps his own age, in a dress of stained green linen. But on her face was a mask made of feathers and tiny seashells that covered all of her face save for her mouth and chin. White quills lined the eyeholes, making her seem like a blend of owl and human.

"Are you . . . Maja?" Abderian asked, recalling the other name the bird had told him.

The girl took a step backward. "How did you know?"

"A little . . . that is, I heard from a friend."

"A friend? And who are you?" Her voice held an edge of suspicion.

"My name is . . ." Again caution made him hesitate. "Darien. Is Apu your grandmother?"

"Not exactly. How did you get into the forest, Darien?"

"I was lost. I had run away from home, you see, and I was hungry and I was told I'd find you and Horaph—I mean Apu here. I didn't know what the forest would do when I went through it."

Maja's eyes narrowed. "I see."

"Ah, getting acquainted, are we?" said Apu from the door.

"Apu! There you are!" said Maja. "I have to talk to you."

"So, talk," said Apu, shuffling into the hovel.

"Look at these beanstalks! They're all twisted in on themselves. Their flowers didn't even open today. The rest of the garden is ruined, too, and not just from the windstorm last night."

"Now, dearie, ye know we just have to weather through this drought."

"It's not just the drought, Apu. Other strange things are happening too."

"That's not uncommon in these parts, dearie."

Abderian disturbingly recalled his dream and placed his hand over the cursemark. "You don't suppose there's some magical cause, do you?"

"If there is," Maja murmured, "I know who's responsible."

Abderian's throat tightened, and he wondered if his foul reputation had come this far.

"Now, dearie, ye can't go blamin' all our troubles on one person. Could be all sorts of circumstances causin' this."

"You don't really believe that, do you?" Maja said softly. She crossed her arms and frowned. "Well, what are we going to do about dinner? We don't have enough to feed ourselves, let alone our 'guest.'"

"We'll just 'ave to kill old Matty, then."

"No! Not Matty!"

"Now, dearie, the old boy's past 'is time already."

"Who's Matty?" asked the prince.

"Shut up!" said Maja.

"If ye can't be civil, child, then be off with ye! Go to yer pallet, or be useful an' find us what greens ye can. An 'ost is duty-bound to serve 'is guest, noble guests in particular. Be off now!"

Maja glared at the prince, then stomped out through the curtained doorway.

Apu clicked her tongue and shook her head. "She's really a fine girl, ye know. But there's one she be fearin', an' though she 'ave reason, she be seein' 'is face behind every bush. Now, Matty, see, is our old goat. 'E's been sort of 'er pet for the past couple of years. But I've lived long enough to know that each thing 'as a time to go. An' if we need a feast, it's old Matty's time. Come along, lad. I might be needin' yer 'elp."

Abderian sadly followed the old woman out of the hovel. He knew what it was like to lose pets. He had once had a pet rabbit that his horse trampled—he still had rueful dreams about it.

As they walked around the outside of the hovel to the back, the prince asked, "Does she wear the mask because of the someone she fears?"

"Very perceptive, laddie. So she does."

"Well, she has no reason to fear *me*."

"Well, now, she don't know that, do she? Ye 'aven't exactly told us much about yerself, 'ave ye?"

"I'm sorry. I can't tell you much right now." He hoped she would think he meant the forest still affected him.

"Ah, 'ere be ol' Matty."

In a tangle of weeds an old brown goat stood tethered to a

stump. It looked up at them with patient dark eyes.

"Would ye like the 'onor of strikin' the killin' blow?" said Apu, handing the prince a cleaver.

"Er, no, thank you. I believe that hosts should always have the 'honor' of slaughtering their own goats. Besides, I, uh, have to answer a call of nature." He gave an embarrassed chuckle and dashed for the cover of the nearest bushes. He dared not admit that he had never killed anything in his life, except insects. And that pet rabbit.

"May the Great Dung Beetle spare me from squeamish noblemen," grumbled Apu. "Maja, come 'elp!"

As he tried to ignore the chopping sounds behind him, Abderian became aware of a warm itching on his chest again. He pulled the pendant out of his tunic. Again, the green stones seemed to have a glow that was fading. Or was it merely the way the sunlight struck the gems? The prince could not be sure.

As he replaced the pendant under his tunic, he heard Maja speaking to Apu. But when the old crone responded, her voice was different—lower and smoother, though still somewhat cracked with age. Most striking, though, was that she no longer spoke with the harsh accents of a peasant. Abderian moved closer, under cover, to listen.

"I just wish we could do something. He'll ruin the whole kingdom before he's through!" Maja said.

Abderian closed his eyes and sighed.

"Calm down, Maja. Until I regain my powers, there's nothing I can do except hide you. We must simply bide our time. Besides, I don't think your father is behind every unfortunate event."

Her father? thought the prince.

"What other wizard would do stuff like this? And what about that noble boy, Darien?"

"What of him?"

"He turns up out of nowhere, knowing our names and not telling us how he knows or where he comes from!"

"Keep your voice down, child. He might hear you. So, you think he's a spy for your father?"

"Don't you?"

"I am going to hold my judgment until I know more. Now, don't just stand there, help me with this."

Abderian decided it was time to return. He was eager to know who Maja's father was, but politesse demanded that he pretend not to have heard the conversation. Instead, he stood aside in discomfort as Maja and Apu worked over the poor beast.

Apu bundled up the meat, keeping the entrails and organs separate, while Maja dragged off the remains of the carcass, tears trickling out from beneath her mask. The smell of blood hung heavily in the air.

Feeling guilty for his lack of courage, he decided to make amends.

"Apu, I'm very grateful for your hospitality—killing your only goat for me and all—and I'd like to give you something in return."

"Eh? What?" Apu looked up from her work.

"I said, in thanks for your generosity, I would like to give you this." Abderian took off the pendant he wore and held it up for Apu.

The old woman's eyes fixed on the pendant as it glistened and sparkled in the late afternoon sunlight. "Where—where did ye find that?"

"In a stream just on the other side of the forest. Do you like it? If so, it's yours."

Her gnarled hand snatched the pendant out of Abderian's grasp and she held it up close to her face. Light beams danced off the gems and the silver, illuminating her sharp features in a pale green glow. Apu seemed transfixed by it, silently standing and staring.

Abderian felt a little uncomfortable with her reaction, but took it as acceptance and strolled back toward the hovel. Stopping by the bag of entrails, he turned and said, "You know, it's a shame you're not familiar with magic. You could take these and do a fortune reading to find out what's been causing your problems. The priests of the Lizard Goddess would often sacrifice lizards and spill them on the ground—well, never mind. It's a disgusting idea anyway."

"No. No, it isn't," said Apu, turning to face the prince. Her voice became smooth again, as it was during her earlier conversation with Maja. She seemed to stand a little straighter and her eyes held a strange light. "It is a very good idea. I think I shall do just that." Apu gave the prince a sly look and placed the pendant around her neck. She picked up the bag of entrails and carried it into an open area of the yard.

Just then Maja ran up. "Apu, what are you doing?"

"Back off, child. I'm going to do an oracular reading."

"But, Apu! We need those sweetbreads for sausage and stew. We can't waste them to make some mystic mess in the backyard."

Apu stopped and looked at Maja. "Where are your wits, child? When was the last time I could do a reading?"

"What? You mean you . . . oh, Apu!" Maja covered her mouth with her hand and obediently backed away.

Apu set the bag down in the middle of the yard and began to weave an odd dance around it, singing:

> Hocus, crocus, toad and newt,
> Cabbage, veg'tables and fruit,
> Show the source of all our trouble,
> That we might not have it double!

Then Apu spilled the contents of the bag on the ground. She stared at the result for some time, frowning. Maja coughed in disgust and walked away.

Abderian watched with a mixture of wonder and confusion. *So she truly is a witch.* Finally, unable to contain his curiosity any longer, he asked, "Well, what does it show? What does our fortune look like?"

Apu drew herself up and declared, "A bloody mess." At Abderian's look of bewilderment she laughed and added, "It's not the answer I expected either. Was there some particular question in your mind as I did this?"

Many questions, thought the prince. "Who is Maja's father?" he asked softly.

Apu laughed again. "I thought you might have been listening. Well, there has been some mix-up in our questions, or my skill has not yet fully returned. It would seem the oracle answers neither of us."

Then she turned and walked back into the hovel.

Abderian stood, uncertain what to make of Apu's words. He approached the pile of incarnadine slop to see if he could read anything there himself. Fighting nausea, he looked as close as he dared. He could swear that some pieces had fallen together to form the letters *O-N-Y-M* and, below that, some intestines twined in a familiar shape. He glanced at his right arm and saw that the shape indeed matched the cursemark. Then Maja came by with a broom. The mess was swept back into the bag and the illusion, if such it was, was broken.

"So, Darien," said Apu, serving him a heaping bowlful of hot goat broth, "has your memory returned yet?"

"Um, a little." Abderian noticed that Maja only picked at her food, fidgeting in her seat and staring at Apu. Hungry as he was, he did not want to appear too eager to dig into what was left of her pet. He took one gamy mouthful and decided it was just as well.

"Have you thought of where you'll be going from here, then?" Apu's voice was now melodious and confident, not cracking at all. And her hair seemed darker, and there were fewer lines and folds on her face.

"I'm not sure. I do not know of any safe place to go. I was hoping I could stay here awhile."

Maja glanced at him in alarm.

"I'm afraid that's not possible," said Apu.

"Why?"

"Because thanks to you, young man, I am now able to return to my tower and continue my life as before. And there are many things I must do."

"Then it's true!" gasped Maja. "You have your power back! Now we can go back to the castle and—"

"Correction, child. *I* can go back. You must find another place of safety. The situation is still far too dangerous for you."

"Apu!" Maja wailed, slamming her spoon down on the table.

"Yes, dear, I know. I'll admit you have courage and spirit, but you haven't the power to face your father again. Simple tricks will no longer work. He's ready for them. It's best if you just stay out of the matter for now."

"Could someone kindly tell me what this is about?" Abderian asked.

Apu looked at Maja, who was glaring at the prince. "Well, child, do you want him to know? It's your right."

"No."

Abderian pressed his lips together in frustration and stared down at his bowl.

"As you wish," Apu said. "Now, I advise you to go to your friends in the mountains and wait until I come for you."

"That's a day's hike up the mountains! Do I have to go alone?"

"No. You can take him with you." Apu nodded at Abderian.

"Him?" Maja's voice was pitched higher in fear. "Apu, please don't make me—"

"We do owe him something, child. And he has said he also has nowhere safe to go."

"Why do we owe him anything?"

"Because he gave me this." She held up the glittering pendant. "He has restored my powers to me. Whatever Darien may be, he is no agent of your father's. I believe you'll find him to be trustworthy enough."

"Your powers came from that? I thought they just returned naturally."

"You know your father would not leave such a thing to chance," said Apu, drawing a circle in the dust on the floor with her finger. "This is a Talisman of Minds-Keeping. He drained my powers into it, then threw it into the Forest of Forgetfulness, where our unfortunate wanderer here found it." She finished her drawing and straightened up. "I must go now. You two may use this cottage tonight. Before you leave in the morning, Maja, you are to destroy it as I have taught you, so your father cannot trace us. And do be kind to Darien, won't you? There's a girl. Good luck to you both." Suddenly there came a wind swirling around the inside of the hovel. Standing inside the circle she had drawn, Apu began to shimmer, then her image blurred into a smear of colors and she was gone.

TEN

"WHERE DID SHE go?" Abderian breathed as the dust settled.

"Home, I expect," Maja said tersely. "She has to restore her spells and . . ." She warily looked at the prince, then seemed to find something fascinating in the wood grain of the table and would say no more.

A long moment of awkward silence passed between them. "I wish you would trust me," Abderian said at last. "I'm not going to hurt you. I don't know who your father is, and I don't really care." This last was not quite true. He was curious about her father, but he hoped to reassure the girl.

Maja only gave him a brief glance in response.

"We seem to have much in common, you know. We're both in trouble with our fathers. Though my father isn't a wizard—"

"How did you—"

"I overheard you talking to Apu. It's nothing mystical. Anyway, we both seem to be having problems with magic."

"If your father isn't a wizard, what's your problem?"

"They all think *I* am one, or ought to be. Some fear me, and some want to control me. That's really all I should say."

"Is that what your cursemark is about?"

Abderian instinctively covered the mark on his arm and looked at Maja in surprise.

"No sense hiding it now. Apu mentioned it to me. Is your curse that everyone thinks you're a wizard?"

"I don't think it's that simple." After a pause he went on. "Maja, do you know who or what 'onym' is? *O-N-Y-M?*"

"Onym? I've heard it before. I think it's some wizard's name."

71

"Another wizard. Wonderful. I get the feeling there are too many wizards in my life."

"Same here. Only for me, one is too many."

"Oh? What kind of wizard trouble have *you* got?"

"I got in the way of one too often," Maja sighed. Slipping her hands under her mask, she rubbed her cheeks. "I hate this thing," she muttered.

"You can take it off, you know. It's not necessary anymore. Even if I was an agent of your father's, which I'm not, I already know who you are. Take it off if you feel like it."

Maja hesitated, and for a moment Abderian feared that perhaps she was hideously ugly and used her father only as an excuse to cover her appearance. Or perhaps she was a beautiful foreign princess in exile. Both possibilities flip-flopped in his mind as Maja slowly reached up to the cord that bound the mask to her head. She undid the knot quickly and in a moment the mask slipped from her face. She was neither ugly nor beautiful. She was, in fact, rather plain, though in a pretty sort of way.

"What's the matter? Haven't you ever seen a girl before?"

Abderian realized he was staring and shook his head abruptly. "No . . . I mean, yes. That is, you aren't what I expected."

"So what did you—oh, never mind. I don't think I want to know." Maja sighed and stood. "I'm going to get some sleep. We're going to have a tough climb tomorrow."

"Climb?"

"Up into the mountains to where my friends live. I hope you're in shape for it."

"Oh. Of course."

"Good. Because I don't intend to drag you. Good night."

"Good night."

Maja walked to the cloth partition, stopped, and turned. "If you try to even touch me—"

"I won't touch you!"

Maja nodded as if satisfied, then passed behind the curtain.

Abderian got up and went to the cot he woke up on earlier. With a sigh he stretched out, wondering how he could make Maja trust him. *Perhaps it will just take time.* He was glad, at least, that she was willing to help him at all.

He relaxed, letting the cool evening breeze from the window beside him flow over him. Soon he was eased into sleep by the chittering of crickets and the songs of distant birds.

He floated in a formless darkness, with no illumination. Yet he could see, below him, other creatures. One was the great white spider he had dreamed of before. Another was a dragonlet like the one that jumped out of his pie at that fateful dinner. The last was a lean black hound, fierce with hungry red eyes. Between the three animals something wriggled and squirmed. Abderian moved closer and saw that the writhing creature was himself.

In the next moment his viewpoint changed to that self surrounded by the spider, the dog, and the dragonlet. They were huge compared to him, and they loomed over him as if he were a fly. They each seemed to be trying to get to him, but each kept the others at bay. The prince felt certain that one would gain dominance at some point and grab him. It was just a matter of time. He wailed, longing for escape.

Suddenly Paralian's handsome face appeared before him, wearing the same look of sad concern as he had the night he left. Paralian pulled from nowhere a pair of wings and placed them on Abderian's back. He took Abderian's hand and pulled, and with a mighty flapping the two rose above the startled creatures, up and up. Feathers slapped Abderian's face, and with a shock he awoke.

Sitting on his chest was the little bird he had met outside the forest.

"Hello? Hello? Are you all right?" chirped the bird, fluttering his wings against Abderian's cheeks.

"Stop slapping me! Yes, I'm awake now."

"Good. You were making some awful noises for a while there."

"I was having a bad dream." The prince sat up. The pale light of dawn filled the window, and the air was very cool and moist. "What are you doing on this side of the forest?"

"I came to see how you were doing. I had this feeling you were in trouble. You're important, you know. I don't know why or for what, but I just know you are."

Abderian viewed this pronouncement with mixed feelings. Just how was he considered "important"?

The prince was about to ask when the little bird's head bobbed up. "Someone's coming!" The bird hopped out the window just as Maja stepped out of the curtained room.

She looked around, puzzled. "Who were you talking to?"

"Uh, myself. I often talk in my sleep I've been told."

"Do they also tell you that you speak in two different voices?"

"Uhhh . . ."

Suddenly the little bird flew back through the window, landing on the table near Maja. "He was talking to *me*, Maja. You are Maja, aren't you? You've removed the feathers from your face. Why? They were your loveliest feature!"

Maja had jumped back a little and regarded the bird with puzzlement. "Er, yes. I'm Maja. I took off the mask because I didn't need it anymore."

"Didn't need it! Since when does one not need feathers to help you fly and keep you warm?"

"Since I'm not a bird like you," Maja said as if talking to a small child. "How do you know my name?"

"I live around here. I've watched and listened to you and Horaphthia now and then."

"Why were you spying on us?"

"I wasn't spying! You're the only people around here, and I was lonesome for conversation. Other birds won't talk to me. I sent the fledgling here"—the bird pointed a wing at Abderian—"to you because you were the only people I knew."

"Oh." Maja looked at the prince with an unreadable expression, then looked back at the bird. "Why didn't you talk to us then?"

"I tried to speak with Horaphthia, but she would only shoo me away, saying she couldn't do anything for me. Do you know what she meant by that?"

"No. Do you have a name?"

"Name? I'm not sure. If I did, I've forgotten it. Say, fledgling, I forgot to tell you that's what the forest does. It makes you forget things."

"Thank you," the prince said dryly, "I discovered that."

"How about if I call you 'Brownie'?" Maja asked.

"That's not very descriptive," said the bird. "How about 'Swift-Winged-Singer-of-Bright-Songs, Who-Survived-the-Forgetful-Forest, and-Speaks-to-Humans'?"

"I'll stick with Brownie if you don't mind."

"Suit yourself."

"Well," Maja sighed, "as long as we're up already, we might as well prepare to leave. Do you want to come with us, Brownie?"

"Oh, no, thank you. I have a territory to keep and protect. But I do wish you luck. And you, fledgling."

Abderian nodded. "Thank you. My luck could use a turn for the better."

"May you have it, then." Brownie flew back out the window toward the forest.

Maja looked at Abderian and giggled behind her hand. "Fledgling?"

The prince shrugged. "So he calls me." Abderian stood up, stretching and yawning. "I take it you don't think 'Brownie' was sent by your father?"

"No," Maja said, eyes focused somewhere beyond the window. "The bird is too cute for my father to have anything to do with him. My father hates cute things. Come on. Let's get ready to go."

An hour or so later Abderian stood some yards from the hovel, blinking in the morning sunlight. He shifted the pack on his back, which contained some dried remnants of old Matty and a waterskin, and waited.

Suddenly Maja came running out of the hovel. She came up to the prince breathlessly and turned to look behind her. They both watched as the ramshackle hut glowed with blue light that became more and more intense, until the house disappeared in a bright burst of blue. When the light subsided, nothing was left of the hovel, not even the foundation stones. Only a bare patch of greensward remained.

"What did you do?" asked the prince. "And why?"

"I merely completed a spell Horaphthia set up long ago. This is so my father cannot trace her or me to this place if he tries. It's just a precaution. Let's go."

They headed northwest along the road, which soon narrowed to little more than a footpath as it wound up the foothills of The Edge. The prince felt a sense of freedom as he walked, breathing the fresh mountain air. He almost forgot his troubles for a time.

Maja did not speak to him much, but Abderian did not feel snubbed. Instead, there was a curious, comfortable companionship in the quiet they shared. And now and then Maja would give him an awkward little smile that said more than words.

By the time the setting sun touched the westmost peaks of

The Edge, the path had disappeared altogether and Abderian and Maja were clambering wearily over bare rock.

"It's around here somewhere," said Maja, scrambling over large granite boulders.

"What is?"

"The entrance."

"Entrance? What should it look like?"

"A big hole in the mountain, mostly. I thought it was right here."

"What's all this noise?" piped a strange voice. A tiny man with a burly beard, wearing rough clothes and a pointed cap came out from behind a rock.

Abderian pointed and exclaimed, "It's a dwarf!"

The little man frowned and said, "So I am. You needn't make an issue of it."

Maja jumped down from a rock ledge above them. "There you are, Nani. Hello!"

"Ah! Lady Maja! Greetings." The little man bowed very low. "It has been a long time since you graced us with your presence."

"Lady Maja?" Abderian stared at her. She smirked back.

"May I ask the name of your . . . companion, My Lady?"

"Oh, this is Darien."

"'Darien,' eh?" said the dwarf, scratching his beard. Then his eyes widened. "Ah, you mean 'Darien' as in Prince Ab-Darien, King Valgus's son?"

"Prince?" Maja exclaimed. She stared at Abderian, then dropped into a curtsy.

"Uh, that's not necessary, really," Abderian stammered. "No one makes a fuss over me at home. No reason why you should."

"Your Highness." Nani nodded deferentially. "We have had an avalanche of visitors lately. Ordinarily we would not welcome more. But the Lady Maja is always welcome. And there are people who await you inside, Your Highness, so you are somewhat expected. Follow me, if you please."

People who await me? thought the prince. *Friend or foe?*

As the tiny figure led them through a maze of boulders, Abderian became more worried that he was walking into a trap.

"What's wrong?" Maja asked him.

"Nothing, I hope. We'll see."

They turned another bend and abruptly came upon a dark opening in the mountainside. It was a tunnel, cool and damp, that widened as it wound down into the mountain, eventually opening into an enormous cavern.

Abderian's jaw dropped in surprise. He had heard stories that dwarves lived in dark, horrible caves . . . stories that did not at all prepare him for the reality. This cavern was airy and filled with light that came in through narrow shafts in the ceiling. Delicate stalactites glistened in the light beams. Along the walls were natural stone shelves on which grew brightly hued plants. Their flowers gave a sweet smell to the air. Tiny waterfalls ran here and there between the plants, filling the room with their soft music.

"It's beautiful!" Abderian sighed.

"Letting the place run down a bit, aren't you?" said Maja.

"Well, we've been a bit busy lately, My Lady. Since you both seem road-weary, I will see you are provided with refreshment."

"Thank you again for your hospitality," said Abderian, looking warily around for some sign of his father's guards or Tingalut's priests. "Er, where are the people who have been awaiting me?"

"I shall inform them you are here. I'm sure they'll be along shortly. They seemed most eager to find you." The dwarf bustled away, leaving the prince not at all reassured.

He turned to Maja, but found her almost hidden among a throng of joyous little people smiling and calling her name. They guided Maja to a table on a terrace overlooking the cavern, Abderian tagging along behind and being largely ignored. They were soon brought mugs of a fruity juice that did much to wash the dust from the prince's mouth.

As Maja chatted with the dwarfs, renewing acquaintances, the prince turned his attention to the rest of the cavern. There were little people everywhere, involved with the humdrum activities of everyday life. Some were entering the far end of the cavern carrying bushel baskets full of fruit and grain. Others carried water buckets in and out of the great hall. Still others sat on a stone platform below, spinning, dyeing, and weaving.

Then, across the room, Abderian noticed a tawny-haired giant stride in. "Burdalane!" the prince cried, jumping up from his seat, startling the small folk beside him.

"Your Highness!" responded the commander as he bounded across the cavern toward the prince. Burdalane reached their terrace quickly and pulled the prince into a great bear hug. "We had hoped beyond hope that you would still be alive and well. We searched for you these past two days and feared the worst when we found no trace of you."

"That warrior woman, Hirci, kidnapped me."

"We know."

"You do?"

"Ahem," said Maja.

"Oh. Excuse me. Burdalane, allow me to present the Lady Maja. Lady Maja, this is Lord Burdalane, Commander of the Royal Armed Forces, and my cousin."

Maja curtsied as best she could in the simple raggedy dress. Burdalane raised an eyebrow, but kissed her hand in greeting nonetheless. Abderian watched as Maja's eyes roamed lingeringly over Burdalane's handsome features, and the prince found that it bothered him. And the fact that it bothered him bothered him. "Er, about Hirci . . ."

"Ah, yes, well—" began Burdalane. Just then a now familiar song came blaring up from below, sung in a voice resembling an out-of-tune hunting horn:

King Thalion's sword earned him worldwide reknown,
It shone near as bright as the King's golden crown.
Imagine how maids of his court watched with dread,
As he gave his sword to his jester instead!

Looking over the low terrace wall, Abderian saw the warrior woman walk unsteadily up the steps to the terrace. On either side of her walked a wary, muscular dwarf armed with a sword. Hirci carried a wooden tankard that spilled wine whenever she gestured. As she came up to Commander Burdalane, she saluted with the tankard, spilling more over anyone near her. "Swordswoman Hirshi reporting as ordered, shir," she slurred.

"You're a disgrace," rumbled Burdalane.

"Well, I seem to have fallen out of your grace, Your Grace." She turned to the prince. "Ah, we meet again, Your Highnesh." Hirci bowed dramatically.

"Who is this . . . person?" Maja asked.

Hirci gasped and stared at the girl. "Is this . . . is this the Lady Maja?" She fell into a one-kneed bow before her.

As Hirci gazed up at Maja, Abderian noticed an unsettling fervor in the warrior woman's eyes.

"I am rewarded," Hirci said softly.

Maja took a step backward, retreating from Hirci's gaze.

"Leave us, Hirci," said Burdalane, taking her by the arm, and pulled her to her feet.

With a second sloppy salute to her commander, Hirci allowed the dwarfs to lead her away. Her eyes were still shining as she swayed down the stairs, and Abderian had the unsettling feeling it was not entirely due to the wine.

"My apologies, Your Highness," said Burdalane. "And to you, My Lady. We brought Hirci here because we did not deem it wise to let her go free. Dolus brought her back to me and—"

"Dolus? Dolus is here?"

"Why, yes. He . . . ah, here he comes."

Approaching them was a handsome middle-aged man with shoulder-length black hair, wearing a robe of deep blue. As the wizard reached the terrace the prince rushed up to him and hugged him hard.

"Easy, lad, you're crushing the velvet."

"Dolus, I thought you were dead!" Hearing a throaty noise behind him, Abderian turned, assuming Maja wanted to be introduced again. Instead, he saw her face go pale and her eyes stare in horror. She was shaking and her fists were clenched. "Maja?"

"You liar!" she screamed at the prince. "You were sent to betray me after all!"

ELEVEN

NANI AND ANOTHER dwarf rushed up to the terrace.

"How could you?" Maja screamed at them. "What did he offer you for my life?"

Nani grabbed Maja's arms. "It isn't *him*, Maja! Truly! He merely looks like him."

Abderian frowned at Maja in confused surprise. "Maja, this is Dolus. He was the court wizard at Castle Mamelon. He won't hurt you, honest."

Maja walked up to Dolus slowly and looked hard at his face. "Oh," she said. And "Oh" again. "I—I'm sorry. I thought . . . Please, excuse me." Covering her face with her hands, Maja ran from the terrace with concerned dwarfs trotting after her.

"What was that all about, I wonder," said Burdalane.

Dolus looked thoughtful. "I regret that I may have distressed the girl. Who is she, lad?"

"I met her near the Forest of Forgetfulness, where she was living with a witch. You must, somehow, resemble her father, whom she's very much afraid of. What disguise are you in now?"

"I had thought," Dolus said, looking down at himself a moment, "that this was my natural appearance. I am 'in disguise,' as it were, as myself."

"Ah, very clever," said the prince. "But tell me, how did you get away from the bullfrog? How did you find me? What's happening at Castle Mamelon?"

"One thing at a time, m'boy," chuckled Dolus. "And first things first. First, I want to sit down." Dolus sat at the table, and Abderian and Burdalane joined him.

"Now, as to the bullfrog," Dolus continued, "I was rescued, in a way."

"By one of your friendly demons?"

"By a very unfriendly Captain Maduro, who had the unfortunate good fortune to find the map of Castle Doom in my chambers."

"But he did rescue you."

"Aye, only to march me into a dungeon cell on charges of kidnapping and treason, and to serve his guardsmen frog legs for supper."

"Oh. So how did you escape?"

"Patience, lad, I'll get to that. That very night I was brought before King Valgus to be tried for treason. Naturally I was found guilty—you know your father's temper—and I believe I would have been executed immediately, had Tingalut not interceded on my behalf."

"Tingalut? He wanted to help you?"

"Alas, hardly. He merely wished to carry out the sentence himself. He was quite upset that I had let you slip from his grasp. And he had ... other reasons. I was taken to the temple and lashed to the floor, in the midst of one of their Great Patterns. I shall not go into detail, but say only that I was then stripped of my magical power ... slowly and painfully."

Abderian felt his stomach tighten. "They stripped your power away? I didn't know that was possible. You mean ... you are no longer a wizard?"

"Well, I retain the knowledge. But my actual power ... But this is not the time or place for a lengthy discourse on magic. It was to my good fortune that the magic of the Lizard Goddess priests is based upon laborious ritual. Before they could bring the spell to its fatal conclusion, the demons I had unleashed from Castle Doom flew in and rescued me, carrying me out to the hills. In gratitude I released the demons from their bond. This means that Castle Mamelon is now without protection from Castle Doom." Dolus chuckled. "A pity I had to leave. It would be interesting to see how the lizard worshippers will handle *that*."

Abderian felt mixed emotions. He was pleased to see Dolus alive, yet at the cost of his magical power ... a fate the prince imagined to be worse than death. "Dolus, I'm sorry. I feel responsible—"

"Do not trouble yourself, lad. The way things were going,

a falling-out between myself and the king was inevitable. And I still have a few tricks up my sleeve."

"You mean like the smoke spell you cast when you rescued me from Hirci? You made a wonderful wraith, by the way. I half-believed you were dead myself."

Dolus bowed his head with a wry smile. "You do my meager acting abilities credit, lad."

"What happened after I ran away?"

"With a lucky blow I managed to stun her long enough to drag her back to Burdalane's camp."

The commander took up the story. "The next morning Captain Maduro rode in with two castle guardsmen and two priests of the temple, seeking you. I was able to truthfully tell him you weren't there, but they were suspicious. The captain implied that if I spoke falsely, I could be tried for treason. I promised him I would do all I could to find you."

"But you can't take me back—"

"Fear not, cousin. With things as they are now I would not take you back. My main concern is your safety, even though I will be called traitor and lose my command."

Abderian stared down at his shoes. *Dolus has lost his magic and Burdalane has lost his position . . . because of me.* He was sure there was nothing he could do to make up for their loss. Guilt settled over him, crushing what joy he had felt upon seeing them again. He wished he had some paper so that he could write a suicide note.

His dark mood was interrupted by a voice at his shoulder.

"Excuse me, gentlemen," said Nani, "but evening meal is about to be served. Would you care to proceed to the table?"

At the far end of the cavern Abderian saw long tables being set with dishes and cutlery. Dwarfs streamed in carrying chairs and bowls of food.

Burdalane put his arm across the prince's shoulders. "Do not be so distressed, Abderian. Worse fates might have befallen Dolus or me. It truly is not your fault."

"At least," said Dolus, "not directly."

Abderian gave the wizard a puzzled frown, but Dolus said nothing more.

They were guided to the central table, at one end of which had been placed an elaborately carved chair. "For the Lady," said Nani. "Ah, there she is!"

Abderian turned to see that Maja had indeed rejoined them. At least he guessed it was Maja. Her hair was tied back in a severe bun, and she wore a gown of startlingly pink velvet. Colored powders had been applied to her face, and she reeked of flower-scented oils. She reminded Abderian of one of his sister's much-abused dolls. Although she carried it off with a certain elegance, the prince decided he preferred her in rags.

Maja gave the prince a small curtsy. Then she turned to Dolus and said, "Please excuse my earlier outburst, sir. I have had reason to be worried lately, and I fear I—"

"It is all right, my dear. Abderian explained it to me."

Maja glanced a moment at the prince, then took her seat. Abderian sat to her right, Burdalane to her left, and Dolus sat next to Burdalane. Abderian briefly wondered if the wizard had deliberately chosen to sit just far enough away that conversation with him during dinner would be awkward. The prince's mind was still filled with questions, but each one seemed to carry a banner warning: "Beware how you ask me. I'm dangerous."

Platters piled high with mysterious mixtures (some of which looked edible) arrived at the table. To Abderian's amazement, there was no grabbing, pushing, or shoving for the food, even in jest. The gentility of the meal was quite a contrast with what he had been accustomed to at Castle Mamelon. There, one could expect food to fly at the slightest insult; eating utensils were strictly optional; one's napkin was one's sleeve; and the sound level rarely dipped below a dull roar. These little folk behaved with such grace that the prince felt oafish and out of place. Even his fork—which seemed to have been made for smaller hands—kept slipping within his grasp.

He did have one consolation—he wasn't having trouble with his chair. It was just a bit narrower than what he was used to and lower to the ground, but he could manage. Burdalane, on the other hand, seemed to be experiencing considerable discomfort.

"Are you all right?" said a lovely little lady across the table from the commander. "Is there some problem?"

"Oh, no." Burdalane smiled heroically. "All is quite well."

Maja rewarded Burdalane with a smile of her own that made Abderian instantly jealous. He turned his back on her and attempted conversation with Nani, who sat at his right.

"Excuse me, sir, but I've understood that dwarves are magical. Yet I've seen no sign of real magic since I've been here. Is—"

Nani was shaking his head. "Well, that's just it, don't you see?"

"What? No, I don't."

"You spoke of 'dwarves.' Those are mythical, magical people of great power. They also don't exist. We are 'dwarfs,' just little people. Oh, there was some small magic involved in the formation of this particular group of us. But other than that . . ." Nani shrugged and returned to his meal.

Eventually the dishes were emptied and the plates cleared away. An expectant hush fell in the great cavern. At the opposite end of Abderian's table a pot-bellied dwarf with receding hairline and keen eyes stood and surveyed the room.

"That," Nani said with quiet respect, "is our mayor, Lord Undertall."

"My lords, ladies, and gentle guests," began the mayor, "it is with utmost joy that I welcome back into our midst our one-time savior and forever friend, the Lady Maja!"

At this there came applause. Maja smiled and nodded in acknowledgment.

Abderian wondered from what this brusque girl could have saved the dwarfs, or how she came by the title 'Lady.' Was it a reward bestowed upon her by these people, or was she born to it?

"—and, of course, we welcome those other guests with her. And now," Lord Undertall went on, "we sing!"

Cheers greeted this announcement and a smile lit up every small face in the cavern. Wineglasses and carafes of golden liquid were passed among the tables. This turned out to be a sweet, fruity wine the dwarfs drank with relish, but Abderian found too cloying for his taste. He would have preferred a mug of strong ale, such as was served at Castle Mamelon. To his surprise, he felt a pang of homesickness.

At the direction of Lord Undertall, the singing began:

> Though men have told of caves of gold,
>   and mountains far away,
> Though heroes die and soldiers cry,
>   "Once more into the fray!"

> Though fools may tread, with bowl and bread,
>> where ne'er an angel dares,
> Let's raise a cup and drink it up
>> and rightly say, "Who cares?"

(Here, the crowd echoed in chorus "And rightly say 'Who cares?'")

> Though dragons roar in tales of yore,
>> and maidens lose their heads,
> Though elves and sprites and barrow-wights
>> steal children from their beds,
> Though treasures gleam and dark gods dream
>> of sacrificial glut,
> Let's drink a toast to Vespin's ghost
>> and loudly cry, "So what?"
> ("And loudly cry, 'So what?'")

This went on for several more verses, finally ending with:

> Though mermaids swim through oceans dim,
>> and monsters haunt the sea,
> Though hydras hiss and vampires kiss,
>> it's all the same to me.
> Though dead gods wake and mortals take
>> their turn at Fortune's Wheel,
> We'll just snore, or sing some more,
>> as we all cry, "Big deal!"

The song ended amid cheers and applause, and calls for other songs. Lord Undertall smiled and bowed. "My thanks, friends. But I should not hog the stage myself. I think I should ask . . . Kanti, why don't you step forward and lead us in a song or two?"

A younger, red-haired dwarf sprang from his seat and went to the end of his table. Raising his arms dramatically, he shouted out a song title, and the room was filled with another spirited tune.

Abderian didn't get much of a chance to hear it, however. For just after Lord Undertall made Kanti song leader, the mayor came around to Dolus and Burdalane and tapped their shoul-

ders. Burdalane then looked at the prince and gestured for him
to follow. As Maja watched with a puzzled frown Abderian
joined Dolus, who had also stood to leave.

"What's going on?" asked the prince in a loud whisper.

"No doubt you've felt you deserve some explanation of how
matters stand. There is news you should hear."

"I fear it's time to speak of darker things, cousin," said
Burdalane.

Maja looked questioningly at them.

Dolus shrugged and smiled at her. "Cats in the coal cellar
at midnight. Things like that, you know."

Maja frowned and turned away.

As Lord Undertall led the prince, Dolus, and Burdalane
toward a side passage off of the main chamber, the commander
said, "Just a moment, Lord Mayor. I wish to check up on
Hirci."

"Certainly, Lord Burdalane. I believe she's over here." The
mayor led them back toward the terrace where, in an alcove
in the cavern wall, the warrior woman lay sprawled between
her two guardian dwarfs. She was snoring loudly.

"Dead drunk," said one of the guardians with a smirk. "I
don't think she'll give us any trouble."

Burdalane nodded in satisfaction.

"Now, this way, if you please," said Lord Undertall.

He led Abderian, Burdalane, and Dolus to a room that might
have been a library in any lord's mansion. At the far end of
the room was a fireplace ornately carved out of the rock, in
which burned a small fire. Books lined low shelves that were
also carved from the rock. A multicolored rug lay on the floor.
Were it not for the fact that there were no windows, Abderian
could easily believe this room was in a house aboveground.

Five small, cushioned chairs were arranged around the fireplace, and Lord Undertall motioned for them to sit. Abderian
had no trouble finding one he could fit in if he stretched his
legs out. Dolus and Burdalane, however, had learned their
lesson. Removing the cushions from two chairs, they sat on
the floor.

Lord Undertall shut the thick oak door, saying, "I trust this
room should be private enough." The mayor sat in the chair
nearest the fire, an earthenware mug in one hand and a briar
pipe in the other.

Abderian looked at his friends expectantly. "Well?"

"Burdalane, do you care to tell the lad?" said Dolus.

"I would rather, good wizard, that he hear this news from you."

Dolus sighed. "Abderian . . . the diners are dressed in black."

TWELVE

ABDERIAN'S BREATH CAUGHT in his throat as he remembered the dining hall ceiling on the day Paralian's death was announced. The mannikins had been draped in black velvet, and the seat directly above where Paralian had always sat had been empty. "Who is dead?" the prince asked when he found his voice.

Burdalane said, "Your father, King Valgus, may he rest in peace."

Lord Undertall slowly lowered his briar pipe. "Indeed?"

The prince stared at Burdalane, then looked to Dolus, who nodded in confirmation. He looked back at Burdalane. "You're . . . certain?"

"We did not see it with our own eyes, but we received word from the Lady Chevaline this morning. And I believe her word can be trusted."

Abderian stared at the fire. He felt no grief, only shock and surprise. He had never felt close to his father, but now it seemed a keystone had fallen from the structure of his life. "How did it happen?"

Burdalane cleared his throat. "Apparently your father was ascending the steps to his tower chambers when he stepped upon a wheeled toy belonging to your sister Amusia. This caused him to slip and fall down the stairs, breaking his neck."

Abderian felt cold at the pit of his stomach. "Then . . . it was an accident?"

"Well, that is an interesting question," said Dolus. "At first glance it seems so. But Captain Maduro is convinced it was murder."

"Murder!"

"And regrettably, according to Lady Chevaline, the nobility at court is not discouraging his view. One duke is claiming that, since it was Amusia's toy that brought the king down, she has played 'the prettiest trick.' Therefore, because of your family's peculiar ideas regarding succession, she has rightful claim to the throne."

"With the duke to act as her regent until she comes of age, of course," added Burdalane.

"That's not being taken seriously, is it?"

Dolus shrugged. "After Paralian died, your father did not designate a new heir. So I suppose all claims must be considered."

If Paralian were still alive, thought the prince, *there would be no question. After all, he bore the* . . . Abderian looked at his arm. "I now bear the Mark of Sagamore," he murmured. He looked up at Dolus. "Is there anyone—"

"Supporting you as rightful heir? Interesting that you ask. Yes, one group is throwing the court into turmoil by putting forth your claim."

"Who?"

"The Temple of the Lizard Goddess, of course."

Abderian swore and stared at the rug.

"And they are leaning heavily on the belief that the Mark of Sagamore indicates the rightful king."

Lord Undertall looked up and glanced at the mark on the prince's arm. His mouth tightened into a smirk and he settled back into his seat, saying nothing.

"Queen Pleonexia is supporting Prince Cyprian, citing the standard rule of primogeniture as basis for his claim. Were it not for the temple's bid, I'm sure Cyprian's claim would not be seriously questioned."

"So if I were to go home now, I would only cause more trouble."

"For yourself as well as for the kingdom, I'm afraid. Maduro believes there is a conspiracy between you, Tingalut, and myself to place you on the throne. He may have gotten this idea from Valgus himself. Should he convince the Council of Lords of this, you might find yourself returning to a dungeon cell and a death sentence."

"Has Tingalut been arrested?"

"There's another odd thing. Tingalut has disappeared. Perhaps he fears Maduro's wrath, or perhaps he is searching for you. His minions at the temple aren't saying."

"Might Captain Maduro already have carried out a private execution?"

Burdalane answered, "Maduro may be ardent in doing his duty, cousin, but he is not rash."

Dolus went on. "It's likely the priest is biding his time, perhaps setting up a major enchantment. They were carving extensive new patterns into the temple floor as I was tormented there. I believe their intent was to place my power within these patterns. That would be necessary only for a spell of grand scale. If you return, Abderian, that may be the trigger for them to unleash their enormous power upon the kingdom."

Abderian stared into the fire, recalling the dream where he sat on a golden throne, king of a blighted wasteland. Was it a foreshadowing of Tingalut's plans for him? "What should I do?"

Burdalane said, "My main concern is keeping us all alive. And my advice to you is to ask Lord Undertall for asylum here."

Suddenly Dolus tapped Burdalane's shoulder and put a finger of silence to his lips. The wizard got up and glided to the door. Grasping the handle firmly, Dolus yanked the door open, and a fluffy pink bundle tumbled in.

"I was just walking by!" said Maja, picking herself up off the floor.

"And the door reached out and grabbed you, eh?"

"Dear Lady," said Lord Undertall, "had I known you wished to join us, I would certainly have invited you. You need only to have asked."

Dolus frowned. "My Lord Mayor, we did ask that this be private—"

"Yes, of course, but we hold the Lady Maja in high esteem here. She is quite trustworthy, I can assure you. If it is her wish, I have no objection to her remaining."

"I still would like to know why the Lady is interested in our affairs."

Maja gave a little shrug. "I was . . . just curious as to why a prince, particularly of Sagamore's kin, should be wandering by himself. And why he would be asking help from me and my friends."

Lord Undertall chuckled. "Isn't it obvious? She likes the boy!"

Abderian looked down, feeling awkward. Despite the dubious expressions of Dolus and Burdalane, Maja sat in the chair nearest Abderian.

Burdalane cleared his throat and continued. "As I was saying, Abderian, you should ask for asylum here until you are certain it is safe to return to Castle Mamelon. Though I fear you must accept the fact that it may never be."

Conspirator. Renegade. Exile. He stared down at his right arm. *All on account of this cursemark. How I wish Paralian had not given it to me. '. . . I must lay a heavy burden upon you,' he had said.* Abderian wondered if Paralian had known just how heavy it would be.

If only I could find out more about it—there's a chance I could be rid of it. Looking at the mark, he saw again in his mind's eye the letters written in goat's entrails back at Apu's hovel.

"What was that, Abderian?" said Burdalane.

"What? Oh, I was just remembering something I saw in an oracle. The word *onym*. I was wondering what it was."

"Onym?" said Lord Undertall. "Faugh!" He threw his mug into the fireplace, where it shattered among the flames. "That for Onym, may he rot in Earthfire forever!"

Maja looked at the mayor. "That's who Onym is! I knew the name was familiar."

"You know who Onym is, then!" the prince said to the mayor. "If it would not cause offense, could you please tell me?"

"No, I don't mind. Although I'm surprised a kinsman of Sagamore hasn't heard the name."

"Much knowledge of his time has been lost," Dolus explained. "Some of it, it is said, was destroyed by Sagamore himself in the madness before his death."

"I'm not surprised," said the mayor. "At any rate, Onym was the court wizard to King Sagamore, and to King Thalion before him. The reason I cursed him is that Onym is directly responsible for our little community here." He chuckled at some private jest.

"Why should that be a reason to curse him?" asked the prince.

"As you recall, my lad, Sagamore was the Jester King."

"Yes, of course."

"And what often appears by the side of a jester at court?"

"Um . . . a dwarf?"

"Quite right, my lad. But dwarfs, you see, are in nature quite rare. And Sagamore saw that there might be a time when his court, or that of his descendants, might be, Goddess forbid, dwarfless! So what do you think he did?"

"I don't know, sir," said Abderian, fearing that he did know.

"Come now, you seem a brighter lad than that. Good King Sagamore had his trusty wizard, Onym, curse a village so that all the villagers' offspring would be dwarfs. And, of course, all their offsprings' descendants as well. This way, no castle would ever lack for a dwarf. Wasn't that clever of him?"

"And if . . . he had not cursed that village," Abderian said tentatively, "you and all your people would have been born . . . normal-sized?"

"Ah, there now! I knew you had some wit about you. But then, you should, being Sagamore's kin."

Abderian nearly winced at the bitterness in the mayor's voice. Suddenly he understood why he had not been given a grander welcome here. He was lucky he had received any welcome at all.

"Of course, we weren't the only jolly idea Sagamore had. There was that forest you passed through, for example. That was Onym's handiwork as well."

"And Castle Doom . . ." Abderian added looking at Dolus. Suddenly the prince felt embarrassed at the admiration he had so openly expressed for his great-grandsire. He looked again at the cursemark. "Is it possible that Onym cast this curse?"

"Well," said the mayor, "that's harder to say, although I wouldn't put it past him. If that is indeed Sagamore's curse, then it is the same that afflicted the Jester King himself."

"Can you tell me anything about what it means or does?"

"Sorry. It must have been a private jest between Sagamore and Onym. Wait, there may be one record of it." The mayor got up and walked to a shelf filled with vellum-bound manuscripts. He searched among them for a moment, then pulled one down. "Here we are. *Ye Memoirs of Master Gromli, Dwarf to Ye Court of His Majesty Kinge Sagamore, Containing Ye Collected Wit and Wisdom Thereof*. Snappy title, eh? Makes marvelous midnight reading. Let's see, I seem to recollect a passage in here..." Some moments passed as he flipped and scanned pages. "Ah! This is it. '... and then His Majesty cried out in great sorrow, "Oh, woe betide me for I am yet beset with this curse. Though I have begged my Onym to strike it from my arm, yet he will not do so. How long will I, my kin, and my kingdom suffer this curse! Hmm. I'm sorry, lad, that's all that he says about it. Although here's another interesting thing I'd forgotten: Apparently it was shortly after this outburst that Onym left Sagamore's court forever. Perhaps the wizard was banished for his stubbornness."

Abderian sighed. "I wish he were still around. I could ask him myself."

With a chuckle Burdalane said, "It has been nearly a century since Sagamore's time, cousin. The wizard is surely only dust in a tomb by now."

"Not necessarily," Dolus put in. "We wizards tend to be vain and like to preserve our lives when we can. Lifespans of two hundred years are not unknown among us. It is possible this Onym may yet live."

Abderian's eyes widened, hope rising again. "You mean— if I could find him, I could—"

"'Twas unfair of you, Dolus," said Burdalane. "See how you have cruelly raised the boy's hopes."

"It's not cruel!" Abderian cried. "It's the best news I've heard yet. Think what good it would do the kingdom if I could get this curse lifted!"

"But you don't even know where to look for him," said Dolus. "And even if you did... if Onym would not remove this curse for Sagamore, what makes you think he would do so for you?"

Abderian paused and looked at his hands. "I have to try."

"If you want to find this wizard of Sagamore," said Maja, "I think I know where you might find a clue."

Lord Undertall's mouth dropped open and he slowly closed the book in his hands. "Of course! I should have thought of that."

"Where?" asked the prince.

"Not far from here," she said. "In Castle Nikhedonia."

"Of course," said Lord Undertall. "Sagamore took that residence after Thalion's death, and lived there until Castle Mamelon was built."

"I may even know where this wizard's study was," Maja

went on. "If nothing else, you could learn more about your curse there."

"Wonderful!" said Abderian. "When can we go?"

"One moment," said Dolus, his eyes narrowing suddenly. He got up and slowly walked toward Maja's chair. "My Lady, I have a brother, a twin, who is named Javel. Some twenty years ago we parted company—I to serve at Castle Mamelon, he to study wizardry on his own. Shortly after that time he was given a small fief in this region of the kingdom. And his seat was to be... Nikhedonia." By this time Dolus had moved behind Maja's chair. She stared at the floor, saying nothing. Placing his hands on Maja's shoulders, Dolus continued. "How is it, My Lady, that you know the location of a wizard's study within that castle? And what is it you see in my face that causes you such terror?"

Softly Maja replied, "Castle Nikhedonia used to be my home. And Lord Javel... is my father."

"It still is not safe for you to go home again, is it, My Lady?" said the mayor.

"Not yet. Though it may be soon."

"I'm sorry," Undertall went on. "Shall I explain to the others?"

Maja nodded.

"You see, Maja's father had no greater love for the remnants of Sagamore's humor than we do. But instead of merely living with it and cursing it, Lord Javel chose to destroy it. He saw our little community as a blot upon the kingdom. Fortunately Maja had befriended us. So, as her father prepared the spell that would destroy us—"

"I interfered," Maja said. "I messed up the pattern he needed to direct the spell, and I stole his magic texts and hid them in a safe place. He was so furious with me, I had to run away."

"And your father would cause problems for us if we went there?" Abderian asked.

Maja nodded. "Unless—"

Suddenly there came a furious pounding at the door, and it slammed open. One of the guardian dwarfs rushed in, panting heavily. "Lord Undertall! The swordswoman! She's escaped!"

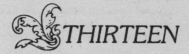 THIRTEEN

"WHAT!" ROARED BURDALANE, jumping to his feet.

"We thought she was drunk!" gasped the dwarf guard. "We left her for only a moment, and when we returned she was gone!"

"Fools!" said the commander, turning to Lord Undertall. "You assured me—"

"Might I remind you," said the mayor, "you saw her yourself and made no comment as to the inadequacy of her guard. Besides, what harm can the one woman do?"

"If she informs Captain Maduro of our location, you may find your little community surrounded and under siege by the royal army."

"In which case, we would simply deliver the prince as requested."

Abderian looked at the mayor in alarm.

"Is this what your people call hospitality?" said Burdalane.

"My people's safety is as much my concern as the prince's is yours. And independent as we are, we do consider ourselves subjects of the Kingdom of Euthymia, loyal to whoever happens to be on the throne currently. If this Captain Maduro is acting in the name of the crown, we cannot but comply. However, so long as no one directly asks us to betray your presence, you may remain with us."

"I am reassured," said Burdalane sardonically.

Dolus touched the commander's shoulder. "Let us not worry yet. It is more likely Hirci will report first to her priestess. Though, I confess, what she will do with the knowledge I cannot say."

"Then I suggest, gentlemen," said the mayor, "that we let the matter rest until we know what we are facing. I will order the highwatch to be extra alert tonight, though nothing could arrive from Mamelon for another two days or so. And I will consult with a couple of my advisors. I know you must all be weary from your wanderings and in need of rest."

"It has indeed been a full evening," said Dolus. "We have found our prince and I have gained a niece."

"And I have lost a father, and gained some hope," murmured Abderian.

"You may bathe while sleeping quarters are prepared for you," Undertall went on. "Now, if you will follow me—"

Although Abderian felt the need for a bath, he did not feel at all tired. Events and possibilities seemed to be falling upon him rapidly. He realized he felt driven to one choice of action that might spare his hosts and friends from whatever danger Hirci brought, one action that might lead to the lifting of the Curse of Sagamore. He had to seek Onym's study at Castle Nikhedonia—alone.

About an hour later, bathed but not rested, Abderian sat on a mat-covered ledge carved from the stone wall of the stark little grotto that was his sleeping room. Though his sore muscles would have preferred a feather bed, and his pride would have preferred finer trappings, he was grateful for the lack of distraction. He was thinking about how he could arrange for travel provisions without arousing his friends' suspicions, when he heard Maja's voice outside the tapestry that served as his door.

"Abderian?"

"Maja? Come in."

She entered, wearing a long muslin nightgown, her hair flowing loose around her shoulders. "I have to talk to you." Her voice seemed shaky and her face was pale.

"What's wrong?"

She sniffed and held out a piece of paper in a trembling hand. "I found this on my pillow. I—I thought I'd better ask someone about it."

Abderian took the note and opened it to read:

To Lady Maja. Greetings. Though I now leave in haste, I shall return to guide you to your

mother, and to the destiny that is rightfully yours,
among the stars.
Your Servant,
Hirci.

"That's strange," said the prince. "What does it mean?"

"I was hoping you could tell me. I don't know this Hirci person, or how she would know my mother. My father sent my mother away when I was younger because she didn't approve of the way he was using his power. When my sister and I had no word from her, we thought she was dead."

"Perhaps she isn't."

"Except that the note refers to her 'among the stars.' I remember my mother telling me that was a place you go when you die."

"Hmm. Dolus mentioned that Hirci was a member of some cult involving stars. Maybe—"

"You see? It's probably some death cult. Maybe they want me as a sacrifice, or something. Maybe my father sent her."

Abderian shook his head, trying to sort out the wild thoughts from the reasonable. "Look, I don't know if Hirci is associated with your father." He took a deep breath. "But I might be able to find out. Maja, I'm going to leave for Castle Nikhedonia as soon as I can. I need you to arrange provisions for me and to tell me how to find Onym's study."

"I'll do better than that. I'm coming with you."

"Now, wait a minute! You said it would be dangerous for you if Horaphthia hasn't done anything about Lord Javel."

"It will be just as dangerous for you. Besides, I know how to sneak into the castle. We might not have to see him at all if we're lucky. The place is built like a maze. You'd never be able to find your own way."

Abderian sighed, knowing she was right. He did need her help. He felt a mixture of elation and disappointment. He felt flattered that she would want to be with him, but he had wanted to do this alone. Perhaps just to prove that he could.

"I see your point. But why do you want to go?"

"One, to have the chance to help Horaphthia in her vengeance. Two, to make sure I'm not around when this Hirci comes back for me. Enough reasons?"

"I suppose."

"Good. Now, provisions are easy to arrange. But what could

we take as protection in case my father finds us?"

"I can use a sword, if you can find me one."

"Silly. A sword is no use against a wizard. He'd fry you before you could draw the blade. The only things that impress my father are political power and sorcery."

"Well, my political power is pretty low right now. And as for magic, all I have is this curse, which I can't do anything with. It just seems to get me involved in other peoples' schemes. So I really don't—one moment. Perhaps there is something."

Maja leaned forward with interest. "What is that?"

"It's . . . I can't tell you. I've been sworn to secrecy about it, but it may help."

"What will help?"

"I can't tell you, I said!" Abderian wasn't sure if it was his oath to Burdalane or his knowledge of the danger that prevented the prince from telling Maja about the Nightsword. But it was certainly the most powerful piece of magic they could bring. "Don't worry. I'll take care of it later tonight."

"All right." Maja gave him a dubious look. "I'll go talk to the stewards about food and things. We should be able to leave before dawn tomorrow. Rest up well. It takes two days to get from here to Nikhedonia, so you'll need to be well rested. Good night."

"Good night, Maja." Abderian waited several seconds after she stepped out to slip out of the room himself. The prince tiptoed down the hall and stopped at the entrance to Burdalane's room. The commander's snores were audible in the hallway.

Carefully Abderian pulled aside the door curtain just enough to let him slip through. He stood totally still in the darkness, praying that Burdalane would not wake up. He waited for the feeling to come upon him, and soon it was there—the yearning, the ache to see, to touch, the Nightsword. Asking the lady in the boat to guide him, the prince moved along the wall of the room. The yearning grew more and more intense, until his feet struck something soft. Bending down, he grasped a long bundle of cloth. There came a warm vibration from within, as if the sword were a living thing, and his hands tingled with its muted energy. Abderian raised the sword slowly and tucked it under one arm.

Turning to go, Abderian looked to where Burdalane lay snoring and whispered, "Forgive me, cousin."

The commander shifted fitfully on the mattress, causing the

prince to start. But Burdalane continued to snore, entranced within some dream, and Abderian left unnoticed. Just outside, he thought he heard Burdalane mutter, "Fear not, My Lady. I shall rescue you!"

The prince returned to his room and undressed, hiding the Nightsword under his clothes. He stretched out on the bed ledge, still feeling the tingling in his fingers. Though he thought himself too excited for sleep, the vibration in his fingers quickly stole up his arms and flowed over his body, and a blanket of darkness softly descended over his mind.

He drifted pleasantly through the darkness until he saw again a starry night sky. Vague wisps of white floated in the void between the stars, and coalesced into a shape at the center of his vision. It was the face of the pale lady in the boat. Her expression was angry, and she seemed to be trying to say something.

Then another shape appeared—a white hand, pointing to something at the prince's left. His field of vision moved in that direction, and a bright yellow star expanded to fill the whole scene. But within it roamed a giant black hound, tearing up peasants' huts with its jaws and scattering people and houses everywhere, snarling and snapping. A cord was attached to the hound's neck, and it was dragging something behind it. Abderian's viewpoint narrowed in on the line, and he saw it was himself being dragged by the hound, by a leather collar around his neck. He struggled to be free of the leash, but he seemed only to become tangled in it further, until it was wrapped around his right shoulder and shaking him to and fro. Shaking him, shaking him . . .

The prince shuddered and sat up. The dwarf beside him removed a rough hand from the prince's shoulder to cover an enormous yawn.

"You sleep heavily, Your Highness," mumbled the dwarf.

"What is it?" Abderian said groggily.

"'Tis the hour before dawn, Your Highness. Her Ladyship said you wished to be waked at this time."

"Already?"

"Beats me why anyone would want to get up at this hour. She says you have some sort of outing planned."

Slowly the prince stretched. He became aware of the aroma of cinnamon and noticed a bowl and spoon in the dwarf's hands.

"Breakfast, Your Highness."

It was a warm, spiced oat porridge with raisins that Abderian found surprisingly good. He wolfed it down and stood up, noticing a set of clean tunic, surcoat, and hose at the end of the bed. "Where did those come from?"

"Compliments of Her Ladyship. I'll be waiting outside."

Abderian dressed quickly, finding the tunic sleeves just a bit tight, and the hem almost short enough to be embarrassing. Still, the clothes were clean and in good repair, which was more than he could say for his own.

Taking his old silk tunic, Abderian tore off two strips of fabric and tied one around each end of the wrapped Nightsword. Carefully he slung the sword across his back, tying the fabric strips across his chest. After making sure the sword was comfortably and securely positioned, Abderian joined the dwarf out in the corridor.

"It's this way to Morning Star Gate, Your Highness."

Abderian was guided through a maze of passages, none of which, he was sure, he had seen before. At last they came to a tunnel that led straight, angling upward. At the top was an ancient-looking stone gate, with the design of stars and mountains carved upon it. On either side of the gate sat two armored dwarfs, drowsily leaning against the wall.

"I heard a good one last night from the swordswoman. You know, the one who escaped?" said one guard.

"Oh?" said the other. "What?"

"The verse went like this:

King Sagamore's sword was a joke, as you'd think.
Must be that his swordsmith had too much to drink.
Too soft to breach velvet, too flimsy to score,
Though hard he might try, it'd just sag all the more!

The dwarfs chuckled until Abderian's guide called out, "Look alive there! This fellow wants out, at the Lady Maja's request."

The guardsmen stumbled to their feet and struggled to pull open the heavy gate.

The guide gave the prince a strange look. "You know, I

don't understand this idea of a breakfast picnic. Seems too cold and dark to me. Well, have a nice time. 'Ware the dragon." He shrugged and waved, then trudged back down the tunnel.

Picnic? Dragon? Abderian wondered just what Maja had told them. With a shrug of his own the prince squeezed through the narrow opening the guardsmen had wrested from the gate. He stepped into a short passage just barely illuminated by pre-dawn light. At the far end the exit was choked with weeds, vines, and bushes, which Abderian had to push through with some difficulty.

When at last he disentangled himself from these, the prince stood still a moment, breathing the cool mountain air. Then, in front of him he suddenly noticed three dark shapes standing and watching him.

"It's about time," said one of them in Maja's voice. "I was beginning to think you had lost your courage and had gone back to sleep."

"Good morning to you too," Abderian grumbled.

"Sorry. I was just getting impatient."

Abderian went closer and saw that the other two shapes were dark ponies whose reins Maja held in one hand. She held one set out to him.

"Here. It'll be faster if we ride."

Abderian got on the pony offered him. "Maja, do you happen to know anything about a dragon?"

"Do you mean in general or one in particular?"

"I'm not sure. The dwarf who led me to the gate told me to 'beware the dragon.' He didn't explain. Do you know what he meant?"

"Hmm. It's probably just a new way of saying 'good-bye,' or something. There haven't been any dragons in these mountains for as long as I can remember."

Maja swung onto her pony and they set off down a narrow track that became wider as they drew farther from the dwarfs' cave. An hour after setting out, the sun peeped over a ridge, illuminating pines and jagged rock formations, and peaks with a thin veil of snow. Though aching from little sleep and shivering from the cold breeze, Abderian found it beautiful.

"What's that thing on your back?" Maja's voice seemed unnaturally loud in the mountain stillness.

"It's the thing I couldn't tell you about."

"It's a sword, isn't it?"

"If you already knew, why did you ask?"

"I just . . . never mind. Why did you ask me to get you a sword if you already have one?"

"No, you don't understand." Abderian gave an exasperated sigh. "It's a magic sword."

"A . . . magic . . . where did you get a magic sword?"

"I borrowed . . . well, I stole it from Burdalane."

"You stole it? You idiot! After all the trouble I went through to make up a story to tell the dwarfs so your friends wouldn't come after us. And now that you stole their sword, they'll be on our tails in no time!" Maja looked over her shoulder apprehensively.

"But I had to take it! We'll need it! Burdalane would never have let me use it if I had asked him. And I . . . and . . ." In actuality, the chance that Dolus and Brudalane would come chasing after him simply hadn't occurred to him. He turned his face away in embarrassment.

"Well, let's hope your friend doesn't discover his loss for a while. What does it do?"

"What?"

"The *sword*. What sort of magic does it have?"

Abderian stared straight ahead. "It's powerful. It's dangerous. I can't say anything more." He didn't dare. He didn't know what Maja would say if he admitted he couldn't even handle the thing.

It was near midday when Abderian and Maja heard hoofbeats approaching from behind. They were crossing a saddle ridge between two peaks, and there was nowhere to hide.

Abderian dismounted nonetheless, and stood looking to either side for cover.

"What now, bright eyes?" said Maja dryly.

"Shut up." Abderian narrowed his eyes. In a minute two horsemen rounded the peak behind them—Dolus and Burdalane. Abderian ran up the road a short way to a narrow pinnacle of rock standing on the ridge. Throwing his reins to Maja, he clambered onto the rock. *At least if I'm here, they can't grab me and drag me back before talking to me*.

The hero and the wizard rode up, their horses panting and sweating from the run. Their eyes went instantly to Abderian standing on the rock. Burdalane pointed at the sword on the prince's back.

"So he does have it!" said Dolus.

"Abderian! Have you gone mad?" cried Burdalane. "Return the sword to me and return with us to the cave at once!"

"No, cousin," said Abderian. He felt stupid and disgusted with himself for not thinking. But most of all, he felt angry. Angry that the one chance he had to gain some control over his own destiny had been ruined. Ruined by his own stupidity. Dear as his friends were, he wished them far away. He hungered to be free to go on as he had chosen, reckless though the choice might be. He felt the anger and frustration build and build within him.

"What was that, cousin? What did you say?"

Abderian's fists clenched. A mighty shout welled up within him and burst out from between his lips. "No!"

He felt a shudder, and suddenly realized the shaking came from the ground beneath him. Rumblings like the deepest thunder roared around him. Dolus's horse shied, tossing the wizard to the ground. A rift opened up in the earth between himself and the others, widening as the quaking continued. The prince felt fear overtaking his anger. "Stop!" he cried out to nothing in particular.

Gradually the shaking subsided and the crack in the earth widened no more. An eerie stillness settled around them, and the prince's breath and heartbeat seemed loud in his ears.

Dolus stood up slowly, dusting himself off. Maja stared at the prince, eyes wide with amazement.

Burdalane said, "Whence came that? You see, cousin, the very land is treacherous here. Will you not—"

"Lord Burdalane," Dolus said, regarding the prince solemnly, "I think we had better do as he wishes."

FOURTEEN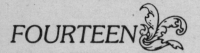

ABDERIAN SLOWLY WENT down on his hands and knees and clambered down off of the rock. His back tingled where the Nightsword lay across it, and his arms ached. Quickly, hands shaking, he untied the silk straps and took off the sword. He placed the sorcerous weapon at Burdalane's feet and jumped back as if afraid it would bite.

"Is that what the sword does?" asked Maja breathlessly. "It causes earthquakes?"

"I—I'm not sure."

Burdalane picked up the black silk bundle, frowning. "I never knew it to do aught such as that."

Abderian rubbed his right arm where it ached, then abruptly pulled back his sleeve. The cursemark was glowing a dull red, though the light was fading. The ache seemed to be radiating from the mark.

"What is it, lad?" said Dolus, walking toward him.

"Dolus, was it . . . could the curse have caused that?"

"Who can say, lad? Until we know the nature of the curse . . ." The wizard shrugged.

Burdalane partially unwrapped the Nightsword, still holding it by the silk shroud, and inspected it for damage. It was spectacular, even in daylight, as the sunshine sparkled against the stars on the blade. Abderian heard Maja gasp in wonder beside him. The commander, with a satisfied nod, rewrapped the sword and tied it onto his saddle. "The next time you want to borrow this sword, kindly ask."

"Yes, sir." Abderian felt no desire to touch anything magical for a while.

Maja said nothing, but her eyes were alive with curiosity.

"You are heading to Castle Nikhedonia, aren't you?" Dolus asked the prince. "Just what do you expect to do when you get there?"

"I hope to see Onym's study, to learn something of the wizard's whereabouts, if not the curse itself. If Lord Javel is there, I might ask his help. From what Maja has said about his hatred of Sagamore's ways, I'd think he'd want to help me."

"Then again," Dolus said, "if he despises the kin of Sagamore, Javel might wish to see the curse continue."

"Oh."

"Or worse, if he knows something of the nature of the curse, he might manipulate it for his own purposes."

"Well, you see, that's why I took the Nightsword. Maja said the only things that impressed her father were magic and political power. The Nightsword is the most powerful magic item I could get on short notice. I thought the sword could be used as an item for parley or threat."

Burdalane shook his head. "Even though you could not wield it yourself?"

"Well, Lord Javel wouldn't know that. Would he?"

The commander sighed and remounted his horse. "He would learn soon enough."

Dolus took the reins of his still skittish horse and patted its flank reassuringly. "Because it is so much your heart's desire, lad, we will follow you to the castle. Perhaps I can speak persuasively with my brother, if need be."

The road became narrower and more rocky as they proceeded eastward. The sound of their horses' hooves echoed loudly between the rock outcroppings and cliffs. Their progress was slow as the road wound up and down, and during the rest of the afternoon they made little real distance. As the sun went down, turning the color of the rocks from gray to golden-pink, the air grew cooler and more still.

They took evening meal in a wind-hollowed alcove, huddled around a small fire. "Lady Maja, could you tell us how we might breach this castle once we reach it?" asked Burdalane.

"Not a wise thought," said Dolus. "If we enter as bandits, we shall be treated as such."

"But there's no guarantee Lord Javel will wish to see us."

Dolus grunted. "He'll see us. From curiosity, if naught else. Am I not right, My Lady?"

"Probably," she said softly. "Though if Horaphthia has had her way, the point will be moot. If you will excuse me." She got up and headed out of the alcove.

"Wait. Where are you going?" asked Abderian.

Maja made a face at him. "To answer a 'call of nature,' nosy one."

"Oh. Of course. Sorry."

As she left, Burdalane gave Abderian a speculative look that only doubled his embarrassment. Fortunately Dolus continued the conversation. "Who is this Horaphthia she speaks of?"

"Uh, she's a sorceress, somehow a relative of Maja. She's quite powerful. And she bears a grudge against Javel because he removed her powers at one point."

"I understand how she must feel," grumbled Dolus.

"The night before Maja and I left her hovel, Horaphthia disappeared, transporting herself somewhere to prepare her revenge. She may have already done it."

"Depending upon if her revenge is swift or slow," Burdalane put in. "If slow, or delayed, we might find ourselves arriving in the midst of a wizards' war—a situation I would not joyfully anticipate."

"It could be awkward, yes," mused Dolus.

The commander snorted. *"Awkward* is a mild way to put it—"

Their conversation was shattered by a scream that came from near the horses. Dolus and Burdalane leaped to their feet and ran out of the alcove, Abderian following after. Out on the road the dim twilight made it hard to see what had happened. The horses and ponies pranced and whinnied nervously, trying to avoid a dark shape lying near them.

"By the Seven Towers of Patridi!" said Dolus, bending down.

"Dear Goddess—!" said Burdalane.

"What is it?" said the prince. "What happened?" He peered over their shoulders and his voice caught in his throat. Maja lay on the road, a cloud of black silk covering her legs and the Nightsword glittering in her hands.

That fool! That silly, stubborn fool! Abderian thought, pacing back and forth across the alcove. Dolus and Burdalane placed Maja on a pallet they had made from their cloaks.

Abderian could only watch, feeling sick and helpless, his arms aching in sympathy. *Oh, Gods, I wish this hadn't happened.*

Burdalane stood up and walked over to the prince, scowling. "Is she—"

"Aye, cousin, she lives. She is fortunate. Sleep will help her, though I envy her not her dreams. Didn't you tell her the sword was dangerous?"

"Yes . . . well, not enough, I guess."

Burdalane glared and sighed with an angry rumble. Shaking his head, he said, "We are making camp here, obviously. You had better sleep as well as you can. Who knows what surprises the morn might bring us."

Abderian went over next to Maja and curled up against the rock wall of the alcove. But he was unable to sleep, and the hours crawled by like snails. The fire burned down to red-glowing embers, and Burdalane's snore rumbled in the alcove. The air was clear and cold, and the sky filled with stars—a sight which did not cheer the prince.

It was well into the night when Maja awoke. Abderian heard her stirring and watched her silhouette stand and stretch and walk out of the alcove. As quietly as possible the prince followed after her.

He caught up with Maja at the edge of the road, where the mountainside sheared away at a steep drop. But Maja was looking at the star-filled sky, not her feet. Abderian grabbed her arm. "Maja! Are you all right?"

"I'm fine," she said, not taking her eyes off the sky.

"Did the sword hurt you badly?"

"It only hurt a little . . . at first." Her voice was vague and distant.

"Did you . . . did you have any dreams?"

"Dreams? Was she a dream?"

"Did you see a woman in a white robe on a boat?"

"Yes, I saw her. She smiled at me and bade me welcome."

"Bade you welcome?" Abderian shivered, not just from the cold. The eerie tone of Maja's voice frightened him. It was clear the lady in the boat was not merely imagined by himself and Burdalane. But what was she? "Why did you touch the sword? Don't you remember that I said it was dangerous?"

"She called to me. I had to touch the sword. When I saw the stars shining in the sun, she called to me."

"She seems to summon everyone," the prince muttered.

"Did she say anything else to you?"

"She welcomed me and called me kinswoman. She said it is prophesied that I and my sister would both marry kings, and thereby each liberate a kingdom."

"Well, that's better than what she told me." Abderian found it hard to accept that raggedy Maja, even Lady Maja, could be related to the beautiful lady of the Nightsword. Or marry a king. "I . . . don't suppose she mentioned me at all, did she?"

Maja turned to the prince, starlight reflected in her eyes. "Yes, she did. She was not pleased with you. She says we have chosen the more difficult path, and will face greater danger. We may fail in what we seek."

"But I only did what—" Abderian blurted out, then calmed himself. It was useless to try to argue with Maja's dream. "You should sleep some more. You'll feel better for it."

"Sleep? Who would want to sleep when the stars are so beautiful?"

Abderian sighed and, as gently as possible, guided Maja back to the alcove. Then he hunkered down beside her with the hope of being able to keep her from doing anything else foolish. He watched her watching the sky until sleep swept over him, filling his mind with whispered warnings and blurry constellations.

The following morning, to Abderian's relief, Maja seemed herself again.

"I'm fine!" she growled at everyone's query. "Even if my arms feel like they've been run over by a hundred horsecarts."

"'Twill teach Your Ladyship not to be poking in strange packages," grumbled Burdalane.

"I hadn't seen a magic sword before. I just wanted to look. Besides, it didn't kill me, did it?"

"It might have."

"Anyway, it was worth it to see the lady on the boat."

Burdalane started, and his eyes for a moment were red with anger. Then he turned away and finished his breakfast in silence.

By mid-morning they had remounted and continued on their way. Maja indicated it was still another day's travel before they'd reach the castle. She rode slightly ahead of the others to scout out the road before them.

Dolus rode alongside Burdalane, keeping a concerned eye on him. Abderian rode by himself at the rear, feeling as if he'd suddenly lost control of events once more.

Some ways down the road, Maja began to sing:

> Oh, Burdalane's sword is all magic and fey,
> A maid need but touch it and she's blown away,
> To a magical place where the stars meet the sea—

"My Lady, cease!" Burdalane rode up beside Maja and glared at her.

"Don't you like the song, My Lord?"

"No! And I insist that you speak of that sword no more!"

"But it was just—"

"No more! Do you hear?"

"Yes, My Lord." Maja sounded confused and hurt.

Burdalane rode ahead alone. Abderian glanced at Dolus, who shrugged. Deciding to find out for himself, the prince cantered up alongside his cousin. "Burdalane, you didn't have to yell at her like that."

"How dare she?"

"It wasn't all her fault. The sword called to her too. I for one am glad to see that she's alive and well."

"I meant how dare she know of things that are in my dreams."

"Oh. I didn't tell you, but I have seen the lady on the boat also, after touching the sword."

"You also? You and then Maja. I thought the Lady of the Nightsword was a creature of my own mind."

"Well," said the prince, "it looks as though the lady has a mind of her own."

FIFTEEN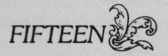

SOMETIME IN THE late afternoon they came to where the road bent around a small hillock, then descended steeply. Maja dismounted, saying, "That's odd."

"What is?" asked Abderian.

"This area doesn't look the way I remember. I'm going to have a look around." She scrambled up the hillock, which seemed to be formed of loose stones. Abderian followed after her.

From the top of the hillock they could see that the road led into a cul-de-sac within a semi-circle of escarpments rising more than twenty feet above it. Where the road ended there stood a great, solid iron gate. In the cliffside to the left of the road was a cave opening from which issued a thin plume of smoke.

"My father must have blocked the road to prevent the dwarfs from striking back."

"How do we go on?" asked the prince.

"You see the chain on the cliff, leading from the gate toward the cave?"

"Aye."

"I think we might be able to pull the gate open."

"That looks difficult. Couldn't we just go around the other side of these cliffs and avoid the gate altogether?" Abderian did not want to add that the appearance of the cave worried him as well.

"Don't you think my father would have thought of that? The slopes on either side are very steep and slippery. We'd

110

have to abandon the horses and make our way on foot. Even then our chances of sliding off the mountainside are great."

She scrambled down the hillside and remounted her pony. "Let's go."

Abderian followed suit, and they all rode single file behind Maja into the cul-de-sac.

Their horses' hoofbeats echoed painfully loudly between the cliffs as they rode up to the gate. It seemed even more massive and immovable up close.

"How are we ever going to raise this thing?" sighed Abderian. He squinted over his shoulder at the cave.

"What concerns you?" Burdalane asked the prince.

"Oh, I don't know. I . . . the last dwarf I spoke to told me to beware of a dragon. That cave looks suspiciously like—"

"A dragon's lair?" Dolus laughed aloud. "Abderian, dragons died out over a century ago. Thalion's father, King Telarian Wormslayer saw to the extermination of all the dragons in Euthymia."

"All but one . . ." a deep voice suddenly boomed behind them. "Do you require some assistance?"

Abderian twisted around, but could not see where the voice came from. Then, slowly, the hillock he and Maja had climbed earlier shook and shuddered and began to rise. Small avalanches of stones cascaded off its sides. Presently he could see squat legs beneath it and the blunt outline of a long snout. Like a wet dog, the creature shook off the last of the debris. Revealed beneath was a reptilian form whose pale leathery skin hung in folds like discarded bedclothes.

"A dragon!" breathed Abderian.

"An imperial dragon," added Dolus.

"I am Kookluk," the reptile announced, "Guardian of Pilika Pass. May I ask what brings you to my humble domain?" He grinned at the party with good-natured malice.

"Good Lord Burdalane, why don't you reason with it?" Dolus suggested, pushing him forward.

"Reason with it? My only experience with 'dragons' was the slaying of several oversized lizards that frightened some overimaginative peasants. You're the wizard. You should know something about talking to dragons!"

"Me? By the daystar, I do not—"

"Master!" Kookluk exclaimed, staring at Dolus. "Why did

you not say 'twas you? Why did you not tell me you were coming? I would not have bothered to disguise myself."

Maja ran over to Dolus and whispered loudly in his ear, "He mistakes you for my father, as I did. You might be able to convince him to let us go on!"

"Ahem. Well, Kookluk," said Dolus, "I was merely testing you. Keeping you on your talons, you might say. Glad to see you're still doing a good job. Now, if you will kindly lift the gate so that we may proceed homeward . . ."

Kookluk frowned. "You have never needed my help with the gate before, master."

"Well, I, uh . . . I'm feeling just a bit weary at the moment."

Suddenly Kookluk thrust his fleshy white snout against Dolus's middle and sniffed. "Odd," said the dragon. "You do not speak or act like my master, yet you look and smell like him. Most confusing."

"Another test, good Kookluk, and you have passed it ably. Now, about the gate—"

"And who is this?" The dragon swung his head to stare at Maja, standing beside the wizard.

"This is my daughter, Maja."

"Ah! Then you have brought her to me as you promised! You meant to surprise me with her, yes? This is sooner than I expected. I am pleased, master."

"One moment . . . I promised her to you?"

Maja stepped back, her face ashen with fear.

"Why, yes! You . . . is this another test, master?" Kookluk sighed. "You know a dragon's memory can be trusted. Because I had been cursed by that wizard of King Sagamore—"

"Onym, you mean?"

"I remember the name, master. Since he had cursed me with the eternal desire to possess a human maiden, you promised me your daughter, Maja, in exchange for my services. And now you have brought her. Do I pass?"

Between his worrying, Abderian decided that Onym had a lot to answer for. *That is, if I get the chance to find him.*

"Well, Kookluk," said Dolus, "you know what they say, 'Maiden now, no maid tomorrow, young man's joy is dragon's sorrow.'"

"A riddle, master? I'm wise enough to have learned that I cannot outriddle you. Pray tell me its meaning."

"It means I've changed my mind. You can't have her."

"What! One does not 'change one's mind' in a promise to a dragon! Methinks," Kookluk snarled, crawling forward, "that you are not my master after all!"

Maja shrieked. "Burdalane! Abderian! Do something!"

"Abderian?!" thundered Kookluk. "Is there someone here named Abderian? Is it you?" The dragon looked directly at the prince.

Abderian could only gulp and tighten his hold on the reins as his pony shied and pranced.

Burdalane drew his plain sword and stood between the dragon and the prince. "Leave His Royal Highness be, or I shall slice you to a pile of bootlaces, you overgrown laundry-heap!"

"Ah, a gallant protector he has too. Well, fear not, Lord Tin-Plate. You may be pleased to know that my orders from my master . . . my *true* master," he added, glaring at Dolus, "are that His Highness is to pass through the gate in safety."

This pronouncement elicited gasps of relief and surprise from everyone until the dragon added, *"Alone."*

"Alone?" said the prince. "I can't do that! I won't!"

"It's all right, Abderian," Maja said softly. "You go ahead. Find Horaphthia and tell her what's happened. You wanted to do this yourself anyway, didn't you?"

"No! I'm not going to just leave you and the others here." Turning to Kookluk, the prince said, "I will not leave unless they, all of them, are allowed to leave with me."

"I *am* sorry, Your Highness," the dragon replied, "but my orders are most explicit. If you choose not to leave, I shall have to treat you and your friends in such a way that you will want to leave. Or that you will no longer have any reason to stay."

Abderian glared at Kookluk, feeling anger mix with his worry and fear. He briefly thought of asking Burdalane to lend him the Nightsword again. He tried to reach for the power he had felt the day before on the rock. But his efforts seemed scattered and he felt nothing but more tension in his back and stomach.

"Go on, Abderian," said Burdalane. "We will do what we can."

"Aye," said Dolus, "then at least one of us will have escaped. Perhaps when you reach Lord Javel, you could explain how his brother's little jest backfired, and ask him to release us from his dragon's custody. Surely he would not let his own brother and daughter suffer if he learned of our predicament." The wizard gave Kookluk a significant look.

"My master mentioned no 'brother' to me, and I no longer trust you, Lord Imposter. However, his instructions regarding His Highness were quite specific. No one is to accompany His Highness to Castle Nikhedonia." Kookluk slowly approached Abderian and guided his pony toward the gate. The pony nearly threw the prince as it reared and pranced in fear. When they reached the gate, Kookluk pulled on the iron ring and the gate rose with loud creakings and rumblings. As soon as the gap beneath it was higher than the prince's head, the dragon said, "Begone! And give my regards to my Master." Then he flicked a talon across the pony's rump.

With a heartrending whinny the pony dashed through the gate, Abderian holding grimly on to its mane for dear life. The prince heard behind him a great clang as the gate slammed shut once more.

The road wound steeply downward with many sharp turns that the pony, in its pell-mell flight, only just barely negotiated. Abderian could think of little else besides staying on the pony and praying that the pony stayed on the road.

Finally, with gentle tuggings on the reins, the prince slowed the pony down to a fast walk, and he could dare to look back over his shoulder. The gate was already far behind them. With a sigh Abderian turned his attention forward.

The road was leading down into a small, narrow valley in which lay a crumbling edifice that the prince assumed to be Castle Nikhedonia. From high above it the castle looked vaguely like an insect that some clumsy giant had stepped upon. Abderian wondered if Horaphthia had already exacted her revenge. If so, he might find neither wizard there. He did not find this thought encouraging.

It was sunset when the prince finally reached the valley floor. The pony's hooves made hollow sounds as they crossed a wooden bridge spanning what had once been the castle moat. Now the moat was filled with silt and choked with weeds.

The outer wall was mostly ruins, with only the gatehouse still standing. But the portcullus gates had rusted open and Abderian had no trouble riding through. The main courtyard of the castle was also overgrown with weeds, and some of the inner buildings had collapsed. Had there been any towers, they must have fallen also.

Abderian stopped his exhausted pony and dismounted, allowing it to graze on the weeds in the courtyard. He frowned, realizing no guards had challenged his presence. No grooms came to care for his mount. No curious faces appeared on the walls or in the windows. The only sounds were the prince's bootheels on the courtyard gravel and the wind moaning through broken stonework. So far as Abderian could tell, the castle was deserted.

Unless Horaphthia has an "instant aging" spell, this decay has nothing to do with her. It's been going on awhile.

"Hello?" he called out. Echoes of his voice came back to him, but there was no other response. The prince walked up to what appeared to be a main door of carved wood. It still seemed quite solid. The door was flanked by a pair of tall black stone hunting dogs, narrow-faced and noble. For a moment the stark memory of a nightmare flashed across the prince's mind— the black hound that dragged him on a leash. Abderian sat on the steps before the door and shook his head, wondering what to do.

"Knocking usually works," said a high voice.

Abderian started, then saw the little bird sitting on the stone dog to his right. "Brownie!"

"Good evening, fledgling. You've chosen a good place to nest for the night. Lots of nooks and crannies here."

"Well, I'm not exactly nesting . . . how did you find me?"

"It was no problem. I've been following you."

"You have? Why?"

"Well, that's kind of difficult to explain. I'm worried about you. I have this feeling that I should look after you even though you're no eggling of mine. There's something I ought to tell you, something you ought to know."

"But you don't remember what it is."

"How did you know? Oh, well, I expect it will come to me eventually, and then I can tell you. I'll just follow you until I remember."

Abderian managed a small chuckle. "Well, all right. As you wish. Actually there's a small favor you could do me, if you don't mind."

"What's that?"

"Find Horaphthia. She lives in a tower somewhere around

here. Tell her that Maja has been caught by Javel's dragon. And tell her I'm here at Castle Nikhedonia. Will you do that for me?"

"Hmm. It's kind of hard to stay by you and find Horaphthia at the same time."

"I'll probably be staying here awhile, so you needn't worry about losing me. Now I think I'd better find out if Lord Javel is here." He stood and turned to knock on the door.

But before his hand touched the wood, the door shuddered and slowly began to open, its great hinges groaning like a tortured man. "On second thought," said Brownie, "I think I will go look for Horaphthia. Take care, fledgling. G'bye!" He took off in a flurry of feathers.

"Wait!" Abderian called, but the bird was gone, leaving him to face whatever lay behind the door alone. In the ever-widening darkness between the door and its frame, the prince saw tiny flames that flickered like candlelight. Wondering what sort of sorcery this was, Abderian said weakly, "Lord Javel?"

He was answered by a sweet feminine voice that said, "Welcome, Abderian, son of Valgus. We have been expecting you."

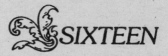

SIXTEEN

CLIMBING BACK INTO his skin, Abderian cautiously approached the door.

"Please, come in," the sweet voice beckoned.

The prince peeked into the dark entry and felt his breath catch in his throat. Standing beyond the threshold stood the most beautiful girl he had ever seen. She stood a little taller than he, dressed in a pale blue silk gown. Her hair was the color of beaten gold, and she wore it in a looser style than that of the ladies at Castle Mamelon. In her left hand she held a sconce set with three lit candles that shed warm light on her face. With a bemused smile she said, "My name is Khanda. Are you all right?" Her tone was reminiscent of Maja's.

"Uh, yes. I mean, no. I mean, I'm fine," Abderian stammered. He stepped into the doorway, not taking his eyes off the girl. "Um, you must be Maja's sister."

"Maja!" Khanda looked back at the prince, a concerned frown on her pretty face. "You've seen Maja? How is she?"

"Not too well at the moment. She's currently in the keeping of a dragon."

"Kookluk has her?" Khanda said softly. Her shoulders drooped a little and she looked away. "I knew it would happen sometime but . . . Maja always did tend to get into trouble."

"I'm hoping your father will order the dragon to release her and my other friends."

"That's not likely. Father has not cared much for Maja since . . . well, it is too late to speak of it now. Come. I'd best take you to him before he becomes impatient. I know you and he have much to talk about."

117

The corridor she led him down appeared as ill cared for as the courtyard. Dusty, broken statues lined the walls and threadbare tapestries covered damp, moldy walls. Abderian wondered how the place could look so abandoned if people still lived there.

As if reading his thoughts Khanda said, "Please excuse the disarray. Father does not expect to remain here much longer, and he dismissed the groundskeepers and most of the servants some time ago. As he keeps mostly to his work, he doesn't notice his surroundings much."

At a junction of hallways they took a left turn into an arched corridor that seemed in somewhat better condition. "Father should be in his study," Khanda said, motioning down the corridor.

"Oh, speaking of studies," Abderian said, suddenly remembering, "do you happen to know where Onym's study is."

"Onym's study!" Khanda whipped around to face the prince, hints of anger and fear in her blue eyes. "Why do you want to see that?"

"I'm hoping to find a clue to where Onym might be. I need to find him for . . . an important reason."

"It doesn't matter. You can't see it." She held her chin up defiantly.

"Why not?"

"Because . . . it's been destroyed! It was in that part of the castle that's ruined now. There's nothing left to see."

"You're certain?"

"Quite certain."

"Oh." Abderian stared at the floor, letting despair wash over him. He had led his friends into terrible danger, on a search that turned out to be utterly useless.

Khanda placed a hand on his arm. "Was seeing the study that important to you?"

"Yes."

"But that's nonsense. Onym would be dead by now." Khanda took Abderian's arm and gently pulled him farther down the hallway.

"Dolus said he might not be."

"And who is Dolus, to know this?"

Abderian frowned at her. "He's your uncle."

With an awkward little laugh Khanda said, "You must be mistaken. I have no uncle named Dolus."

As Abderian stared at her, confused, Khanda guided him to an elaborately carved door on which she knocked once, then she pushed it open. Directly across the room a fire roared in a huge fireplace. In the middle of the room, facing the fire, sat a man in a plush velvet chair. His features held an unmistakable similarity to those of Dolus. Yet the court wizard's eyes had never been so icy, or his brows so severe.

Without looking up the man said, "Well, Khanda, you've arrived with our guest at last. We were beginning to worry."

"I'm sorry, Father. I did bring him directly here."

"Of course you did. Now let us not keep old friends separated. Show the boy in."

"Yes, Father." Khanda motioned for Abderian to enter, then curtsied and hurried away.

"Old friends?" said the prince, stepping into the room. "I don't believe you and I have met, Lord Javel."

"You and I have not. But I was referring to my . . . associate here." He gestured to Abderian's right.

The view of that portion of the room was blocked by the open door, so the prince reached over and pulled it shut, then stopped. And stared, his jaw dropping open. For there, looking elegant and composed in his lizard-skin robes, stood the high priest Tingalut.

"Good to see you again, Abderian," said the high priest, giving a curt bow. "I am glad to see you are well."

The prince found he could say nothing in reply. The realization struck him that not only was the trip to Nikhedonia unnecessary, so was his leaving of Castle Mamelon. He was right back where he started . . . almost.

"Come, come, no need to look so shocked. We can explain it all quite easily, can't we, My Lord?"

Abderian turned and saw Lord Javel regarding him with a face full of dark concern. "Of course," the wizard said with no trace of friendliness. "Come sit, boy."

"You may address me as 'Your Highness.'" Abderian surprised himself with this haughty tone. He had never insisted on formal address before.

"As you wish . . . Your Highness." Javel said it as though speaking to a mad child. With a cold smile he held out his hand to indicate Abderian should sit in the chair before him, giving a cynically deferential nod as the prince did so. "For now," Javel added, settling back in his chair.

"And, we hope, in future," said Tingalut, approaching the back of Abderian's chair. "Perhaps, in future, it will even be 'Your Majesty.' That is, if you allow us to help you."

Abderian shut his eyes and felt his stomach sink a little lower.

"You do know what has happened at Castle Mamelon, don't you?" Tingalut went on.

"Yes. My father is dead."

"I am surprised to hear you so disconsolate. Your father loved you little, you know."

Abderian knew, but still felt oddly hurt at the bald mention of it. "And I suppose you know who killed him?"

Tingalut seemed surprised. "But . . . it was an accident."

"A fortuitous accident," Javel murmured.

"Just like the fortuitous plague that took Paralian?" asked the prince.

"Plague?" Javel raised an eyebrow in amusement and looked up at the high priest. "Is that the story at court?"

Tingalut pressed his lips tightly together a moment, then said, "That was the official explanation, yes. But if you are trying to imply, Your Highness, that I or my temple had anything to do with either your father or your brother, I must disappoint you. Your father's death came sooner than is truly 'fortuitous.'" Tingalut shot a glare at Lord Javel. "We have been caught ill-prepared. As for your brother's disappearance, I was as sorry to hear of it as you were."

Abderian turned and stared at Tingalut, astonished. "Disappeared? Is that what happened?"

As the priest began to answer, Javel held up a hand to silence him. Looking back at the prince, the lord said, "We will gladly tell you the details . . . *if* you agree to cooperate with us."

It was not the bargaining point Abderian had hoped to use, though he burned with curiosity to know about his brother. He decided to deal with the living before the dead. "My friends are being held by the dragon Kookluk. Order him to release them, and I will cooperate."

"Friends?" snorted Javel. "Those peasants became your friends?"

"Peasants?"

"I suppose I should not be surprised that a descendant of the Jester King should befriend himself with the likes of . . . what were their names, Gruff and Dismal?"

The prince's mouth dropped open. "You! You sent those two to kidnap me! But . . . how . . ."

Javel nodded with a cynical smile. "At last, the light dawns. Yes. With Tingalut's plan to flush you from the castle, and knowing my dear brother's tendency to help the unfortunate, it was simple to have men waiting at the right place and time."

"So they could knock me out and cart me off." Abderian nodded slowly as he realized just how easily he had been manipulated.

"They were supposed to 'escort' His Highness, not treat him like a side of beef," Tingalut grumbled at Javel.

"Well, you know how hard it is to find good help these days."

"Indeed."

Abderian felt himself becoming numbed to the surprises being flung upon him. *Perhaps it is time I spring a surprise of my own.* "It may interest you to know that those two peasants you sent died in Commander Burdalane's camp."

"Did they?"

"Yes, at the hands of a warrior woman who's a fanatic of the Star Goddess cult." Abderian added these for, he hoped, convincing detail. From the suddenly serious expressions on his hosts' faces, he realized he had elicited far more.

"Fanatic of the Star Goddess cult, you say?" said Javel. The lord and Tingalut exchanged dark glances. "How very interesting."

Now, why is that important? That's not the item I thought would catch his attention. "Yes. So you see, my friends in the dragon's lair are not 'peasants.' They are none other than General Burdalane, your brother, Dolus, and your daughter, Lady Maja."

To Abderian's great surprise, Javel smiled. "Well, at least the news isn't all bad then, eh, priest?"

"Apparently not."

"You'd give your own daughter to a dragon," the prince said, sickened.

"She chose to ignore that kinship some years ago. Now I am merely returning the favor. I no longer consider her my kin."

"But your brother, Dolus—"

"—could be considered trouble if he were running around loose."

"Not after what Tingalut did to him." Abderian glared at the priest.

"That was to be a formal execution, Abderian, ordered by the king. My intention was that the wizard's sizable talent should not be wasted despite his transgression. You should be thanking me, not condemning me."

"Fortunately," Lord Javel said dryly, "my dragon has achieved what Tingalut could not. Under Kookluk's gentle care Dolus and Lord Burdalane are no longer a problem. This simplifies things greatly."

Abderian sighed, realizing, too late, his mistake. Now the only hope for his friends was their own resourcefulness. *I'm caught in a trap of my own*. Except . . . there was one more bluff he could try. "I've learned some things about this curse I bear since leaving Castle Mamelon. I know I can use it to destroy. If you do not release my friends, I shall unleash its power upon you."

Javel stroked his chin thoughtfully and frowned. Tingalut, however, gave a small smile. "Excellent, Abderian. It pleases me that you are more . . . informed. Pray, give us a demonstration of your awesome abilities."

Damn. Abderian decided to continue the bluff anyway. He balled his hands into fists and squeezed his eyes shut. With all the will he could summon at the moment he wished another earthquake to occur. A detached part of his mind noted, however, that the experience this time felt like flailing at a mechanism, not knowing which lever to pull to make it work. Nonetheless, after a few moments a vase on a shelf began to rattle and shake. Lord Javel looked anxiously around him, and Tingalut's eyes grew wider. Then, just as suddenly, it ceased.

In frustration, Abderian relaxed, letting his breath out with a whoosh. As if in response, a cool breeze blew around the room and up the chimney flue.

Javel frowned and turned to the priest. "Is that all? You led me to believe this curse was powerful!"

"I assure you, it is," Tingalut said with a smug smile. "Somewhere in Euthymia, thanks to Abderian's work, something interesting has happened. Perhaps a plague has killed all the fish in Penchot Harbor, or a fresh crop of giant mushrooms sprang up in the southern plains . . . or perhaps he has merely made your vase dance. The Curse of Sagamore is indeed powerful, but it has not yet been controlled. For all his bluster, His

Highness had no idea what he was doing."

Abderian stared at the floor, chagrined.

"But take heart, lad," Tingalut went on. "Agree to throw in your lot with us and I shall teach you how to control it. With my assistance, of course."

Abderian felt like he had tossed his last coin in a game of Demon's Square . . . it was time to give up. He thought of bolting for the door and escaping the castle. *Both of them are powerful wizards. How far could I get before they stop me? Not nearly far enough,* he decided. Very quietly he replied, "I agree. What do you want me to do?"

"Excellent!" Javel said with a smile. "We will do this; we will bring you forward as the next true heir, by virtue of your mark. Through our influence, the priest and I should be able to win you the throne. You will rule purely as a figurehead, of course—"

"A lad as young as yourself has yet to acquire the wisdom necessary for leadership."

Javel gave Tingalut a disgusted smirk, then continued. "You will marry my daughter Khanda. Don't look so dismayed. I'm sure you will find the marriage as pleasant as I find it politically expedient."

"She is a pretty girl, isn't she?" said Tingalut.

"What if she doesn't like me?"

"It hardly matters, so long as she does her wifely duty by you. In this way, our families will be joined on the throne, which should quell most opposition."

"How is that?"

"Has my dear brother not told you? I am the son of Famlus, son of Thalion."

"King Thalion the Wise?"

"Tsk. Is that what he is called now? How history forgives. Yes, the very same Thalion the Fool, who gave his crown to his jester instead of to a kinsman."

Suddenly Abderian understood Javel's hostility to any of Sagamore's relatives. "You feel he denied you your birthright to the throne."

"Bravo. It appears the boy has some intelligence after all."

"The story I heard was that King Thalion considered his own family unfit to rule."

"And I'd heard that well before he died Thalion had gone mad," Javel shot back. "But once Khanda has borne you a child, who will presumably have the cursemark, Euthymia will again have an heir of Thalion's blood."

"If that is what concerns you," Abderian said carefully, "why don't you bid for the crown yourself? Why use me?"

"That thought had occurred to me. And should anything . . . happen to you, I will certainly try. But Tingalut has convinced me that this is not the wisest course. Your brother Cyprian has too strong a claim. But with you to wear the crown and my daughter as your queen, our claim becomes much stronger."

Abderian nodded and sighed softly. "I didn't want to be king."

"Then you need not remain so long. In a few years, when you've come of age, you may, if you wish, abdicate in my favor. I would see that you are well-supported in whatever sort of life you choose, so long as you do not make trouble for me. But I would not allow you to abdicate until you have sired a child to bear the cursemark."

"I see," said the prince. *Thus depriving me of the one weapon I might use against you.* "And now that I've agreed, will you have Kookluk release my friends?"

"If it is not too late, I shall have him release all but Maja. I'm afraid I have promised her to him, and it is most unwise to renege on a promise to a dragon."

Abderian felt a flash of anger at Javel's lack of concern for his daughter. But he had to hope that Horaphthia would get his message, or that Burdalane and Dolus could somehow help Maja. "And my brother Paralian? What will you tell me about him, now that I've agreed."

"Very well, Abderian," said Tingalut, "you are entitled to the truth. Quite simply, we don't know what happened to Paralian. He disappeared one day, leaving all his clothes and possessions behind. There was evidence in the temple that he had worked some sorcery there, but we were unable to determine its nature."

"Then he might still be alive!"

"It is possible. Though this brings up an interesting question. How could the cursemark have transferred to you if not in death?"

Abderian said, "Yes. Interesting," and nodded a trifle too fast.

Raising a suspicious eyebrow, the priest asked, "You wouldn't happen to have any ideas concerning that, would you? If something occurs to you, please let us know. It could be most useful later."

Javel rested his face upon his steepled fingers. "If Paralian lives, might he not become a problem for us?"

Abderian stared at Javel, shocked.

"Oh, I think not. If he had wanted, or were able to cause trouble, we would have seen signs of him by now . . . particularly since the events at Castle Mamelon. He's likely exiled himself to the Gorgorran Empire, so I doubt that we shall see him again."

Somewhere in the distance a bell chimed twice. "Ah," Javel said, "that will be dinner. Come, Tingalut, shall we introduce Khanda to her newly betrothed?"

SEVENTEEN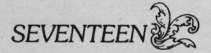

DINNER WAS SERVED in an enormous dining hall that showed signs of serious neglect. Dust coated the floor and the draperies, and seemed to hang in the air. The prince, the priest, Lord Javel, and Khanda were seated at one end of a long narrow table. Candelabra had been set near the diners, but the rest of the hall was left in darkness.

Khanda had been told her fate as they sat, and at first her blue eyes had flashed defiance. But her father's tone had indicated he would accept no dissent, and she had quietly acquiesced. Now she regarded the prince with an expression that might be worry, or speculation.

Their dishes were brought by two servants who came and went in utter silence, which only added to the eeriness of the setting. Abderian picked at his food, though he was hungry, trying not to look at Khanda and trying not to think of Maja in Kookluk's grasp.

Numerous questions drifted through the prince's mind. *Is this what my dream meant? That Javel would ultimately control me? Is this what the Lady of the Nightsword warned me of? The more dangerous path?*

Javel and Tingalut were chatting amiably about preparations for the move to Castle Mamelon. Seeing Javel in a good mood did not endear him any more to the prince. Though the nobleman smiled, his eyes glittered like knifeblades in moonlight. *He has so much hate,* Abderian thought, *I wonder if he truly enjoys anything.* Tingalut wore an air of pleasant reserve. It was clear the two men did not quite trust each other. Abderian wished he had the wits to use that fact to his advantage.

Finally Khanda pushed her chair back from the table, the scraping of the wood on the stone floor echoing loudly in the hall. "Father, I wonder if I might be permitted to speak privately with His Highness for a while."

Javel frowned. "Why?"

She gave an embarrassed smile. "If he is going to be my husband, Father, I should like to know what behavior he will expect of me, and how I should comport myself at Castle Mamelon. It would not do well for our bid for the throne if I were to arrive unprepared to be queen."

Javel stared at his daughter a moment, then gave a bark of a laugh. "You are a bright girl, Khanda, and sensible. Of course. You may take a sconce and sit with him at the far end of the table. You understand—I'd like to keep an eye on him for now."

"Yes, Father." Nodding to Abderian, she rose and took a candelabrum in hand, then guided him down the hall. At the far end of the table she sat opposite the prince, placing the candles to her left. The light and shadow cast by the candle flame made the statues lining the walls seem to be leaning inward, as if to listen in on the private conversation. Abderian felt no more comfortable here than he had at the other end of the table.

Khanda leaned forward on her elbows, but just looked at the prince awhile, saying nothing. Uncomfortable with the silence, Abderian said, "If you're wondering about the marriage, it wasn't my idea. I mean, I don't mind that we have to get married, you seem nice enough, but if you aren't excited about it, well, I won't be offended or anything."

"You don't have much experience with women, do you?"

The prince briefly considered boasting about previous non-existent conquests. It was what Cyprian would have done in this situation. That in itself was almost reason enough for Abderian to tell the truth. "No, not really."

"I always thought princes were allowed to sow their wild oats early and whenever they wanted."

"My brother Cyprian is like that. And Paralian was, too, a little, before he . . . left. But I'm . . . well—"

"You're shy."

"Yes, I suppose."

"You haven't had any official betrothals?"

"No. I'm not important enough in my family. At least, I wasn't until I got this cursemark."

To his surprise, Khanda smiled. "Good."

"You mean . . . you don't mind if—"

"No. In fact, I consider it a bonus. If you will excuse me, I need to ask my father something." Taking the candles with her, Khanda left Abderian in the dark in more ways than one. He scratched his chin and waited, wondering.

At the other end of the table Lord Javel said, "You want to *what?*" Khanda leaned over to whisper in his ear once more. Lord Javel's expression softened. "I see. Yes, that's a good point. Well, well. My little Khanda has grown up after all. Very well, my dear. As you please."

Khanda returned to the prince, her expression almost smug. "Father says I may escort you to your room. I trust you are weary from your journey and would like to lie down."

Abderian realized he was indeed tired, having risen early that morning and slept fitfully the night before, watching over Maja. "Yes, I believe I would, thank you."

Abderian heard Javel's coarse chuckle down the table and wondered what he found amusing. Khanda did not seem to notice and led the prince out of the dining hall. As they walked down another bleak, dusty corridor Abderian said, "You know, it's funny. Maja told me of a prophecy she heard that said both you and she would marry kings. At least you will fulfill your half of it."

Khanda was silent a moment. "Yes, I suppose I will." She put her hand through the crook of the prince's arm and smiled up at him. "Ah, here we are at your room."

She opened the door and led him into what was once a sumptuous bedroom. Now the gilt molding was flaking, and the velvet bedcovers were wrinkled, and the draperies were sagging. But clearly his residency was expected, for some of the dust had been cleared away and only one or two cobwebs remained. Abderian turned to wish his hostess and bride-to-be good night, and found her standing very close to him indeed, her face tilted upward—expectant.

Perhaps I am supposed to kiss her, he thought, a little surprised. He did so, finding it only a little awkward . . . and very pleasant.

Khanda sighed and said, "That was a nice beginning."

"Beginning?"

"Of course. If Father expects me to present him with a royal heir as soon as possible..."

Abderian gulped. *This* he had not been prepared for at all. His voice cracked embarrassingly as he said, "But Khanda, I'm not sure I'm ready—"

"Don't worry. Father owns several marriage scrolls. I've read them all, though he doesn't know it. I can teach you all you need to know."

"No, I mean, I don't *feel* ready."

"Leave that to me." Her delicate hands undressed him, smoothly caressing his shoulders, his chest, his abdomen. Abderian found himself scarcely able to breathe from mingled anticipation and fear as her hands drifted lower and lower. "My, what a fine, upstanding young man you are," she cooed.

Somehow Abderian found himself on the bed, and then Khanda was upon him and he forgot everything but the girl in his arms.

In one of the quiet hours before dawn Abderian woke to a sound he had not heard in a long time. Outside, a gentle rain was falling, and the breeze from the window brought in the sweet smell of damp grasses. *After so long a drought,* the prince thought. He felt Khanda beside him and hugged her closer, feeling happier than he had in a very long time.

Khanda stirred and gazed up at Abderian. With a breath-taking smile she said, "You've done something very special for me."

"And you for me!"

Khanda laughed and rolled out of his arms. Getting out of bed, she flung a dressing gown around her. "I don't think we mean the same thing." She leaned over the bed and kissed him on the forehead. "But come with me and I'll show you what I meant." She took up a candle and headed for the door.

"What? Where are you going?" Dressing awkwardly in the dark, he followed her. He padded down the hallway behind her, wary for any observers. Then Khanda selected one particular arras and slid behind it. Somehow she opened a section of the wall and pulled Abderian through with her.

For a moment the prince stood in near darkness until Khanda had lit some oil lamps that hung on the walls. The illumination revealed a small room lined with shelves from floor to ceiling.

The shelves were bursting with scrolls and tomes and bottles and doodads assembled in disarray. In the center of the room a circle of translucent stone was inlaid on the floor, and within it was carved an intricate design.

"What is this place?" asked the prince.

"This is what you've come all this way to see. This is Onym's study."

Abderian took another long look around him. "If this is it, why did you tell me it was destroyed?"

"I didn't know your reasons for asking. And I was afraid you might tell Father that I know where it is. He doesn't know that I've been studying sorcery on my own. After tonight, however, it won't matter if he knows or not."

"Why is that?"

"You'll see," Khanda said, smiling. She took down two vials from a shelf and began to mix their contents slowly.

Abderian wandered the room, scanning the shelves. "Do you think somewhere here might be a clue to where Onym now lives, if he lives?"

"It's quite possible. I couldn't say. You would probably have to search a long time, and even then it's probably encrypted in some odd manner. But there's a much faster way to find out."

"How?"

"Wait a few minutes and you'll see."

The liquid Khanda had mixed was giving off a pale yellow vapor and a very strange smell. She took up the vial and began pouring its contents into the circle on the floor, controlling the flow such that it fell in a pattern. As the liquid hit the floor it turned black and gave off gray smoke. Khanda hummed a sing-song chant as she poured, the eerie tone of her voice raising the hairs on the back of Abderian's neck. He felt a small thrill at thinking he had just made love to a sorceress. He also felt a modicum of worry, hoping Khanda knew what she was doing.

Taking some powder from another shelf, she threw it into the circle. There was a flash, and a gray column of dust and smoke rose from the floor. A red glow appeared in the column and spread outward to fill the area within the circle. A male figure appeared within the glowing column and solidified into an almost human form. The creature was tall, with a well-endowed physique, and eyes like shining scarlet opals.

A demon! "Khanda! Watch out, it's—"

"Fear not, Abderian. All is as it should be."

The demon turned and gazed at Khanda. "You know the price for summoning me again."

"Yes, Belphagor," she exclaimed, her face radiant with joy. "I am ready!"

"Then come, and be my queen." The demon stretched out his hand to her.

"What? Khanda, what are you doing?" The prince started around the circle to grab Khanda, but before he could reach her, she stepped into the circle and took the demon's arm. Abderian flung his arms toward her and felt white-hot sparks sear his skin.

"Do not interfere," said the demon.

"Be kind to him, Belphagor. It was this young gentleman who prepared me for this honor."

The demon stared at Abderian. "An unlikely liberator." He gave a deferential nod, although his expression did not change.

The prince felt hot tears well up in his eyes. "I don't understand, Khanda. Why are you doing this?"

"Don't you? Father intended to make me his pawn, using me to control you and your curse. To be a breeding cow for the sake of politics. Tonight I achieve a power of my own."

Abderian could see the same sort of defiance in the tilt of her chin that he had seen in Maja. "But why did you sleep with me if you're running off with . . . him?"

"It was necessary, I'm afraid. Demons have peculiar requirements. To wed Belphagor, I had to be a virgin whose virginity was taken by a virgin. That was rather difficult, since we have few visitors here, and Father kept a watchful eye on me. But you gave me the perfect opportunity. Father even encouraged our union."

"But what will I tell your father? What will he do to me?"

"Belphagor, I think Abderian deserves some sort of reward for his trouble. Can't you help him?"

Abderian felt as much as saw the demon's eyes upon him. His lungs seemed to fill with hot air and the back of his neck grew damp. His eyelids felt held open by force, and the demon's eyes blazed into his.

"Your problems come to you from the past," said the demon. "Therefore you must seek the answers in the past." Without turning his head, the demon pointed at the wall behind him. A section of the wall opened out, leaving a three-foot-square hole. "That way you shall find what you seek. You may call upon me once again if you create the circle and speak my name."

"Good-bye, Abderian," said Khanda with a sweet smile. "And thank you. I hope you get what you are looking for."

The demon and the girl shimmered out of sight, leaving the circle dark and empty. Abderian sank to his knees before it, overwhelmed with emotion. Though he had not yet come to love Khanda, he ached for losing her—for losing what might have been. He shuddered in fear and fatigue, and heavy sobs began to shake his body. Outside, the gentle rain became a torrent, and angry thunder rolled across the sky.

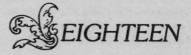

EIGHTEEN

THE STONE FLOOR was cold beneath Abderian's hands. He did not know how long he had knelt there, watching the circle for some glimmering, some sign that Khanda was returning. But the circle remained utterly black, illuminated only by the flickering lamplight on the wall. To his left, the hole the demon opened in the wall beckoned.

As the prince tried to collect his thoughts into some semblance of rationality, he heard faint footsteps from behind the wall on his right, where he and Khanda had entered the room. Then he heard voices, soft and unintelligible, but one was definitely that of Lord Javel.

Escape, said part of his mind, *before they find you*. He went to the wall and took down the lamp, the vial of strange liquid, and the magic powder, then carefully crawled into the hole. Suddenly he was sliding, face first, down a steep incline, rubble rattling around his ears. He struggled to keep the lamp upright and to keep himself from tumbling as he slid faster and faster. Finally, some seconds later, his elbows struck a hard surface and he stopped with a bone-jarring jolt.

The prince groaned and coughed dust out of his lungs. Slowly he crawled off the slide onto firmer ground. "Sagamore must have designed parts of this castle too," Abderian murmured, looking back up the slide.

A cold breeze blew onto his back, disturbing the lamp flame. At the top of the slide Abderian heard more than saw the section of the wall of Onym's study close once more, sealing off that route of return.

133

As the breeze died down, a hollow voice whispered into Abderian's ear, "Quite right, my boy. Come this way, if you please." The skin tightened at the base of the prince's neck and he shivered as he slowly turned around. He saw only an empty tunnel stretching away before him into darkness.

Standing on rubbery legs, Abderian headed down the tunnel, lamp held high in front of him. "Imagination," he grumbled to himself. *Or perhaps that demon is having fun with me.*

Further along, marble slabs were set into the earth walls. Some bore elaborate, carved scrollwork, others had names or short verses inscribed on them. Still others had sculptured faces and figures and an occasional grinning skull. *Catacombs.* Countless noble lords, ladies, and lesser castle residents were buried here, including—the prince noticed—a royal pet or two. He might have found it amusing if fear had not gotten hold of his throat, making it tight and dry.

He heard faint clicking sounds behind him and he whipped around, but saw nothing except the tunnel. *Beetles,* he thought, *or falling rocks.* He turned and continued walking, a little faster now.

Some paces down he heard the sound again and turned once more. He thought he could just barely make out something moving in the darkness behind him. His throat caught even tighter, making it hard to swallow. "You've had your little jest, demon," Abderian said softly, his voice wavering. "Please stop."

The prince walked on, striding as fast as he comfortably could. *It's nothing, you know,* he assured himself. *Fear and imagination, nothing more. Take another glance behind you and you'll see.*

The prince did so, and a scream caught behind his tongue. He nearly stumbled. Skeletons! Skeletons, whole, upright, and walking filled the tunnel behind him. They seemed to be marching, and some carried daggers, and some carried double-edged swords.

Abderian broke into a run, rushing headlong into the darkness before him. He heard the clickety-clacking behind him getting closer and closer. He uttered a strangled cry, uncertain whom to pray to or beg for help from.

Suddenly the tunnel opened out into a large cul-de-sac with a great marble door at the end. The prince rushed to it and struggled to open the door, finding it locked solid. *Dead end.*

Literally. He turned to face his doom, holding his lamp high as if its light might ward off his pursuers.

The skeletons stopped a few yards away from him and stood erect, weapons forward. Then all at once they saluted him.

Abderian stood gasping, wondering what was possibly happening.

"Welcome, O kin of Sagamore!" the hollow voice boomed. "I have been awaiting you!"

"You have?" Abderian squeaked. "You too?"

In answer, the marble door slowly opened inward and the voice said, "Come in!"

Keeping one eye on the ghastly army, the prince tiptoed through the marble doorway. Beyond it he found a magnificent tomb, with pillars and niches all carved in golden-veined marble. In the center lay a row of stone sarcophagi on whose covers were sculpted the likenesses of those interred within. Above one of these a column of pale light shimmered and twisted.

"Who's there?" said the prince. "Where are you?"

"I am here." The column of light formed into the shape of a thin gray-bearded man in royal robes and a crown. The crown encircled a three-pointed jester's cap.

Abderian's mouth dropped open in disbelief. "K-King Sagamore! King Sagamore's ghost!" he whispered.

"Boo," the spirit said with a wry smile. "Yes, I am a shade from the Fields of Those-Who-Have-Passed-Beyond. Don't you hate euphemisms such as that? One of my fellow travelers insists on calling our abode the 'Home for the Currently Bodiless.' It's most annoying." The ghost tilted his head to one side and regarded the prince with a puzzled frown. "Tell me, which one of my descendants are you? I was expecting someone . . . older."

"I am your great-grandson, Abderian," the prince said with a small bow, "and I am honored to meet you."

"If you are 'honored' to meet me, then you are a fool, which of course proves you are of my kin, so I thank you."

"I beg your pardon?"

"As king, I could certainly give you a pardon, although as a dead king I'm not certain where or how such a pardon would be valid. And do you really think a prince like you ought to be begging?"

Abderian was puzzled a moment, then understood. *Of course.*

This is the Jester King. "Why were you expecting me?"

"We of The Beyond are permitted to see somewhat into the past and future. It is very nearly our only recreation. Take my word for it, son, you don't ever want to become a spirit. Become a wizard and discover a spell for immortality. You'll be much happier for it. Being a spirit is a ghastly bore. Heh-heh, get it? Ghastly?"

Abderian groaned. This conversation was going to be difficult. "So you saw I was going to be here."

"Well, I saw that one of my descendants would be coming. This pleased me, of course, since no one has ever bothered to visit my tomb except for Famlus, Thalion's son, who only came to spit on it."

"Then you know why I'm here?"

"To discover your roots, boy! To learn about the grandeur that was your past and is your heritage! To see for yourself the resting place of the famous—or is it infamous now?—Jester King of Euthymia. To—"

"To learn about the cursemark!" Abderian yelled, exasperated.

"To learn about the cursemark," Sagamore added softly, bowing his head. "I feared it would be that."

"Why? What is it?"

Sagamore held up a spectral hand. "Let me explain. During the last year of his reign I watched my beloved King Thalion waste away into infirmity and madness. He came not to trust any of his children, seeing them as cruel, or greedy—which they were no more than any usual royal family. It was all I could do to lighten his heart during those last days, given the pain I felt at his condition. I fear I did my job too well."

"What do you mean?"

"Thalion came to see me as the only soul he could trust. I remember his saying to me, 'Sagamore, thou art my greatest royal treasure. How canst thou have such joy and jollity that thou couldst sustain me all this time?'

"And I replied, 'My Lord, it is in the very being of a jester, for nature hath given us the mirth to sustain a kingdom, which is what we do through its king. Without us, kingdoms decay into eternal solemnity and sorrow.'

"And he was amazed, asking, 'Hast thou truly, dear Sagamore, the joy to sustain a kingdom?'

"And in reply, I boasted, 'Aye, Your Majesty, the boundaries of my merriment are no less than the borders of Euthymia itself!' It was only a jest, damn me, it was only a jest!" Sagamore's voice caught, and he made little gasps as if about to weep.

"But King Thalion took you seriously," Abderian guessed.

"Aye!" wailed the Jester King. "That very day he called in Onym, the court wizard, to make my foolish boast a reality. so it happened that my happiness, and that of my heirs, would be tied to the health of the kingdom. And to cap off the honor, so to speak, Thalion chose to make me king."

"So, when I am happy, Euthymia is well? Is that it? Somehow that doesn't feel right. Perhaps because I've so rarely been happy."

"Just so. My Lord Thalion assumed a simplicity of emotion that does not exist. He did not see, could not see, that my jollity covered anguish. That my jesting nature hid much deeper hurts and fears. So what Thalion intended as a blessing became, instead, a curse." Sagamore lapsed into sobbing once more. "When I saw the horrors this brought about when I became king, my guilt and sorrow only made matters worse. I was not a good king. Did they tell you I went mad before I died?"

"Yes."

"It's true. I did. The weight of the curse became too much. That is why the knowledge of its nature became lost. To know what it means causes more damage than the curse itself."

"Why, then, didn't you have Onym remove the curse?"

"I tried! He refused. He loved Thalion as well, and would not go against his command. I suspect Onym was slightly mad himself. Finally, in anger, I sent him away."

"Where is he now? Is he dead?"

"Dead? No, I have not seen him in The Beyond. If he were, I would give him an eternal tongue-lashing."

"How might I find him? Perhaps by now he has seen the error of his ways and I could talk him into removing it."

"That is unlikely, my boy. But if you wish, I will try to help you. It is the least I can do."

The spirit shut his eyes and seemed to concentrate a moment. "The vision is . . . somewhat blurry. It's like the way one's eyes get as one grows old—the things near in time are blurred and hard to see. Only distant things are clear. A pity no one makes scry-lenses for seers . . . he could earn a small fortune. Heh-heh-heh, get it? Fortune?"

Abderian gave a loud sigh. "You're not helping, Your Majesty."

"Oh, dear. I'm sorry. No wonder Euthymia is in such sad shape. You should find a wizard to bless you with a sense of humor. Hold on, I see . . . a dragon with some people standing near it. Does that make any sense to you?"

"Kookluk? Why would you be seeing him? He was guarding the gate above Castle Nikhedonia. He let me through but kept my friends hostage. Does this mean they are still alive?"

"I'm afraid I cannot say what point in time this is. It may be. Do any of these friends of yours know something about Onym?"

"Only Maja, and she knew only that I should look in Castle Nikhedonia. By the way, was it you who ordered Onym to make Kookluk need a maiden to possess? The dragon claims he is holding my friend Maja for that reason."

Sagamore closed his eyes. "So, you know of that. I am ever amazed at my own cruel folly. I was even the one to suggest that Kookluk be raised from his century-long slumber. Does not the perfect kingdom require a dragon? And does the perfect dragon not require a maiden? I am sorry my madness has touched you so personally. In my years as king, I thought only of what would be 'appropriate' for my kingdom, not what would be beneficial for its people. Unfortunately Onym was all too willing to humor me. I am pleased to see you have a better sense of responsibility than I."

Abderian wasn't sure if that was true. "If you can help me find him, it may not matter."

"Hmm. I cannot determine what this vision means concerning Onym. Perhaps you will have to ask the current keeper of the castle for more information."

"Lord Javel? He isn't going to be too friendly to me now that his daughter has disappeared."

"Is that so? Hmm. Let me look again. No, I'm afraid your only route seems to be to speak to this . . . Lord Javel, did you say? Him. I haven't much to offer in the way of protection for you. I doubt any of Thalion's kin would be impressed by me. But you may take this." Sagamore gestured at the wall to his right, and an object floated through the air toward the prince.

As Abderian reached out for it he saw it was a golden sword. Its hilt, however, was the shape of a jester's stick, complete with a face and three-pointed cap at the end.

"My Lord Thalion had it made for me as a coronation gift. It was intended to be purely for ceremony, but it has other uses. Commanding that small army out there, for example."

"The skeletons?"

"Certainly. I remember one of my best generals, Mungo the Sloppy, once said, 'Use whatever is ready to hand.' Only, I believe that is how he finally died. When attacked in his quarters one night, instead of taking the time to grab his sword, he tried to fight off his assailants with the glass of warm milk on his bed table. I'll have to ask him the next time I see him."

Abderian almost laughed this time. Then another thought occurred to him. "Have you, by any chance, seen my brother Paralian in The Beyond?"

"No, I've seen no close kin of yours except your father, my grandson, and he's not speaking to me."

Abderian smiled and bowed. "Thank you, Great-Grandfather. I shall make the best use of your gift, and information, as I can."

"You are welcome, Abderian. And if you cannot convince Onym to remove the curse, may you use it better than I did. And please do not think unkindly of my Lord Thalion. It was the act of a sad old king who wished only to help his people." Sagamore's image began to fade.

"I shall remember." Abderian gazed at the golden sword, his eyes captured by the lamplight glimmering on the blade. The reflected flames brought back a faint memory of a dream—where he sat on a golden throne, surveying a devastated kingdom. Was it a scene of what was to come if he let his sorrow and guilt drive him mad, as Sagamore had done? The sword felt very heavy in his hands. *Did I cause the drought?* He wondered how many of Euthymia's ills might be his fault. *Perhaps the old prophet at Castle Mamelon was right. In any case, I'm not worthy of this responsibility. I will cause only further misery.*

With renewed determination to rid himself of the curse, Abderian turned and went toward the marble door. Then suddenly he turned back. "How do I get out?"

Though his image was gone, Sagamore's voice said, "There are stairs to your left."

"Thank you," Abderian said, and went out to the tunnel,

where the skeletons still waited. He wondered a moment how one could command such an army. With a shrug he tried the first thing that came to mind.

"Atten-tion!" ordered the prince. Instantly the skeletons snicked erect and saluted. Abderian smiled. "Forward, march!"

The ghastly army began to march toward him. With more hope than he had felt in a while, Abderian turned and started up the stairs.

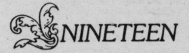

NINETEEN

ABDERIAN EMERGED FROM the crypt into bright morning sunlight. He wondered briefly if his skeletal troops might balk at the daylight, but they marched proudly behind him, never missing a step.

Looking around, the prince saw that he was in a courtyard behind the castle. There was a narrow window in the wall just ahead of him, but no entrances. He paused a moment, wondering what to do.

"There he is!" called a voice. Abderian turned to see one of the servants gesticulating in his direction. *No need to go looking for trouble,* thought the prince, *trouble is coming to me.*

In a moment Javel and Tingalut came around the corner, walking very fast. Javel's fists were clenched and there was thunder in his brow. Not even the sight of the skeletons slowed him. Tingalut came just behind the lord, tugging at his sleeve and urgently trying to tell him something. They both stopped a few yards away.

"What is the meaning of this?" growled Javel. "Where's Khanda?"

"If there was something you disliked about our agreement, Abderian," said the priest, "you should have told us sooner. We had planned to leave within the hour."

"I'm not going with you."

"It appears we have a misunderstanding somewhere. I thought you agreed—"

"I changed my mind. Khanda decided to marry a demon, and I have decided to go help my friends and seek Onym."

141

"You expect us to believe your lies?" snarled Javel. "What would Khanda know of demons? I despair of working with kin of Sagamore. I shall seek the crown myself!" Javel drew back his arm and golden flashes of light appeared between his fingers.

"No!" cried Tingalut, grabbing the lord's arm. "Think about what you're doing! You'll destroy everything if he is harmed!"

"He has disrupted my plans and done gods-know-what with Khanda. I would gladly endure chaos and ruin than try to rule with this . . . this . . ."

"Wait! Abderian, be sensible. Have we not told you that those in Kookluk's lair are beyond help? That Onym has not been seen for decades? Be a smart lad. Give us the sword, tell your fine fetid friends good-bye, and we'll be on our way, all forgiven."

"No."

"Then I can no longer be responsible for what Lord Javel will do." Tingalut let go of the nobleman's sleeve.

The golden glow brightened in Javel's hand and it leaped toward Abderian's face. Quickly raising the sword, the prince managed to deflect the magical orb. The skeletons hissed and chattered in anger. "Charge!" Abderian ordered, pointing the sword at Javel's middle. Clattering and rattling, the skeletons advanced upon the lord, weapons at ready.

"Oh, hush!" Javel said impatiently, waving his hands.

The skeletal army collapsed in its tracks—bones, weapons, and armor falling into a disordered heap. Abderian looked at the jumbled pile, then back at the wizard, feeling fear creep up his spine.

"Please reconsider, Abderian," said Tingalut. "Think of what you are doing to yourself and to Euthymia."

"It is too late for talk, priest. This Son of Clowns has caused me too much trouble." Another glowing sphere flew from the sorcerer's hand.

Abderian swung to bat it away, but missed. The orb struck him full in the chest. The prince felt as if he had been run through with a firebrand as the pain rushed through his upper body. His lungs felt about to burst. He reeled and staggered, barely able to hold on to the sword. The air around him grew bakingly hot.

Suddenly there came a wind, blowing dust and sand in swirling eddies. Abderian had to close his eyes to keep the dust from stinging them. Oddly, instead of blowing him over, the wind seemed to be holding him up.

"Where is he?" the prince heard Lord Javel cry. "Damn this dust!"

"I do not like this, My Lord," said Tingalut. "Let us go on to Mamelon and leave the boy be."

"No! He will only continue to cause us problems. We must be done with him now."

Abderian heard the sound of a fiery orb go whizzing past his ear, missing him. The prince wondered dazedly how much longer he had to live.

"Javel, you *idiot!*" roared a voice through the whistling of the wind. "Stop what you are doing immediately!"

"Horaphthia! You! By the Crown of Thalion, it cannot be you!"

"Well, I'm not the Lizard Goddess incarnate, ratface. Thought you'd safely keep me an old woman forever, eh?"

Horaphthia? Brownie found her! As dust and sand still obscured his vision, the prince could not see her. And though his pain from the first fire orb had subsided, he still felt the need to be wary for the next one. He awkwardly shifted back and forth, sword held at ready.

"I shall not tolerate any more interference from my family! Not even you, Aunt Horaphthia. None of you wanted to fight for the crown, yet you would try to keep me from attaining it!"

"We had our reasons, Javel. And all this foolishness you do shows why. You're beginning to make me think your grand-father was right in giving his crown to Sagamore."

"No!" Javel shouted, quite near to the prince now. Abderian swung the sword defensively and struck something firm. He heard a sickening groan, and he struggled to pull the weapon away from what, the prince feared he knew, he had hit. Abderian staggered backward and opened his eyes a little . . . enough to see dust-covered blood running down the golden blade.

Indefinable noises surrounded him for a moment, and the prince felt disoriented and sick. Finally the sorceress called out over the wind, "You can stop the hurricane now, Abderian, they're gone."

"What?" At first Abderian did not understand what she meant. Then something deep within him relaxed, and the wind began to die down.

Without the wind to support him the prince fell forward on his hands and knees, dropping the sword. Before him he saw Lord Javel's robe, crumpled and heavily stained with blood. "Is—is he dead? Did I kill him?"

"I don't know."

Abderian heard the approach of light footsteps and looked up. Beside him stood a woman wearing a loose red and purple gown. She seemed perhaps forty years of age, with a strikingly attractive, angular face that was framed by thick black hair.

She really has changed. The only thing about her that's like Apu are her eyes.

She picked up Javel's robe. "It certainly seems that you dealt him a healthy blow. Much as that is a contradiction in terms," she added with a wry smile. "From the marks on the ground, I'd guess the lizard priest transported him, or his body, somewhere. You know, I ought to be furious with you for ruining the surprises I had planned for him. It would have been a lovely revenge. I sincerely hope you have a good explanation for this mess."

"I'm sorry." Abderian caught a whiff of the blood on Javel's robe and felt his gorge rise. Though he did not at all care for the man, Abderian found himself fervently hoping Javel was still alive.

"Hmm, you're looking rather pale. Perhaps we ought to retire to someplace more comfortable. Just stay right there. That'sa boy."

Abderian had no problem complying. He didn't feel like moving at all.

Horaphthia walked around him, uttering strange words and drawing in the dirt. The prince looked down between his hands and saw, beneath the dust, flowers that were now withering and dying. He wondered if his curse had caused them to be, or caused them to die . . . or both. He felt as guilty over them as he did for the wounding of Lord Javel.

Suddenly the world around him blurred and swirled dizzyingly. When everything straightened out, the prince found himself lying on a rough stone floor. Horaphthia's strong hands helped him stand. Then she looked into his eyes. "Oh, dear. Not used to sorcerous modes of travel, I see. The window is that way." She guided him quickly to a narrow window, where he leaned out and relieved his stomach of its contents.

When he raised his head at last, he looked out upon a beautiful view of mountains. But above them a bank of dark clouds roiled over the peaks. They seemed to move of themselves, their churning not caused by any wind. From the interior of the clouds came a greenish glow that flickered as they moved.

Abderian backed away from the window, staring aghast at the scene.

"What is it?" Horaphthia said, coming up behind him.

"It's me. It's this curse. I caused that." The prince pointed a shaky finger at the clouds.

"Your curse? Ah, the Curse of Sagamore. I recognize it from when I was growing up in Sagamore's court. Those were exciting times, let me tell you. Now, come have a seat and relax."

Abderian let the sorceress guide him to one of the two chairs in the room. The only other furnishings were a folded bedroll in one corner, a cabinet with many drawers against one wall, and a small hearth in which hung an iron teapot.

Abderian rubbed his face as he sat, feeling miserable. He felt something warm on his lap, and saw that Horaphthia had given him a steaming mug of tea. A few sips of the warm liquid and he felt much better.

"So, you are the new bearer of the Curse of Sagamore. No wonder Javel was so interested in you. It's a good thing I showed up when I did. You are forgiven for spoiling my revenge."

"Thank you. Um, where are we?"

"This is my home," Horaphthia said, "but, of course that doesn't help you, does it? We are some miles to the north of Castle Nikhedonia. Would you care for some late breakfast? No, I see you wouldn't. Mind if I indulge?" The sorceress covered a bowl of biscuits with cloth and placed it on a little bed of coals in the hearth. She took a second mug of tea and cradled it on her lap as she sat in the other chair. "So what brought you to Castle Nikhedonia? Were you that eager to find out about Maja's father?"

"No, I came to learn something about Onym."

"Onym?!"

"Yes. The dwarfs told me he was responsible for this curse, and Maja told me his study was in Nikhedonia."

Horaphthia began to laugh. "Oh, dear. Yes, it is. But what

on earth would you want with Onym?"

"I want to find him. I want him to lift the Curse of Sagamore from me and my family forever."

"Oh, no." Horaphthia covered her face with her hand, still laughing. "Good luck."

"Thanks. As I told Maja—" Suddenly Abderian looked around. "Where is Maja, by the way?"

"How would I know? The last time I saw her was in the hut near the forest. If she didn't stay with you, my best guess is she's staying with her dwarf friends."

"No! Didn't Brownie tell you?"

"You mean your little feathered messenger? He wasn't terribly clear in his message, I'm afraid. I could only discern that you were going to see Lord Javel and the bird was worried about you. Poor fellow. Transformance cases usually do have messed-up minds, particularly with so drastic a change."

"What? Never mind. Didn't he mention Maja at all?"

"The only other thing he babbled about was a dragon."

"But that's it! Maja is caught in the paws of the dragon Kookluk, who guards the pass above Castle Nikhedonia. I hope that Burdalane and Dolus have been able to free her, but I don't know. If they haven't, they may no longer be alive."

Horaphthia frowned with concern. "Hmm. Caught by Javel's dragon? I don't like the sound of that at all. Maja is a tough little cookie, but I don't think she's up to handling dragons. I'd better pop over to Kookluk's gate and have a look myself."

"Good. Let's go!"

"Now, wait a minute, young man. From the sound of things, it isn't a good idea to put you anywhere dangerous. You may stay here while—"

"No!" Abderian stood up. "I was responsible for putting my friends there. I want to help them get out."

"A noble sentiment, but impractical, as many such are."

"But I have to do something! I can't just sit here."

Horaphthia frowned, studying the prince a moment. "Very well. You say you wish to find Onym. I may be able to help you there. He has put up several spellblocks to ensure his privacy, but there are ways around that."

"How do you know this?"

"Simple. Onym is my father."

Abderian felt his jaw drop open. "Why didn't you tell me?"

"I was about to when you brought up Maja. Not that my

relation to that stubborn old wizard will help you. He has hidden himself even from me, and I haven't had much urge to find him. You understand, he may be quite mad."

"So I've heard. But it doesn't matter. I must see him."

"To remove your curse, yes. I suppose you must try, though I recall King Thalion demanded that the spell be permanent. But we are wasting time." The sorceress stood and went to the cabinet. She pulled from a lacquered box a white stone and began drawing on the floor. "I will send you to the location of someone who knows Onym's whereabouts. It is a way around my father's hiding spells that I've thought of trying. This may be risky, but it's safer than taking you to a dragon's lair."

"But what if there is no one who knows Onym's whereabouts?"

"Come now, you wouldn't be searching for him if you truly believed that, would you? Besides, the spell will simply not take you anywhere if there is no place to go. There. Now give me a lock of your hair."

"What? Why?"

"So that I may find you later. Here, I'll do it." she whipped out a slender dagger and deftly whacked off a lock of his brown hair, which she then knotted onto her belt. The sorceress wiped the blade of Sagamore's sword on Javel's cloak, then handed the weapon to the prince. "Here. Just in case. Now step in the circle."

Abderian reluctantly did so. "You'll come get me as soon as my friends are freed?"

"Yes. Now, don't worry. With your condition it would only make matters worse. Until we meet again . . ."

The prince watched her wave her arms and chant again, and the world beyond the circle became a kaleidoscope of colors. He fought his vertigo and nausea this time—not liking the thought of another eerie cloudbank, or something worse, appearing somewhere in Euthymia.

When the view before him settled down to a solid hue once more, Abderian dizzily fell over against something soft. Slowly looking around, he saw what he had fallen against was the fleshy white snout of the mighty Kookluk himself.

TWENTY

ABDERIAN SCRAMBLED BACKWARD until he ran into the cave wall behind him. *By the Goddess! Horaphthia must have made a mistake. She must have sent herself to the one who knows Onym, and she's sent me to the dragon. Now what do I do?*

Kookluk, who had apparently been sleeping, brought his head up with a snort. Rubbing a talon across his injured nose, the dragon said petulantly, "What did you do that for?"

"I—I'm sorry! I didn't mean to."

"But, say, aren't you the young prince I let pass yesterday? Why have you returned? Few care to visit me a second time."

"I, uh, Lord Javel sent me to tell you that you are to let Maja and the others go."

"Indeed?" said the dragon, raising the muscle above one eye ridge. "And why does he not give me this order himself?"

"Well, uhhh, he couldn't make it today. You see, he's been . . . injured."

"Mere injury would not stop a wizard intent upon giving an order. I'm sorry, little prince, but you cannot pull the leather over my eyes that easily. Now, why are you really here, hmm?"

"I came to res—see that my friends are all right."

"I thought it might be something like that." Kookluk sighed. "Well, I suppose you can join those who are left alive."

"Those . . . left . . . alive?"

"Yes, though I don't recall which ones I've eaten and which ones are left."

"You've eaten some of them? And you don't remember?" Abderian felt his heart sink as his stomach rose.

"Come now, boy, be reasonable. Do you remember what *you* had for yesterday's lunch?"

"It's not the same thing!"

"Perhaps to you it isn't. Ah, yes, now I recall. It was the four-legged ones I ate."

"What?"

"He means the horses, Abderian."

"Maja, is that you?"

"No, I'm an enchanted talking rock. Of course it's me." Her head peeked out from behind Kookluk's tail. "I'm glad you made it back. I think he was going to start on Dolus and Burdalane next. Where's Horaphthia?"

"She should have been here instead of me. I wish I knew where she went. I'm glad to see you're all right." He walked toward her, only to be blocked by a dragon's paw.

"That is quite far enough. She is my maiden now. I'll accept no interference from you."

"I see. Well, mighty Kookluk, does this make you think any differently?" The prince poked the golden sword toward Kookluk's neck. "Now will you let her go?"

"My, my, what pretty thing have we here?" Kookluk deftly plucked the sword out of Abderian's hands and examined it. "Yes . . . quite a nice item this is. I'll be pleased to add it to my collection." He tossed it onto a huge pile of weapons, armor, and bones. "But someone should have told you, young man, that I do not take bribes. The Lady Maja will stay in my keeping."

Maja shook her head. "Some rescuer you are." Then in a loud whisper she added, "But thanks for trying."

Abderian turned away, fists clenched, and kicked a rock in helpless anger. He briefly considered trying to collapse the cave with the power of the curse, but knew it would be foolish. Particularly if he were to succeed. "Where are the others?"

"Down that passage, in another room."

Abderian ran down the stony tunnel until he came upon a small chamber in which Burdalane and Dolus stood manacled to the wall. "Hello! Is everyone all right?"

"Abderian!" They shouted nearly in unison.

"I am glad to see you, cousin, yet I am not. 'Tis not safe for you here. We all yet fear for our lives."

"Aye. You will be lucky to escape with your skin, like the

rest of us," said Dolus. "Despite the fact that I'm pleased to see you, Abderian—why do you stare at me like that?"

"You do look like him." Had the prince not known better, he would have sworn that the person chained next to Burdalane was a greatly disheveled and worn Lord Javel. After shaking his head and looking closer at Dolus, the resemblance seemed not so great. But now Abderian saw why Maja had reacted as she did when she first met the wizard.

"Javel, you mean? There is still that much resemblance? How interesting. A pity Kookluk didn't think so. Even with my few tricks and Burdalane's strength we haven't been able to free ourselves."

Suddenly there came a loud *fwoomp!* from the main cavern behind the prince. "That might be Horaphthia," he said, and ran back down the passage.

When he reached her, the sorceress was standing and dusting off her gown. She carried a large satchel under one arm.

Kookluk said, "Dear me, another guest. No one told me I would be giving a party."

"Greetings, O mighty Kook—Abderian, what are you doing here?"

"Apparently you sent me here."

"I did not. I sent you to the person who knew Onym's hiding place. I sent *me* here."

"You must have made some mistake. We're both here."

"Impossible. The spells are quite distinct from each other. I'm certain there was no mistake."

"Horaphthia?" Maja called out from behind the dragon's tail. "Horaphthia! It is you!"

"So it is. Are you all right, child?"

"So far. I feel much better now that you're here."

Horaphthia gave Maja a reassuring smile. "Now, where are the others?"

"In another chamber," Abderian answered. "They're fine, though a bit tired and hungry."

"Pardon me for interrupting this charming conversation," Kookluk broke in, "but seeing that this is my domain, could you please do me the courtesy of explaining who you are and what you are doing here? I like to know who it is I will be destroying."

"Certainly, O mighty Kookluk," Horaphthia replied genially. "I am Horaphthia, daughter of Princess Pavonnine, grand-cousin to your late master, Lord Javel, Great-grandcousin to your captive Lady Maja, and sorceress without portfolio. I am here to relieve you of the burden of these people by removing them from your territory."

"And as I was telling His Highness—did you say my 'late' master?"

"That I did, great Kookluk. Lord Javel is dead. As his closest adult relative, it is my duty to hereby so inform you and release you from your bond to him."

"Father . . . is dead?" Maja said softly.

"Yes, child. You have my condolences or congratulations, whichever you feel appropriate."

Maja's expression was thoughtful. Looking at Abderian, she murmured, "Now we have one more thing in common."

Abderian wondered if she wanted him to console her. *Perhaps it's just as well that I cannot. It would seem wrong, since I am her father's . . . murderer.* His stomach twisted with self-loathing, and he had to look away.

"I assume you have proof of this," said Kookluk.

"Of course." Horaphthia put down her satchel and removed from it Javel's blood-stained cloak. "Here is the proof." She placed the cloak at the dragon's feet, then stepped back.

As Kookluk put his snout to the cloak to verify it was his master's, Horaphthia took Abderian's arm. "Take me to your friends quickly!"

The prince led her down the passage, asking in a loud whisper, "You are now sure that Lord Javel is dead?"

"No. I still don't know, and I'm gambling that Kookluk doesn't either. But we must hurry to get the others out before he starts asking questions."

They ran into the other chamber, and Horaphthia stopped. "You didn't tell me they were chained!"

"You didn't ask!"

The sorceress sighed and looked closer at the captives. "This is going to take longer than I had hoped. Why, if it isn't my sister's son, Burdalane!"

"I beg your pardon, madam. I don't believe we've met."

"But of course. I don't think I've seen my sister Chevaline in, oh, twenty years. And here is my other grandcousin, Javel's brother."

"Horaphthia!" Dolus murmured in wonder. "I've not seen you since I was a lad. You haven't changed a bit."

The sorceress laughed. "Would you, of all people, expect me to? I taught you the preservation spells. Doesn't appear that you've used them yet."

"I've been more concerned with looking aged and wise than young and pretty."

"Ah. You know, when I decided to come here, I didn't expect it would be a family reunion. But, to work." The sorceress raised her hands toward the chains and began to sway and chant.

"Excuse me," said Kookluk from the chamber entrance. "One moment, please."

Maja sat with a worried expression on the dragon's back. She gestured something to Abderian, but the prince did not understand what she meant.

"Before you so kindly 'relieve' me of my 'burden,' there is one bit of unfinished business I must attend to."

Horaphthia slowly turned to face the dragon. "Which is?"

"One final instruction I was given by my master. Should he be killed while I serve him, it is my duty to seek vengeance on his behalf. So I ask you, kin of my master, who is responsible for his death?"

Carefully not looking at Abderian, she replied, "No one is 'responsible,' O mighty Kookluk, save perhaps your master himself. He died by accident."

"A most curious accident, I should think, madam sorceress. I have examined his garment closely, and I see the wound was cut into him, and I smell the tang of sword metal in his blood. Therefore, I ask again . . . who?"

Abderian felt himself begin to tremble. He steeled himself to not move a muscle until he was certain the situation was dire. But he felt the back of his tunic grow damp with perspiration.

Kookluk swung his snout in the prince's direction. "I smell fear—greater than before. Does someone *here* have reason to dread my accusation?"

Abderian swallowed hard, clenched his fists, and waited.

"You, little prince?"

Despite himself, Abderian's eyes shot wide and his shoulders twitched.

"I see. I wonder at my late master's wisdom in letting me send you through my gate. Nevertheless, I must fulfill his final request."

Time seemed to slow down as he watched the white claw rise and then fall toward him with assured death. Some part of Abderian heard Maja screaming in the distance. A last fantasy drifted across his mind—Paralian on a shining steed coming to rescue him, lifting him up and carrying him away to safety. Then the vision passed, the claw still descended, and Abderian waited to die.

TWENTY-ONE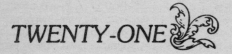

SUDDENLY THERE CAME a flash as lightning flew from Horaphthia's hands. Kookluk jerked back as the bolt struck his paw, bellowing in pain.

"Run!" cried the sorceress.

Time regained its proper speed and Abderian felt the legs beneath him come to life. Just as a paw crashed down beside him, he jumped aside and began running down the tunnel. He managed to reach the center of the larger chamber and quickly looked around. The only other exit was just beside the one he came out of, and Kookluk swiftly came in and blocked them both with his massive body.

"Do not incur my wrath further," growled the dragon, "or your death will not be swift, nor will your friends'."

Abderian looked to his right and saw, atop a pile of bones, Sagamore's golden sword gleaming. It was a chance . . . all he had.

Scrambling up the mound, the prince though, *Kookluk must have slaughtered an army to have this many bones*. As he grasped the shining hilt, he realized, *Bones! Army!* He held the sword high as the dragon advanced.

"Atten-tion!"

The mound beneath him shuddered and slithered and began to collapse. Bone snicked against bone and ancient weapons flew into skeletal hands. Armor clanged onto ossified frames and shields rose at ready.

Somehow the prince managed to keep his feet as the sorcerous army assembled out from under him. In scarcely a minute, at least fifty troops strong surrounded him and saluted with intense martial spirit.

Kookluk paused, surprised and uncertain. This gave Abderian his chance. He pointed at the dragon with the sword and ordered, "Forward, charge!"

An unearthly, grating groan, like bone grinding bone, arose from the skeletal troops. As one, they rushed at the dragon. "Try and swallow *these*, Kookluk!"

The troops quickly moved in, sticking their swords and spears into the reptile's leathery hide. With a disgusted sneer Kookluk swept several skeletons away with one paw—only to see them reassemble and join the fight once more. He brought his foot down atop another set of soldiers, only to bellow in rage and pain as they stabbed him from beneath. He tried to bite them as they slashed at his lips and tongue. Dark, bloody cuts began to appear in his flank, small but numerous. Presently the dragon was roaring in frustrated anger, moaning in wounded pain. At last he said, "Very well! Very well, I surrender! Please call off your sorcery! I submit!"

With a victorious smile Abderian called, "Cease attack!"

Again as one, the skeletons stopped and stood at attention, awaiting his next command.

"You will let us go free now?"

"Yes, yes. You may all go." The dragon began to lick at his wounds.

"Maja as well?"

For a moment Kookluk glared at the prince with eyes radiating hate. "She was promised to me! The death of my master does not change that."

"I can always order my army to complete the job it began." Abderian wondered if Kookluk's sense of self-preservation was stronger than his sense of duty.

It was apparently so, since a moment later the dragon said, "And Maja as well."

A cheer resounded from the people gathered at the chamber entrance. The skeletons responded with a ghastly roar of their own and clattered their weapons against their shields in praise. On a whim, Abderian bowed to them. And, of course, they all bowed in return.

Maja rushed through the skeletal troops and hugged the prince hard. "Thank you!" she gasped. "You know, for a dumb prince, you're kinda clever." She kissed his cheek.

"Uh, thanks. I think." Had the moment been more private, Abderian might have kissed her in return, full on the lips. He considered it anyway, but chose a one-armed hug instead, so that he might still keep his sword ready. *She is not as lovely as her sister,* he thought, looking down at her, *but her face has more . . . character.*

"Excellent work!" called Burdalane from across the room. "I could not be a finer commander myself."

Abderian looked over at his friends and noticed Dolus setting a limp form down on the stones. "Horaphthia!" He rushed over to her side. "Is she all right, Dolus?" He felt sick that this woman might have been harmed by helping him.

"So far as I can tell, lad, she's merely stunned."

Abderian saw that the right side of the sorceress's face was bloodied, but she was otherwise unmarred. "What happened?"

"She tried a restraining spell on the dragon at the same time as she worked a spell to release us. Working these simultaneously took time which, unfortunately, she did not have. Only the release spell succeeded. And before she could complete the restraint, Kookluk dashed her against the wall."

Maja joined them and began dabbing at Horaphthia's face with a scrap of cloth. Presently the sorceress came around.

"Ohh," she moaned, "that's the last time I underestimate the speed of an angered dragon." With Dolus's help she stood, a trifle unsteady and leaning on the wizard for support. "This hurts too much," she mumbled, and with some waving of her hands, she healed herself until only a small bruise remained. "Ah, that's better. Abderian, I'm glad to see you managed without me. I was not in a state to be much help."

"So I see." The prince managed a rueful smile. "Well, you can make amends by finally sending me to where I was supposed to go in the first place. To the one who knows Onym."

Horaphthia gave an exasperated frown. "I told you, I made no mistake. The spell was simple enough, I could not have possibly botched it. Face it, someone here must know the whereabouts of Onym."

"But I've asked all of them. Not even Maja knows."

"Then someone is holding back," the sorceress said, folding her arms with finality.

"Who?" cried the prince. "Who here could possibly know where Onym is?"

Everyone looked at one another warily. They almost didn't

notice the wounded Kookluk raising a tentative claw.

"You!" said Horaphthia. "Of course. I should have guessed."

"The dragon?" said Dolus. "Oh, no."

The sorceress gave Abderian a glance that said *I told you so.*

The prince sighed. "Great. Just my luck. Now what?"

"I believe you shall have to convince our reptilian host that it is in his interest to tell you."

Kookluk bared his teeth. "Not by the tail of the Lizard Goddess."

Abderian turned toward his skeletal troops, still standing at attention. "Company—"

"Very well! I'll tell you." Kookluk cleared his massive throat and intoned, "He lives in the Tower of Shame, west of The Edge of the World, east of The Pit of Forever-Dark, south of The Veil of Giant's Tears, and north of Demon's Teeth."

"Father always had a flair for the melodramatic," Horaphthia sighed.

"Father?"

"Later, Maja."

"Well, now that we know where we are to go, let's go!" said Abderian. "Is it far?"

Burdalane was shaking his head. "Several weeks travel, I fear, and through difficult terrain."

"Hmm. Then we ought to get started right away."

The commander chuckled sadly. "We no longer have horses, Abderian. And very little food. It simply isn't possible."

"But I can't have come so far to give up now!" The prince turned to Horaphthia. "Now that you know where he is, can your spell send us there? Or near there?"

The sorceress shook her head. "You don't understand, Abderian. The spell can only transport you to a person, some talisman of a person, or to a place you know very well. None of those conditions apply to what you are suggesting."

"But don't give up hope yet," said Dolus, eyeing Kookluk intently. "A reasonable source of transportation may be standing right before us."

"What do you mean?" asked Burdalane.

"Correct me if I am wrong, O mighty Kookluk," said the wizard, "but is it not true that your leathery hide can be shaped into wings when you have need of them?"

The dragon whuffed disdainfully. "What of it?"

" 'Tis well and good, Dolus, that you know such trivia about dragons," said Burdalane, "but—nay, you do not mean to suggest that Kookluk *fly* us to Onym?"

"Why not?"

Horaphthia smiled slowly in appreciation. "I see you have Javel's cunning as well as his looks."

"No!" cried Kookluk. "I have submitted to enough indignity. I shall do no such thing."

"Remember, I can call on my guard again."

"So you can, little prince. But you cannot bring your guard along with you. Once we are away from here, I might not be able to resist the temptation to drop you from a convenient height. Forget the idea, if you are wise. And leave me to take solace in the frustration of your quest."

Abderian sighed, feeling angry at another delay. The sooner the cursemark was gone from his arm, the easier he'd sleep. Who knows what destruction was being wrought through the kingdom as he was subjected to various frights, dangers, and frustrations. When this was done, he would be surprised if there would be any Euthymia left to be ruled.

Abderian looked back at the dragon. "I'll chance it."

"What?" gasped Burdalane in horror.

"Think about what you're saying," said Horaphthia.

"I have thought enough. Kookluk is my only avenue to Onym, and he will take me there."

"Do you seek death so soon?" asked Kookluk, a hopeful gleam in his eyes.

"Not at all. Maja will come with me. Should you try to unload me during the trip, Maja will fall too. You wouldn't wish to harm your maiden, would you?"

With a look of regret toward Maja, the dragon replied, "But I have already lost her as my maiden, as you ordered. Therefore her death costs me nothing."

Abderian frowned, momentarily outwitted. It was time for drastic measures. He looked at Burdalane. "The Nightsword?"

The commander shook his head angrily. "So that my lady of the boat may end up on a pile of bones? The pain it would give him would only anger him further, and do us no good. Face it, Abderian—"

But the prince cut him short with a curt wave of his arm. He had one last gambit to play, and he was determined to prevail over Kookluk's stubbornness.

"In that case, O mighty Kookluk, how do you feel about demons?"

"Demons?" In an oddly human gesture Kookluk rubbed his chin with a paw. "Demons and dragons are both protected by the Lizard Goddess. I would expect any demon to be my ally, not yours."

"Shall we find out?" Abderian took out the vial of liquid and removed the cork stopper. Yellow vapor drifted out of the bottle and spilled over the side. Dolus and Horaphthia each took a step back.

"Where did you get that?" Dolus breathed.

"Onym's study. My visit to Nikhedonia was not entirely fruitless." The prince poured out the liquid in a rough circle on the cave floor. Again, as the liquid struck the stone surface, it turned black, giving off a thick gray smoke. Abderian set down the bottle and pulled out the packet of powder. He tossed a handful into the circle and said, "Belphagor!" A column of smoke rose out of the circle toward the ceiling. In moments it glowed red from within, and a figure formed in its midst. Another moment, and the demonic figure of Belphagor stood before the prince.

"Greetings, Lord of Demons. About that second favor you offered me . . ."

"Consider well before you ask. This is the last aid I will give you."

"I have no choice but to ask you now, Belphagor. If I do not find the wizard Onym, the curse I bear might destroy myself and the kingdom. This dragon, Kookluk, knows where to find Onym and has the means to get me there, yet he refuses to help me. Could you, perhaps, persuade him to accommodate me?"

"Yes. It is important that you find Onym. I will gladly do this." Belphagor turned to face Kookluk, who reared back his head, offended.

"How dare you! In the name of She who serves us—"

"You mean, dragon, She whom we must serve. My people bear no love for the Lizard Goddess, who would dominate us. I feel no kinship with you, avatar of Her domain. It gives me no qualms to do as this one asks."

The demon gestured in the air, and a rope of fire appeared

in his hands. With a deft toss Belphagor threw the flaming cord in a fiery lasso over the dragon's head. It solidified into a harness of scarlet rope.

"Remember, Kookluk," said Belphagor, "this bridle was once fire, and fire it can become again."

The dragon pawed dejectedly at the bridle a moment, then simply glared sullenly at the demon. "You will pay for this indignity, both of you," he snarled as Belphagor led him out and up the righthand tunnel.

Horaphthia shrugged at Maja, who was looking worried and confused. Taking her hand, the sorceress led the girl after the dragon.

Abderian was about to follow, but Dolus caught his attention and pointed at the skeleton army, still standing awaiting orders. "Shouldn't you take care of them first?"

"Oh. Right." As Dolus and Burdalane went up the passage Abderian raised the golden sword toward the troops. He felt a touch of regret at giving this last command. They had served him well. "Dis-missed!"

With a final salute the skeletons separated once more, falling with a hollow clatter to the ground. "Rest in peace," the prince said softly, then he turned on his heel and dashed up the passage.

TWENTY-TWO

OUTSIDE, ABDERIAN WITNESSED a startling transformation. The passage had led out onto a high, broad ledge. There, Kookluk stood, bending his forelegs to lie straight back along his body in what looked like a painful angle. Twisting this way and that, the dragon worked his arms deep into the folds of his skin. For a time he shrugged and wriggled like a child putting on a too-tight coat. Then he stretched his arms out from his body to display a magnificent pair of leathery wings.

Belphagor stood waiting beside Kookluk, holding the crimson harness like some nightmarish stablemaster. Maja pulled Abderian aside and asked, "Where . . . how did you find that . . . thing?"

"That 'thing,' Maja, is your new brother-in-law."

"What? Stop joking, Abderian."

"I'm not joking. Remember the prophecy that both you and your sister would marry kings? Well, Khanda fulfilled her half. Belphagor is King of the Demons. He's willing to help me because I helped, uh, assist their elopement."

"That's ridiculous. Father would never have let Khanda marry a demon."

"He didn't have any say in the matter."

Just then Horaphthia walked up. "I thought you were eager to leave," she said sardonically. "We've been discussing logistics. You, of course, will ride Kookluk. I can then magically transport myself and two others to you. The problem is, that leaves one left behind. Someone else will have to ride the dragon with you."

Abderian turned to Maja. "Will you come with me?"

161

Horaphthia began, "I don't think—"

"I'll go," Maja said even though her eyes still held fear. Abderian smiled.

Horaphthia asked, "Are you sure? Yes, I see you are. Well, Belphagor isn't exactly a proper chaperon, but I suppose he'll have to do."

Chaperon? Abderian wondered just what the sorceress thought he and Maja could do atop a dragon in flight. He was almost sorry he would probably not have a chance to find out.

"Now, when you arrive," Horaphthia went on, "you must tug on your hair three times. Then I will find you with the lock of your hair I carry, and transport the rest of us to you."

Abderian nodded and approached Belphagor. "Well, I'm ready."

The demon leaped onto Kookluk's back and lodged himself at the junction of the dragon's neck and shoulders. Abderian cautiously clambered up the dragon's side, lending a hand to Maja, who came up behind.

"Take hold of my belt," said Belphagor. A loose leather band appeared around the demon's waist, and the prince took hold of it, noting that the demon's skin radiated intense heat.

At least my hands will be warm, he thought. He felt Maja slip her arms around his waist, and he smiled to himself. *And my back will be too.*

"Good-bye, children," said Horaphthia, "Abderian, remember three tugs when you arrive!"

"Be careful, cousin!"

"Luck be with you, lad. Have fun."

Abderian and Maja waved. Then Belphagor slapped Kookluk's brow with the scarlet rope, and the dragon lifted his mighty wings and leaped off the ledge. The sudden lurch and drop in altitude nearly sent Abderian sliding into Belphagor's back. Maja clung tightly to the prince's waist. Abderian felt her bury her face between his shoulder blades, shaking with fear.

The wind whistled past the rider's ears and whipped their hair behind them as the dragon picked up speed. "Well now, Master Belphagor," Kookluk's voice boomed in the wind, "as we are airborne, tell me, how you will keep me from throwing the lot of you against a cliffside?" At this, Abderian felt Kookluk's back fall out from beneath him and lurch to the side. The prince felt his stomach rise to his throat and he squeezed his eyes shut. Maja shrieked behind him.

"You forget, dragon, that your harness is made of fire. You pay a painful price for your trickery."

Abderian felt heat and brightness against his eyelids and heard Kookluk bellow in agony. The dragon's back slammed up painfully against the prince's loins, then dropped away again. But he himself felt no sensation of falling. Opening his eyes, Abderian saw that he was seated on air with Kookluk's writhing body not far beneath him. The prince quickly shut his eyes again.

"You see, dragon," said Belphagor, "we are not easily shaken. Should you try any more tricks, I will find it easier to take possession of your body, overpowering your will. And I assure you that would be far less enjoyable than your bridle of fire."

The prince felt the dragon's back come up again beneath him, but gently, and the ride became smooth.

"Abderian," Maja moaned between his shoulder blades, "are we all right now?"

"I think so."

"Then why am I still scared to death?"

"Try to distract yourself. Do problems in your head. Or think of a song."

"Hmm." In a quavery voice Maja began to sing:

King Vespin the Sneaky lived up to his name,
Instead of one sword, he had two, he would claim.
Though we don't believe him, we have heard it said
That maids lined up for miles when his swords he displayed!

"I didn't mean aloud," Abderian grumbled. "Where did that song come from anyway?"

"I don't know. But I've heard bits of it everywhere."

"So have I . . . unfortunately."

As the miles sped by beneath them Abderian managed to summon the courage to look around. The land below was rough and rugged, filled with chasms and canyons and swift-running rivers. The prince could see that trying to traverse such country on foot would have been very difficult. From above, however, he could appreciate its wild beauty.

On their left Abderian could see where the snowy peaks of

The Edge began to run north-south instead of east-west. To his right he saw hilly, dusty farmland stretching away to the sea. He wondered if a dark spot in the distance slightly behind them was Castle Mamelon, but he couldn't be sure. With a strange pang he realized he was farther from home than he had ever been before.

A rumbling in his stomach reminded the prince that he hadn't eaten yet that day, and it was already early afternoon. "I wish I had thought to bring some food with me."

"What was that?" said Maja.

Abderian repeated himself, shouting against the wind, over his shoulder.

"Oh. Just a minute." Maja removed one arm from the prince's waist and fumbled in her dress. "Here, have some of this." Maja pulled out of her pockets some beef buns and a small wine flask. At Abderian's surprised expression she added, "Kookluk was so full with our ponies, he overlooked our meal sacks. I grabbed some of the stuff on our way out."

Abderian took some, slipping one arm through Belphagor's belt to free his hands for eating.

"Do you think," Maja asked, "that our demon would like some?"

"I don't know. Belphagor?"

"Thank you, Prince. I would indeed."

Abderian handed a couple of beef buns forward, and watched as the demon warmed them with fiery breath before popping them into his mouth. The prince was amazed at what an amusing picnic could be held atop a dragon's back, a mile in the air.

Another hour or so passed until, ahead of them, they saw an enormous waterfall where a river rushed over The Edge. At its base the water fell into a deep, misty chasm.

"The Veil of Giant's Tears," announced Kookluk. "We are close to Onym's home." The dragon began a slow, spiraling descent into a tiny vale just south of the waterfall. It was a spectacular view, making the prince almost sorry they had to land. Down and down the dragon glided, swooping close to the slopes surrounding the vale. Now a small tower with a moat was visible below them. A few more circuits of the valley, and Kookluk was able to bring them to a surprisingly gentle landing just across the moat from the tower.

Maja quickly slid down the dragon's side, followed by

Abderian and Belphagor. Kookluk swung his ugly head toward them and snarled, "Now, princeling, I may complete my late master's orders. Your demon cannot aid you further, having finished the task you gave him. You will not escape my wrath this time."

Belphagor stood between the dragon and the prince. "Though I shall no longer follow the prince's requests, I can give you information that you will find in your interest. You are acting in error, dragon. Your master is not dead. In fact, he and a priest of She whom you serve are, at this moment, attempting to summon you. Search your mind and you will find that it is so."

Kookluk shut his eyes, then snapped them open again. "So they do. And I must answer. But I will not forget any of you. Soon I will claim my vengeance." The dragon turned, and with a ponderous beat of his wings raised himself into the air, flying away to the northwest.

"I, also, will leave you now," said Belphagor. "But beware, Prince. More hangs upon your fate than you know."

More than the well-being of Euthymia? "Thank you, Belphagor." With a jocular wave he added, "Give my regards to Khanda."

As the demon became a dark column of smoke he said, "That I will." In a moment the smoke spun into a tall black needle, then sank into the earth.

Maja looked at Abderian. "Khanda?"

"I told you—"

"I don't think I want to know." She turned and walked toward the tower, then suddenly looked back at him. "Abderian! Your hair!"

"My hair?" Abderian's hands flew to his head. "What about it?"

"You were supposed to tug three times, remember?"

"Oh. Right." Sheepishly the prince pulled on his forelock. A minute passed and nothing happened. Then a shimmering appeared in the air, circular and blue-edged. In a moment Horaphthia's face appeared within it.

"Well, it's about time!"

"Sorry, we just got here. Where are you?"

"By a waterfall . . . I assume it's the Veil of Giant's Tears. We ran into a spellblock. I should have expected it. Looks like we'll have to walk from here. Go on ahead, if it seems safe enough. We'll be there before long."

As the shimmering vanished, Abderian and Maja shrugged at each other and headed for the tower.

As they crossed the moat over a rickety bridge, Abderian noticed how the area seemed alive with animals. Geese and ducks sported in the weedy moat, watching the fish leaping here and there. Rabbits and squirrels romped through the bushes. The eyes of shy creatures observed the visitors from behind rocks. Though the scene was charming, the feeling of being watched made the prince anxious and wary.

The Tower of Shame was, quite appropriately, unimpressive. It was short and squat and built of large gray stone, overgrown with vines and ivy. It seemed that the builder hadn't decided if he wanted a cottage or a tower, and got a structure that was a bit of both.

"It doesn't look dangerous," said Maja.

"Most of Onym and Sagamore's creations don't. Which is exactly what makes them dangerous."

They approached the front entrance, where a black and white kitten sat washing itself after giving the visitors a casual glance. With surprise they saw that the door was wide open.

"Do you think he's expecting us?" Maja asked.

"It wouldn't surprise me. But if he is, he's been waiting a long time. The threshold is covered with dust."

"Maybe he just isn't very tidy. Maybe he doesn't live here anymore."

"Don't say things like that. Let's go inside."

Cautiously they stepped through the doorway. "Hello? Anyone to home?"

The hallway they entered seemed much larger than what the exterior implied. It had a high, vaulted ceiling that echoed their footsteps. The walls were smooth gray marble. At the end of the hallway stood a pair of massive bronze doors.

"With a barrier like this," Maja said softly, "I can see how he wouldn't mind leaving his front door open."

"WHO DARES TO SEEK THE WIZARD ONYM?" boomed a deep voice.

The pair jumped and stammered in fear.

"ENTER, AND EXPLAIN YOURSELVES!" The great bronze doors swung slowly inward. Beyond lay an enormous room. Abderian was certain this wasn't part of the tower he had seen from outside. But he wasn't sure which was the illusion, this room or the exterior.

Against the far wall was a dais topped by a great stone throne, flanked by blazing braziers of iron. On the throne sat a man wearing robes of pale blue satin, studded with flashing gems. His hair and beard were long and of a steely gray. His eyes were the same shade of blue as his robe and affixed the visitors with a penetrating, inhuman stare. He sat utterly still as Abderian and Maja approached the dais.

"O great and mighty mage," the prince began, "we come from afar seeking your assistance. I am Prince Abderian, son of King Valgus of Euthymia. This is Lady Maja, daughter of Lord Javel of the line of Thalion. Long have I sought you regarding a matter of grave concern both to myself and the Kingdom of Euthymia. I most humbly beg you to hear my petition." Abderian bowed his head before the mage and awaited a reply.

"Meow," said the wizard.

TWENTY-THREE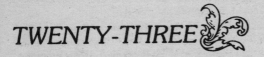

"I BEG YOUR pardon?" Abderian said.

"Mrrow?"

The prince and Maja looked at each other. Then they looked back at the wizard, who was staring at them with wide, curious eyes.

"What's going on?" Maja whispered.

"I don't know."

"Ho there, are you looking for me?" said a small voice by the prince's right ankle.

Glancing down, Abderian saw the black and white kitten looking up at him. After all he had been through, he was almost not surprised to encounter a talking cat. "That depends. Who are you?"

"Why, I am Onym, of course!"

"You are Onym?" Maja and the prince said in tandem.

"Well, yes, why—oh, I understand. You thought that fellow on the throne was me." It was very odd to hear a kitten laugh. "It's quite simple, really. The past few decades I've been practicing soul exchanges. In this case, I have merely thrown my mind, as it were, into the body of this kitten. The kitten's mind now resides in there."

"So that . . . person on the throne is your real form?"

"Oh, heavens no! I never looked so grand. That is my brother Osvog the Intimidating, who was not a good wizard, but looked the part marvelously. I sometimes wonder where *his* mind went. Perhaps it was a frog . . . Oh, well. It was so long ago, it hardly matters now."

"If that isn't your body, where—"

"Is my real one? Why it's . . . hmm. You know, I've forgotten where I left it. Don't go away, I'll be right back." The kitten dashed off through a small doorway to their left.

"No wonder Sagamore liked him," Abderian said softly.

"He's mad."

"I know."

"What are we going to do?"

"Wait, I suppose."

Some minutes later they heard footsteps descending a stone staircase and, off to their right, a door opened. What emerged looked nothing like the mage on the throne. Instead, he was a short, bald-pated, pot-bellied gnome of a man. His eyes were bright and his nose small and bulbous. He wore a too-voluminous, gaudy yellow robe, and carried a huge book under his left arm. "Ta-daa! Here at last!" he said, as if expecting applause. He received none.

"Good to see you again," said Abderian. "It is really you this time, isn't it?"

"So it is, my boy, so it is. Now, if you'll follow me, please." Onym led Abderian and Maja into a small adjoining room that was completely bare except for a high table. Abderian noticed with a slight shudder that the door they entered through vanished into the wall as soon as it shut behind them. The only door that remained was directly across from where they stood. *How much of this tower is sorcerous and how much of it is real?*

Onym set the book he carried down on the table and opened it randomly. "Since you are Prince Abderian, and I have not heard of a new line of kings upon Euthymia's throne, I presume you are here regarding Sagamore's curse. Am I right?"

Abderian's heart leaped with hope. *Perhaps he regained his sanity with his old body?* "Indeed, sir. I am. I wish it removed."

Onym absentmindedly wiped a cobweb off his nose and thumbed through the book he held. "He wants it removed . . ." he muttered. "He wants it . . . removed?" Onym looked up at the prince in horror. "I thought you just wanted to know what it is!"

"I know what it is."

"You do?"

Abderian sighed. "Sagamore himself told me. That is, his

ghost did. The curse makes conditions in Euthymia dependent on my emotions."

"Quite right, my boy! So how can you shirk this tremendous responsibility that is the heritage of your family?"

"That's just it. I'm not often cheerful, and my life has been anything but stable lately. Much of the mess the kingdom is in right now is probably my fault. My bearing of the curse is dangerous for the kingdom, if not for me as well, and everyone will be better off if it is dispelled."

"But . . . but that's—"

Suddenly there came a booming knock at the door. "One moment!" called Onym, and he went over to open it.

"I'll bet that's Horaphthiá," said Maja.

"Oh, dear," Onym was saying as he peered around the door. "Couldn't you have waited?"

The door was shoved open wide, and in strode several figures in pearl-gray robes. At their head, in a silver-gray robe, was the warrior Hirci. She held a bow drawn full back, within it a silver arrow aimed right between Abderian's eyes. With a satisfied smile Hirci said, "I shall not let you escape again, Your Highness."

"I was going to deliver them to you eventually!" Onym whined.

"Shut up!" snapped Hirci. "You see, Your Highness, though twice you have tried to thwart our plan, you have come to us in the end."

"Whose plan? I haven't tried to thwart anything! I just wanted to find Onym." Turning to the wizard, he whispered, "Onym, do something!"

"Meow," said the wizard.

"This is no time for jokes, Onym!"

"I don't think he's joking," said Maja.

Abderian looked at the wizard's eyes that darted about in wild comprehension. *His mind has snapped back to the cat and vice versa.*

"Now what?" the prince said to the robed warrior in front of him. His question was answered by a gust of cold wind that carried a swirling white mist through the door. Within it walked a female figure in a pure white robe, with a hood pulled low over her face. The woman stopped and pulled the hood back, revealing a gentle-face of middle age with blond and silver hair.

She smiled at the prince. "Welcome, Your Highness." To Maja she said, "Welcome, my daughter."

"Mamma!" Maja rushed into the woman's arms.

"Child," the woman said with deep affection as she held the girl.

Eyes brimming with tears, Maja looked back at Abderian. "This is my mother!"

Not sure what to do, the prince bowed. "I am honored, Lady Javel."

"Thank you, but that is no longer my name. It was torn from me when I was cast out of Castle Nikhedonia. You may call me Entheali, and I am known as the Star Mother by the members of our temple." To Hirci she said, "Put your weapon down! This one is welcome among us."

Slowly lowering her bow, Hirci said, "I am sorry, Star Mother, but this one escaped me twice."

"No doubt your aggressive manner frightened him. I should have expected it—'tis what one gets if one sends a warrior instead of a diplomat. Forgive her, Your Highness. She is merely zealous in her duty. I sent her because our people are not safe in Euthymia currently, and I had to send one who could defend herself."

"I see. But could you please tell me why you sent someone after me at all? What do you want of me?"

"Of course. Come with me and all shall be explained."

"What about Onym?"

"Poor Onym," sighed Entheali. "We look after him, but there is little we can do for him. We shall leave him be and perhaps he will recover himself."

"But he was going to help me with my curse!"

"He cannot help you, Your Highness, but we may." She turned, with her arm around Maja's shoulders, and walked with her through the misty doorway.

With a worried sigh Abderian followed, hearing the footsteps of Hirci and the others fall in behind him. He hoped he could keep from directing his irritation at Entheali, at least for Maja's sake. As kind as the Star Mother seemed, he did not like being a game piece in someone else's plan. And he wished he knew what Onym had been about to say about the curse before Hirci had burst in.

He heard the door behind them close, and they descended a ramp that was shrouded in mist. After a minute of walking, the mist parted and they were standing in a cavern. The walls had been deeply stained by minerals, and the ceiling was covered with tiny stalactites that sparkled like the stars in a night sky.

I seem to be spending a lot of time in caves these days, the prince thought.

From another entrance some women in gray robes entered, escorting Horaphthia, Dolus, and Burdalane. Upon seeing the Star Mother, Horaphthia exclaimed, "Entheali! So this is your doing! Is this any way to treat an old friend?"

"Horaphthia! My dear, I *am* sorry." After a brief embrace she continued. "But you know there are enemies of this temple, and we cannot be too careful. Ah, but who is this? Lord Burdalane, we have heard of you. You are also most welcome. And this? You must be Dolus, my once-husband's brother. Even you are welcome, though I know not your feelings for him."

"The point may be moot, My Lady, for Horaphthia has told us Lord Javel is dead."

Entheali threw back her head and laughed. "Oh, dear. Has Javel tricked even you, Horaphthia? Oh, no. My once-husband is not dead. I have watched him most carefully these past few days. Wounded he was"—she shot a glance at Abderian—"but dead he is not."

So it's true. Belphagor wasn't just tricking Kookluk to make him leave us. The prince felt a rush of relief, followed by worry. Would Javel seek revenge for his wounding?

"But I see you all have questions of me. Come sit and be refreshed, and I will answer all I can."

Gray-robed acolytes brought in cushions and dishes filled with fresh fruit and vegetables. More lamps were brought in to give more light. Maja sat eagerly at her mother's side, and the others sat around them. A pale wine was served that Abderian found tolerable and Maja seemed to relish.

After some time was spent eating and relaxing, Maja asked the first question. "Why didn't you ever send word to Khanda and me to tell us where you were?"

"I dared not, child. Especially since your father allied himself with the Cult of the Lizard Goddess. If he were to learn I was here, it would mean doom to this temple, and to our plans."

"And just what are your plans?" asked the prince.

Entheali hesitated. "Because you are not an acolyte of this temple, there is much I cannot reveal to you. But as you are favored by our Goddess, and are to play an important role, I will tell you this much. Seventy-three years ago, at the beginning of King Vespin's reign, our temple in Castle Mamelon was ruined. It was given over to the Cult of the Lizard Goddess. This was surely meant as insult, for that cult has long been in competition with us."

"Why would King Vespin want to insult you?"

"The Star Mother at that time apparently gave him ... unwelcome advice. He took strong dislike to her and her teachings."

Abderian noticed out of the corner of his eye that Horaphthia wore an expression that might be doubt, but she did not say anything. Dolus stroked his chin thoughtfully, but also remained silent. Burdalane was listening with avid interest. The prince asked, "And what is this 'role' I have to play?"

"You're an impatient one," Entheali chided him gently. "Simply, we want our temple back. And our rightful place as advisors to the throne. You will achieve this for us."

"Me?"

"Yes. And in return for your service we shall give you that which you seek. We shall remove from you the Curse of Sagamore."

"You will? You can do that?"

"Of course. Onym is in our care, remember? We have coaxed from him some of the secrets of the curse. I assure you this load can be taken off you. And we will gladly do so once the temple in Castle Mamelon is again ours."

Abderian felt some of his apprehension drain away. *Perhaps all is not lost, after all.* "What am I to do?"

"You must return to Castle Mamelon. Alone."

"Alone!" cried the prince. "But if Tingalut has returned there with Javel, they will just recapture me!"

"That," said Entheali, "is precisely what we want."

TWENTY-FOUR

"I DON'T UNDERSTAND," said the prince.

"I protest!" shouted Burdalane. "Lady Entheali, with concern for His Highness's safety, I must tell you that there are other threats to him in Castle Mamelon besides the lizard priests. Captain Maduro, for example, may yet wish to bring Abderian to trial for the death of King Valgus. As the crown has not yet been settled, any number of noble factions might see Abderian as a threat to their interests. How can you suggest sending him alone into such a quagmire?"

"Yes," said the prince, "why does it have to be me alone? Why don't we just have Horaphthia transport some of your warriors to the temple and have them clean it out?"

Entheali raised her hands for silence. "Please, do not make hasty judgments, my friends. Abderian, sensible though your suggestion may sound, it is not possible. Tingalut and his minions have protection spells on their temple more powerful than even those on Onym's tower. We would not get through that way. And Burdalane, do not think we will be abandoning His Highness to his fate. He will have our help. You have the Nightsword, do you not?"

Burdalane frowned. "Yes, but how—Star Mother, is the one we see in dreams after touching this sword your Star Goddess?"

"Yes, She is our own Tritavia. Once a powerful sorceress, She was so well-loved by Her apprentices that when She chose to leave this world, they built for Her a world of Her own, as eternally beautiful as She. The members of this temple maintain that world for Her now. By touching the Nightsword, you open

174

a pathway in your mind whereby She may reach you in this world."

The commander went to his pack and pulled from it the silk-shrouded sword. Returning, he reluctantly placed it at Entheali's feet. "If this sword belongs to your temple, then I presume you wish it returned?"

Entheali gave him a compassionate smile. "Although this temple created the sword and sent it out into the world, it is not to be returned to us. That would be a failure of its mission. You should now give it to Prince Abderian to carry."

"But, My Lady, the sword is dangerous!"

Entheali laughed. "Yes! It is meant to be."

Abderian said, "But your Goddess, in my dream, said the sword was not for me."

"And she spoke truly, for you are certainly not the Nightsword's intended victim."

Abderian paused a moment, realizing he may have been making the wrong assumption all along. "But I can't wield it either."

"It is meant to be used only once. You will know the moment when it arrives."

"If you please," Burdalane said, almost pleading, "if your Tritavia is the one in my dreams, I am most eager to serve Her, if She will have me. May I please do this one thing for Her? Carry the sword?"

"I am sorry, Lord Burdalane, that is Prince Abderian's task. Fear not, however. I know She has an important task for you, else She would not have spoken to you."

"Then I must rest content with that." Slowly Burdalane placed the sword before the prince.

Abderian regarded the silk bundle warily. "I presume I will know who the sword is 'for' when the time comes as well?"

"You understand perfectly."

Just then an acolyte in silver-gray robes came rushing in. "Star Mother! There is news!"

"Yes? You may as well tell us all."

"Our agent at Castle Mamelon has just sent word that Lord Javel's dragon has arrived and is in residence in the Temple of the Lizard Goddess."

Entheali nodded. "Good. Then all is in readiness."

"What?" Abderian said. "Wait a minute! You want me to

be captured and taken into the Temple of the Lizard Goddess, where Kookluk will be waiting? The dragon will kill me!"

Entheali smiled and shook her head sadly. "You have not allowed me to finish, Your Highness. We do not intend for you to face those in the lizard temple alone. Once you are inside you must take the Nightsword into the Hall of Patterns, which was once our Hall of Stars. It will be easy to find, for it is the largest room in the temple and it is where all the work of the lizard priests is done. When you get there, search for an inlaid star of silver on the floor. There may be more than one left, but any one will do. Place the Nightsword upon it and Tritavia will open a pathway from you there to us here, and we will join you."

"Fine. Then what happens?"

"You are an impatient one. I cannot tell you exactly what will happen then. There will be a ritual, and at one point you will be called upon to act. But you will choose what your action will be, depending on what has gone on before. How you choose will determine the outcome of the ritual."

"So it's . . . like a game?"

"More like a formal duel, but yes. Now, we will allow you to rest this night, and then we shall send you home tomorrow."

"Tomorrow?" Abderian said. "But won't I need more preparation?"

Entheali raised her hands toward the ceiling. "You have already done all the preparation we need!"

Looking up, Abderian saw thin filaments between the stalactites begin to glow with a silvery light, until they appeared as a huge, intricate, luminous spider web hanging over his head.

"Thanks to your wit and bravery," Entheali went on, "connections have been made that assure our success. You have no need to fear. Our temple has been preparing for this time for decades, and we will not let the opportunity pass. That is, assuming you agree to aid us."

"If you can truly take this curse from me, then I am at your service."

"I am relieved and gladdened at your acceptance. And you, Lord Burdalane? Will you help us in our hour of need?"

"With joy, I would do all I could for the lady of the Stars."

Entheali acknowledged this with a small bow. "Horaphthia, you have a grateful mother's thanks for looking after my daughter and bringing her to me. But there is no need for you to risk yourself in this final conflict. We do not ask your participation."

"But I offer it nonetheless, Entheali. Javel is no friend of mine. And"— she gave Abderian a rueful smile—"I was interrupted in my personal vendetta against him. I wouldn't miss this for the world."

The Star Mother gave a slight worried frown. "If that is your wish. And you, Dolus, you also need not come along."

The wizard shrugged. "But I, like Horaphthia, wish to assist you, Star Mother. You need not fear that I will take my brother's side in the conflict. There is little love between us. My powers were stripped by his allies, the lizard priests, perhaps at his suggestion. He knows I have as much claim to the throne of Euthymia as he, and he no doubt fears I will declare it."

Abderian looked at his wizard friend, seeing him in a new light. "Is that why Father stopped asking your advice and kept you stuck in the cellar?"

"It is the very reason I was brought to Mamelon as a young man. King Vespin wished to keep an eye on me. Javel, he felt, had already been bought with a duchy. Little did Vespin realize he was watching the wrong grandson of Thalion."

"If you could make reasonable claim to the throne, perhaps you ought to."

Dolus laughed. "Oh, no, lad. Like you, I've no wish to be king. I'll keep to my study of sorcery, thank you, and let others do the ruling. Though, I fear, my study of magic now will be mostly academic."

"Well," sighed Entheali, "if I cannot dissuade you, then we will find some way for you to assist us. Now, Maja, we have much to discuss. If the rest of you will kindly excuse us. You will be shown to guest quarters. May stars shine in your dreams." The Star Mother took Maja's hand and led her away.

"What is it, Horaphthia? You look worried," said Abderian.

The sorceress was staring after Entheali and Maja. "Hmm? Oh, perhaps it's just that I don't trust leaders of cults. I remember hearing stories that Tritavia gained Her powers through subtlety and craft. I suspect Her temple does likewise."

"I recall reading in Vespin's memoirs," Dolus put in, "that the reason the Star Goddess cult was expelled from Mamelon was that he feared they were becoming too powerful, not that he disliked their advice."

"You would take Vespin the Sneaky's view over that of these folk?" said Burdalane. "Surely you know better, Dolus. These kind people have offered to grant Abderian his dearest wish—to remove his curse. How can you suspect them of duplicity?"

"And what have they offered you?" Horaphthia asked.

Burdalane looked away and remained silent.

"Well, like it or not," said Abderian, standing up, "the Star Mother is the only person who has offered to remove my curse rather than use it. If it should suit her temple's purpose as well as mine, what does it matter?"

"I hope you are right, lad," said Dolus.

"I suppose I'd better get what sleep I can before I have to do . . . whatever it is I will have to do." Abderian bowed good night to his friends and allowed an acolyte in a charcoal-gray robe to guide him to a guest room.

The 'room' was scarcely better furnished than his grotto at the dwarfs' cave, and with a sigh he sat on the ledge bed to pull his boots off.

Just outside his curtain door, a voice called softly, "Abderian?"

"Yes, Burdalane, what is it?"

"May I speak to you a moment?"

Fearing that he knew what the commander would speak about, the prince stood up and pulled the curtain aside. "Of course. It's about the sword, isn't it?"

Burdalane slipped in and looked down at the prince. "Fear not, cousin, I am not here to take the Nightsword back from you. I wish only . . . only that you would allow me to hold it once before I go to sleep. So that I may dream of Her."

"But, Burdalane, you know what—"

"She will not harm me, cousin, not here of all places. And I will gladly endure what brief pain the sword gives for the chance to see Her again."

Abderian was worried, but he saw no reasonable way to argue his cousin out of his request. Particularly remembering how he had insisted on touching the sword himself back at Burdalane's camp. "Very well. But be careful."

"My deepest thanks, cousin."

The prince watched him unwrap the black silk bundle reverently and raise the sword. There came the familiar green bolts of energy from the blade into Burdalane's hands, but despite his agony he wore an ecstatic smile. After a brief time Burdalane dropped the sword and sagged against the wall, breathing hard. Abderian quickly rewrapped the sword, watching his cousin with concern. But Burdalane waved off all offers of help and, with a smile, staggered out.

Abderian sat heavily on the ledge again, worrying. Several things he had done since leaving Castle Mamelon had seemed, in retrospect, reckless or foolhardy. But none of them struck the prince as quite so . . . blindly idiotic as walking right back into Tingalut's temple, alone, and armed with a sword he could use only once. *Have I become so desperate I will do anything to have this curse lifted? On the other hand, do I wish to keep it and eventually go mad, like Sagamore, and destroy the kingdom? Or become the game piece for every power-hungry wizard, lord, or what-have-you?*

Abderian lay back on the mat, arms behind his head, and sighed. He had already made his decision. But he recalled what the lady in the boat—the Star Goddess, Tritavia—had said. *You will gain what you wish, but lose that which you do not value.* There had been times, Abderian remembered, when he did not value his life.

He was flying over the sea again. The night was just as dark and starlit, but there was a wind that stirred the waters below him. The eddies, ripples, and foaming swells reflected the starlight in myriad lines, that continuously formed new patterns. It seemed to the airborne prince that the reflections below were like a glowing spider web seen through a kaleidoscope and, oddly, he was at its center. He felt almost as though the reflections guided his movements, and he changed his flight according to their whim. Something in this frightened the prince, and he sought to escape somehow.

Then, just ahead of him, he caught sight of the boat with a shining white figure standing in it, and he headed toward it as if it were a beacon. As he flew directly over the boat the reflection patterns seemed to catch and gather against its sides and remain there. The Star Goddess flung out Her arms, and the patterns shifted to appear as though they radiated from Her. Something in the way She stood, or perhaps it was another refection, made Abderian think of a white spider in the center of Her web.

Tritavia raised Her arms toward him and he felt a blast of wind come straight up at him. Suddenly he was tumbling up and up, away from the boat and the sea. He felt *free!* Free as an uncaged bird, free as a wind-tossed leaf, free as a disembodied soul.

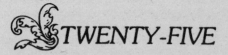

TWENTY-FIVE

IT SEEMED THE sheerest cruelty to the prince that after hours of tossing and turning he should be forced awake only moments after finally achieving sleep. But the hand on his shoulder was insistent, and at last he allowed himself to be roused.

He dressed groggily, having no feel for what time of day or night it might be. As he went to take up a sword, he found himself in a quandary. Leaning against the wall, side by side, were the Nightsword and Sagamore's sword. He knew he must carry the Nightsword, but what should he do with the other? Feeling slightly silly, he tied the Nightsword onto his back and carried the golden sword in his hand. Thus armed to face the day, he went out and made his way to the main chamber.

Squinting in the bright torchlight, Abderian saw that a table had been set in the center with bowls of fruit and nutmeats. As he picked up a bowl and began to eat, he noticed Hirci standing near one wall, polishing a breastplate of silvery metal. She began to sing an all-too-familiar tune:

> King Valgus's sword is too gross, I'm afraid,
> It's more like a bludgeon instead of a blade.
> Though he'd like to use it to lop off maids'
>   heads,
> The maids run away when they see it, instead.

"Have you no respect for our departed king?" said Burdalane, entering behind the prince. "Or at least for the feelings of his son?"

Hirci gave an annoyed shrug and returned to her polishing.

The prince turned and grinned at his cousin. "Good morning. Burdalane. Did you sleep well?"

"Indeed I did, cousin."

"And did you . . . have pleasant dreams?" Abderian asked softly.

"Aye, cousin." His face seemed to glow with inner happiness. "My Lady said if I were to serve Her well this day, I would be granted my deepest heart's desire."

The prince was about to ask what this might be, when Maja came into the room. By the time he had finished saying good morning to her, she was in his arms, face pressed close to his.

"Abderian! I'm glad I caught you before you left."

"What is it, Maja? What's wrong?"

"I'm just . . . worried for you. And me. I don't think . . . Things aren't going to go the way we wanted."

"What do you mean?" Abderian suddenly heard a sound from the entrance and looked up to see Entheali standing there.

"Ahem. Maja, haven't you other things to think about now?"

Maja looked at the floor. "Yes, Mother." Then in one swift movement Maja kissed the prince and turned back to the entranceway. "Good-bye, Abderian," she said softly, and she ran back up the passageway past her mother.

Entheali watched her go by, then approached the prince. "No doubt she is grateful to you for your part in bringing her to me." The Star Mother smiled, but her eyes were cool. "But you should not expect anything more from her than that."

What? Oh, of course. She doesn't know my intentions and she's protecting Maja. "She seemed worried about something," the prince said.

"Maja has an important role to play in our ritual to remove your curse. I imagine she is preoccupied with that."

"It won't hurt her, will it? This . . . role?"

"No. It should not harm her in the least. It merely confers a heavy responsibility. Something Maja is not used to, being so young. But come"—Entheali gave Abderian a brilliant smile—"there is no need for you to dally any longer with us. Are you ready to embark on your brave mission?"

"Since you have said all preparations have been made, I suppose I am. Oh, Burdalane, I have an extra sword here. Perhaps you might want to use it. It has some interesting abilities."

"I thank you cousin, but no. I'll trust my own ordinary blade of steel." He patted the scabbard at his side.

Abderian then turned and handed the golden sword of Sagamore to Entheali. "May I leave this, then, for Dolus or Horaphthia? Perhaps one of them can use it."

The Star Mother accepted it, nodding. "Certainly. I will see that they get it. Now, you ought to be going."

As Entheali led them down a tunnel Abderian asked, "By the way, where are Dolus and Horaphthia?"

"Horaphthia is resting from designing the transport circle for us. Dolus is in our library, studying tomes of ritual magic with Onym. They're preparing the spell to lift your curse. You will see them all again later. Ah, here we are."

They had arrived at a small, totally bare room. The floor, however, had drawn upon it an intricate design of interwoven circles, with symbols and writing scattered around the edges.

"This circle will take you to our agent in Castle Mamelon, who will be waiting for you. She does not know the nature of your mission, however, and you must not reveal it to her. You may understand why when you arrive."

"Very well."

As Abderian crossed into the center of the circles, he saw that one green arc in the pattern had not been completed. Only after he stood in the exact center did Entheali pull a piece of green chalk from within her robe and finish the circle. The prince had barely enough time to hear Burdalane say, "Good luck to you, Abderian," and to see him wave, when the world spun around him, blurring to a brownish-gray, then black.

When the air around him settled into solid colors and forms, Abderian found himself standing in a familiar room. Certain wall hangings were smudged, and the bed draperies were torn, but the queen's bedchamber still looked much as it did before he left.

Behind him, the prince heard his mother say, "Abderian!" As he turned he found himself pressed between his mother's arms and her great girth. "Oh, my son, I'm so pleased to see you returned to me safe and whole!"

All Abderian could mumble was, "Hullo, Mother. Yes, I'm glad too."

"When I heard that Dolus had stolen you away, I thought

all was lost. But now I see it has all been part of Her wise plan."

"Her?" Abderian stared at his mother in surprise as he pulled out of her arms. "You mean *you* are the agent of the Star Goddess?"

"I am sorry that it must be a surprise to you now, but I could not have told you before. Your late father, of course, would not have approved and I would have been in severe trouble, had he known. But my long years of silent faith have been vindicated now, my child, and I may rejoice openly with you."

Abderian managed an awkward smile as his mind spun. He thought back to the disastrous dinner at which the king had discovered his cursemark, and how the queen had prevented Lady Chevaline from telling him anything about it. "So you helped Her plan along."

The queen smiled and held the prince's chin in her hand. "Is my lad perceptive or has he been told? Yes, though it has been hard, the tasks I have performed in Her name have all shown their worth in full measure."

"Tasks?"

"Ah, then you have not been told." The queen walked to a narrow window and pensively regarded the sky. "Your father was ... not a kind man, Abderian. It is true that he had his reasons. The kingdom was not stable. He feared the cursemark that he wore, and then feared it more when he did not wear it. He would not listen to those who would guide him, and he feared them also. He struck out against his fears with violent rage. I was, at times, the focus of those rages. I hope, therefore, that you will forgive your mother when she says that she is not sorry for placing that wheeled toy upon the tower stairs."

Abderian could barely get words out for the tightness in his throat. "You ... killed ... ?"

"Yes. You do understand, don't you?"

"Yes," the prince managed to say. He had not ever been close to his father, but the mere shock that one of his parents would murder the other stunned him.

"And you will not tell anyone, will you? It was for our cause, you know."

"Of course not." Abderian didn't know whom he might have told anyway. He couldn't imagine sending his mother to Captain Maduro's dungeons.

With a sigh Abderian joined his mother at the window, which overlooked the courtyard. He was startled to see it filled to overflowing with people, most of them female. "What's going on, Mother?"

"Haven't you heard? I decided that before I hand over the crown to Cyprian, he should choose a bride. He cannot continue galavanting about as he does if he expects to be king. Once he marries, he should settle down a bit, don't you think?"

Abderian stifled a dubious snort.

"So, nearly everyone has sent a sister or daughter for Cyprian's perusal. It has made things rather awkward. Our resources were stretched tight enough when Dolus unleashed his demons upon the castle. They created such a mess. The priests of the Lizard Goddess have made themselves useful by guarding the portals through which the demons enter. But I feel nervous with the lizard priests working their magic within our living quarters, and they don't seem all that effective. And now I hear they're keeping a dragon in the temple." The queen sighed. "So much has changed. I wonder if Euthymia will ever be a happy kingdom again."

Though Abderian doubted that Euthymia had ever been completely "happy," he still felt a personal pang of guilt and was sharply reminded of his mission. "If you will excuse me, Mother, your Star Goddess has set for me a task that I must fulfill. If I succeed, all things may take a turn for the better."

"But of course! I am so sorry to delay you. What is the nature of this task? Perhaps I can be of help."

"I'm sorry. I was instructed not to tell anyone."

Pleonexia looked slightly hurt, but she acquiesced. "I understand. Be on your way, then. My hopes and care go with you."

Abderian bowed to her and strode toward the chamber door. But at that moment the door opened and the Lady Chevaline stepped in. "Pleo, the steward says you—Abderian! When did you return?" She greeted the prince with a brief gentle embrace.

"Just now, Aunt Chevy. And I'm afraid I must hurry on."

"What is happening? Can I be of any help?"

"No, Aunt Chevy. I'm afraid it may be dangerous."

"Dangerous?" Her bright, aged eyes glinted with interest. "Then you should definitely have help."

"I said no, thank you." Abderian walked past her, through the door. The last thing he wanted was to bring more innocent people into his destructive sphere of influence. He started down the tower's narrow spiral staircase, Chevaline's soft footfalls following behind him.

"Please, Aunt Chevy, I have to do this myself."

"Things have changed since you were last in Mamelon, Abderian. If you are headed somewhere in particular, you might like some guidance."

When the prince reached the bottom of the stairs, he stopped, suddenly understanding what she meant.

The first thing he noticed was the smell. It was the musty, fetid odor of Castle Doom, faint but unmistakable. As Abderian stepped into the hallway he noticed splotches of slime and mold on the floor and walls. Whatever hangings there had been were torn to tatters, and bits of broken furniture lay here and there. Strange symbols were scrawled on the walls in filth. "What in the name of—"

"Oh, didn't you hear? After you left, Dolus unleashed the demons of Castle Doom on us. It's been quite exciting since then. The demons don't harm anyone, really, but they do love to make a frightful mess. The servants fled some days ago, refusing to work around the monsters, so no one has been here to clean it up."

Abderian turned to his right, heading for no particular reason to the dining hall.

"Now, if you will indulge your aging aunt a little, please tell me what you are up to."

"I can't, Aunt Chevy." He turned right at another corner and stopped short. There was a priest of the Lizard Goddess walking in tight circles next to a huge hole in the wall that had been sloppily boarded up. The priest mumbled and moaned, making frantic, repetitive gestures as he stared at the floor.

Abderian whispered, "What's he doing?"

"Keeping the demons out," Chevaline chuckled.

The priest, startled by their voices, looked up. His eyes widened as he recognized Abderian, and he momentarily stopped his noises and gestures. Then a board suddenly popped off the wall and a grimacing green face appeared at the hole. With a shudder the priest moaned again and, with a few gestures to drive the demon away, continued his vigil.

Abderian walked on until he reached the doors of the dining hall. They hung broken on their hinges as if a great wind had shattered them open. The prince stepped in, Lady Chevaline padding after, finding the floor littered with pewter plates, broken chairs, and bits of old food among the straw. In one corner a steward nervously sat eating something out of a wooden bowl. His eyes now and then darted to the ceiling.

Abderian could not resist looking up also. The "diners" on the ceiling were scarcely recognizable. Most of their clothes had been stripped away, and their bodies splattered with bright pigment. Heads had been switched, and attached upside down, and arms and legs jutted out at incongruous angles. Then one of the figures moved.

It wore the jester cap of Sagamore that normally was mounted on the wall behind the king's chair. As it looked down at Abderian, it emitted a piercing, shrieking cackle. *Another demon*. But as it crawled across the ceiling toward him Abderian was certain he'd seen its face before . . . It was the demon Dolus had spoken to in Castle Doom.

"Liberator! Liberator!" it jibbered at him.

Does it call me that because I was with Dolus when he set the demons free?

Out in the corridor a voice said, "You've seen Prince Abderian, you say? Where is he?"

"Captain Maduro!" Abderian said to Lady Chevaline. "I mustn't be taken by him! It'll ruin everything!"

"I'll delay him for you." The elderly lady turned and planted herself in the doorway as Abderian rushed to the far end of the hall.

"Ah-ha! There's the scoundrel!" Maduro shouted from the doorway.

"Just a moment, young man," Chevaline said to the guard. "Do you think you can just barge into this hall because it has been defiled by demons? Have some respect for the royal property, if you will."

"Out of my way, My Lady, or you may be subject to arrest for harboring a traitor."

"I don't know what you're talking about!"

Abderian, meanwhile, was searching frantically for an exit. The one he remembered at this end was blocked almost completely by rubble. Above him the demon screeched, "Free! Free! That's what you would be! So I will free you so that you can free me!"

"You'd make a lousy jester," Abderian grumbled. He looked behind him to see Maduro push Lady Chevaline aside and stride into the hall, followed by two of his men.

The demon flew to the niche for Sagamore's cap and pulled on the jester's stick that still hung there. Directly beneath it a hidden door swung open, revealing a short passageway out to the courtyard.

I never knew that was there! thought the prince. Hearing Maduro break into a run behind him, Abderian dashed through the passageway, the rustle of demon's wings following closely. Once into the courtyard, however, he was confronted by a mass of mostly feminine faces, staring back at him in surprise.

"What's going on?"

"Are you Prince Cyprian?"

"Oh, Your Highness!"

"Eeek! A demon!"

Ignoring the babble around him, Abderian plunged into the mass of people, knocking over tents, tables, and people alike in his scramble to escape Maduro. Within a few yards it was clear he was not going to outdistance the captain of the guard, who was nearly upon him. Then there came the rustle of heavy leather wings, and a pair of clawed talons fastened on Abderian's shoulders. The prince found himself suddenly flailing in the air above a sea of faces, Captain Maduro shouting in frustration below him.

"Cease your squirming, liberator. It makes it harder to keep aloft," said the demon.

"Oh. Sorry." Abderian tried to relax.

"Better. Now where would you go?"

"Uh, the Temple of the Lizard Goddess, please."

"Hmp. It's your sacrifice."

The demon dove toward the mud domes of the temple, depositing the prince on the doorstep. Abderian pounded on the temple door, seeing Maduro still pressing through the crowd toward him.

As the door finally opened, the prince threw himself inside, slamming the door shut behind him.

"What is the meaning of this?" asked the robed acolyte before him.

"I am Prince Abderian," he gasped, "and I come to seek asylum from the wrath of the court. Please tell your High Priest Tingalut I am here."

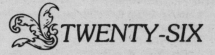 TWENTY-SIX

"TINGALUT IS THIS WAY," said the bewildered priest. Abderian was led down the same corridor as his first visit to the temple.

"By the way," the prince asked, trying to sound casual, "I understand Kookluk has come here to roost. This is an awfully small temple to hide a dragon. Where did you put him?"

"Only the Chamber of Patterns was large enough," said the acolyte, nodding his head toward a corridor on their left.

"Thanks," said the prince, and he dashed in that direction as fast as his legs could take him.

"Wait!" he heard faintly behind him—more of a pleading warning than an order. Abderian found a flight of stairs leading down and descended. The stairs led beneath a carved red sandstone arch, beyond which the air became dark and heavy with the smoke of incense. As he passed through, the prince had to cough a little, and the smoke stung his eyes.

At the bottom of the stairs Abderian had to blink a few times before he could see clearly. He was in a roughly circular room with a high dome overhead. A few priests wandered the room, watching Abderian but not ceasing their movement. The floor, the prince saw, was a confusion of lines, colors, diagrams, shapes, and symbols. Some gleamed of gold or silver, and some glowed with magical light. Abderian stepped carefully into the room, wondering how he was going to find a silver star in this mess.

Over to his right something huge and pale shifted, and he saw Kookluk swing his mighty head around to face him.

"Well," growled the dragon, "if it isn't the Prince of Lies.

189

Have you wearied of your life enough that you come seeking the death I will surely give you?"

"Hold, Kookluk!" Tingalut called from the archway. "You shall have the chance to avenge your honor soon enough. But we have uses for the boy first."

"What a surprise, Abderian," said Lord Javel, who stood beside the high priest. "I could not have imagined you would be so foolish as to seek us out again." Javel held his left arm tightly against his side as he approached the prince. Abderian wondered for a moment if that was where he had wounded the nobleman. "It is our good fortune, I suppose," Javel went on, "that I was wrong."

Hah. For once they weren't expecting me. Abderian backed up a few paces and began scrutinizing the floor again.

"Indeed," said Tingalut, "watch where you step, Your Highness. The patterns in this room contain the power of many sorcerers and countless enchantments. Any pattern you follow could easily destroy you. Walk softly now. We wouldn't want you . . . prematurely damaged."

The prince suddenly felt a tingling on his back where the Nightsword lay, and his feet seemed frozen to the floor. Slowly lifting his left foot, Abderian saw beneath it a four-pointed silver star inlaid in the stone. Swiftly the prince unstrapped the sword and laid it on the star, flicking aside the silk wrapping.

"What is this?" exclaimed Tingalut.

A beam of green fire shot out from the sword, striking the curved part of wall across from the entrance where Javel and Tingalut stood. Just in front of the wall the air began to shimmer and ripple like disturbed water. Within the disturbance there appeared a gray spot that grew and shifted, then turned to white and resolved into four human figures—Burdalane, Hirci, Maja, and Entheali. The Star Mother stood perfectly calm, a slight smile on her face. "Greetings, Tingalut," she said evenly.

"Greetings, Entheali," the priest replied. "So. It is now, is it?"

Entheali nodded. Lord Javel, an expression of deep concern on his face, looked at Tingalut. "It is too soon!"

"Nonetheless, the challenge must be faced when given. Do as I instructed you. We shall not fail."

Lord Javel nodded once and walked forward to the center of the room. Abderian noticed that the nobleman's path was not quite straight. Javel's feet followed one particular line and stopped on a small design in the center of the room.

"Greetings, my once-husband," said the Star Mother.

"Entheali," said Javel with the barest inclination of his head. "Are these the only ones you could find to defend the cause of your 'Goddess'?"

"We are enough, for She protects us."

"This is no longer her territory, Entheali. Her incompetent followers lost it for her. And she did not come to aid them then. But I am not surprised. Tritavia was never the most noble of sorceresses."

"The Scaly One herself was once a demon," Entheali reminded him.

"Yes, but Tritavia, it is said, was the castaway bastard child of a Shufethan whore—sold to a wizard to keep her mother in wine. It is said that Tritavia used her training to become a succubus, and used to lie with mules for her mentor's sport."

"Fiend!" cried Burdalane, rushing forward. Drawing his sword, he stood before Javel and said, "Take back those words or in her name I shall twice cleave your worthless carcass!"

With a condescending smile Javel said, "Oh? Has she played succubus to you also?"

"Enough!" Burdalane's lips drew back in a snarl, and he brought his sword down across Javel's chest, then back across his abdomen. Javel clutched his middle and fell forward to the floor, eyes wide with shock. He looked back at Tingalut, whose eyes held only mild contempt for the dying nobleman. "You . . ." Javel breathed, "you said . . . I would be . . . safe."

Tingalut gave no reply as Javel's blood flowed freely into grooves in the floor, creating a new pattern.

Abderian saw a white blur shoot out from the right side of his vision and he shouted, "Burdalane, watch out!" But it was too late, and Burdalane was firmly in Kookluk's grasp.

"It remains my duty," Kookluk hissed, "to avenge the death of my master."

Abderian reached for the Nightsword on the floor, looking to Entheali. "Is now the time?"

The priestess said nothing.

At first Burdalane's arms were pinned within Kookluk's encircling grasp. But with a twist of his body the general managed to wrest his sword arm free. As Kookluk brought Burdalane up to his jaws the commander slashed out at the dragon's throat, causing a crimson river of blood to cascade down the

pale leathery hide. Kookluk roared in anger and pain, and
squeezed his talons tight. Abderian heard bones cracking and
Burdalane groaning in agony. The prince turned away, unable
to watch, fighting the nausea and sorrow that welled up within
him. Then he heard a gasp, and the floor shook as Kookluk
collapsed, still holding Burdalane, dying, in his claw.

For the next few moments the room was silent, and the
sickly-sweet smell of blood was heavy in the air. Then, to
Abderian's horror, Entheali smiled. "Now it begins," she said
calmly.

"Yes," said Tingalut, also smiling. "So it does."

Abderian looked wildly back and forth between the opposing
sides. *What in Sagamore's name is going on? The Star Mother
ought to at least try to heal Burdalane! Why couldn't I wield
the Nightsword to save him?* Tears blurred the prince's vision
and he tried to speak to Entheali, but she silenced him with a
wave of her hand. Abderian was painfully torn between wanting
to rush to his fallen cousin's side and wanting to curl up against
the wall and weep. Something in the atmosphere of the room
at that moment told him he should not move at all.

"The sacrifices have been made," Tingalut intoned. "One
of ours and one of yours. The patterns are completed with the
blending of their blood." The lizard priest pointed at the floor,
where the winding grooves were now filled with red liquid.

Entheali merely nodded in acknowledgment. Abderian was
certain he was going to be sick.

A noise to his right distracted him. Kookluk's body shuddered as if still in death throes. The rivulets of blood on the
floor seemed to catch fire, and flames raced through the patterns
surrounding the dragon. For a moment Kookluk's body seemed
bathed in flame, but without being burned. His skin changed
from white to a metallic green. And as the dragon lifted his
head once more, his face changed to resemble something hideous, halfway between human and reptile. Abderian recognized
the face from the statues he had seen adorning the temple. It
was the Lizard Goddess herself.

The acolytes of the temple kneeled on the floor in obeisance,
murmuring softly. Tingalut bowed from the waist. Entheali's
eyes became narrowed and flinty, but she did not move.

"So," hissed the creature in Kookluk's body, "the one who
calls herself the Star Goddess wishes returned to her that which
she lost." The voice was higher pitched and softer than Kook-

luk's, and had the effect on one's nerves of metal scraping on stone. "Yet she herself is not here. Is your 'Goddess' such a coward that she sends her servants to face me instead?"

"Your taunts are foolish. You are aware that Tritavia never leaves her home. She has no need to. We have been appointed her representatives, and we shall triumph in her name."

"So be it, unfortunate ones," said the Lizard Goddess. "Have you selected your champion?"

"Yes. He is Prince Abderian, third son of King Valgus, bearer of Sagamore's mark."

"What!" said the prince as Entheali gently pushed him to the center of the room. As he looked up at the Lizard Goddess his knees trembled, and strength drained from his legs. He looked back at Entheali in confusion and despair. *What am I supposed to do?* Nervously he reached down for the Night-sword, determined not to hesitate to use it this time.

"Excellent," hissed the Lizard Goddess. "Here is mine."

Between her extended paws there rose from beneath the floor a woman with hair of fiery gold, whose voluptuous body seemed clad in a gown of flame. Atop her head sat a crown of fire, and her eyes glowed like hot coals. Abderian's mouth dropped open in shock as he recognized her—for she was the new Queen of the Demons . . . Khanda.

It was Maja who reacted first. "Khanda! What happened to you?!" She took a few steps away from her mother's side.

Greetings, sweet sister," said Khanda, her voice low and melodic. "Do not be alarmed for my sake. I am now queen of a kingdom of power and beauty. The Demon Realm is not as horrible as the stories say."

Maja gasped and whispered, "The Demon Realm! Then it is true."

"Come join me, sweet sister. I have saved a place for you by my side. Power and glory unknown in the world of mortals awaits you. Come to me." Khanda extended fire-wreathed arms toward Maja.

Abderian looked at Entheali, and for the first time saw fear in the Star Mother's eyes. She stood absolutely still, but her mouth formed the words *Oh no*.

Maja ran over to Abderian and clutched his right arm. "You knew all along!"

"I tried to tell you."

"Do not cling to him, sweet sister. It was Abderian who lay

with me so that I could become the Demon King's wife. He has already been my lover. Come to me and I shall find you one more worthy among those in the Demon Realm."

Maja looked up at the prince, her eyes searching his. "She's lying, isn't she?"

Abderian wished he could lie. He wanted to shout *No!* at her, to reassure her. Instead, he made only a strangled sound in his throat as he stared at her.

Maja let go of his arms and backed away from him, her hands hovering in front of her mouth as if to prevent words from escaping. "You . . . my sister . . . oh." Abderian felt ready to explode with anger and shame, but he still could say nothing. Maja turned to look at Khanda once more. Slowly she began to walk toward her.

"No!" Abderian cried, and he tried to grab Maja's arm. With surprising strength she shook him off and continued toward the flaming figure.

You will know the moment, a voice said in his mind. He looked back at Khanda, more lovely than ever, and he felt a shudder run through him as he realized what he had to do. He closed his eyes briefly and whispered, "May this be what you want, Tritavia," as he raised the Nightsword off the floor.

Maja was only a few paces from Khanda's waiting arms when Abderian finally summoned the courage to act. Feeling the sorcerous energy vibrating between his hands, he rushed forward. He roughly shoved Maja out of the way with his hip and, running between the claws of the Lizard Goddess, plunged the Nightsword toward Khanda's breast.

In the next instant the Demon Queen stepped to the side and grasped the prince's hands on the hilt. Her eyes glowed inches away from his as she whispered, "Thank you." Then, together, they rammed the Nightsword into the chest of the Lizard Goddess.

There came a wall-shaking roar as the dragon stared in horror at the weapon. Abderian staggered back, terrified.

Green flame flowed out from the blade of the Nightsword, flowing over the dragon's body. The Lizard Goddess wailed in agony as she clutched at the sword, trying in vain to pluck it out. Her tail lashed against the wall, dislodging some of the clay. The domed ceiling shuddered and a chunk of it smashed onto the floor. In minutes the body that was Kookluk and the Lizard Goddess was covered in green flame. The pale skin was charring to an ugly brown-black, and the ribs began to show through. Oddly there was no odor of searing flesh, and the flames were eerily silent as they ate into the reptilian form.

The acolytes of the Lizard Goddess were fleeing in horror. Tingalut and two other priests remained, staring grimly at the holocaust.

The green fire flowed into the grooves in the floor, racing around the patterns, consuming the spilled blood and turning it to a fine black powder. The flames reached Burdalane's still form, but left it untouched. Instead, they raced on to Lord Javel's body—consuming it until there was nothing left but black powder and bits of bone.

"What have you done?!" Tingalut shouted at Khanda. "You have destroyed your protectress! She who would have given you power in this world."

"She who would have given you and your followers power over us!" Khanda retorted. "She who wished to wield us as pawns in her search for dominion! We prefer to remain independent in a world of our own choosing. You and she would be wise not to attempt to command us again." With a bow to Abderian the Demon Queen seemed to fold in upon herself and disappear with a flicker of flame.

"We have won," Entheali said, smiling.

TWENTY-SEVEN

TINGALUT LOOKED AT Abderian and said, "You have made a grave error, Your Highness, in supporting these people. Things would have gone well for you, had you taken our side. I would not have allowed Javel to make you his puppet. I would have made a mighty sorcerer of you. You would have commanded two realms and held the power of the demons as well as your own. But there is no more use to discussion, is there? You will understand your mistake, in time, but it will be too late." With that, Tingalut spun on his heel and strode from the chamber, the other priests in tow.

Abderian sighed and walked toward his fallen cousin. With a start the prince noticed that one of Burdalane's hands was moving. With a low moan the commander reached out an arm and slowly rolled onto his side. Blood trickled from his mouth and his face was ghastly pale.

"Abderian," Burdalane rasped, "would you do me one last favor?"

The prince rushed to his side. "You're still alive! You mustn't move. We'll—"

"The sword," Burdalane went on, ignoring him, "Please bring me the Nightsword. I would leave this earth with it in my hands. Please."

"But I don't want you to die—"

"As you do love me, cousin, *please!*"

Reluctantly Abderian searched among the dragon's charred bones until he found the Nightsword, its black and silver blade gleaming as if never soiled. When he picked it up, he noticed no sensation of sorcerous energy. *It must have spent itself in defeating the Lizard Goddess*. He carried it over to Burdalane, gently placing the hilt in his cousin's hands.

"I thank you, cousin," Burdalane said with a ghost of a smile. "And I bid you farewell. May your heart's desire someday be given you, as I shall be given mine." Gripping the sword tightly, Burdalane closed his eyes.

"No," Abderian said softly. At first the prince thought it was only tears that made the Nightsword seem to shimmer more than before. But then the shimmer flowed over Burdalane's body and grew in brightness until he seemed to be lying in a cloud of silver light. The image of his body seemed to become less distinct, as if sinking deeper and deeper into clear water. And then there was no more body, but a river of silver light that flowed toward the hole in the ceiling like a waterfall in reverse. Rippling and shimmering, the liquid light flowed into the sky above. Abderian blinked, and all the light that had been Burdalane vanished.

"Heart's desire . . ." Abderian murmured.

"Move it there, lazybones," said Hirci's gruff voice behind the prince, shaking him from his reverie. From somewhere Hirci had acquired a broom, and Abderian had to do a quick sidestep to avoid a swipe at his feet as she swept the temple floor. The prince walked away from the dragon's remains and went over to Entheali.

Behind her there formed a gray blur. Others had arrived at the temple, a group of women in gray. As they stepped out of the circle Abderian saw Onym in their midst, carrying the golden sword of Sagamore. The wizard carried the blade to Entheali, saying, "Here, I think this will do. And I have brought silver wire for the binding."

"Excellent, Onym. Then we will be ready tonight." The Star Mother patted the wizard's head as if he were a well-behaved child.

Abderian turned to Maja, who stood not far away. He wanted to talk, to hug, to console—something. But she only glanced up at him sadly, then swiftly ran out of the chamber.

"She is no doubt upset over watching her father die, and seeing her sister as a demon," Entheali said. "Let her be. She will need rest and peace of mind for the ritual to come."

Abderian felt annoyed that the Star Mother continued to interpret Maja's feelings for him. Particularly since there was so much she wasn't saying. Certainly her father and sister were a part of Maja's despair, but the prince was sure there was more involved . . . much more.

"Is it truly over?" Abderian asked. "The lizard priests will not fight us further?"

"For what? Their goddess is gone, their temple is desecrated. What could they hope to gain?"

"Revenge?"

"The cost would be too high for too small a gain. They will save their vengeance for a more opportune time, as we did."

"Even though their goddess is dead?"

"It is unlikely she is dead, but she is not in a place from which she can strike back at us for a very long time."

"Where are Dolus and Horaphthia? Why didn't they come with you?"

"Their presence was not necessary, as you have seen. They would have endangered us, by making our opponents more cautious. We had to seem weak in order to succeed. Putting them in danger by bringing them would have served no purpose. So I gave them drugged wine after Horaphthia drew the transport circle. Now let us hear no more about it. I must help cleanse the temple. I suggest you rest while you can. You will need strength to endure the ritual tonight."

"There will be pain?"

"For you? Yes, briefly. But it will be a small price to pay for the loss of your curse, will it not?" Entheali walked away.

The prince wearily left the Chamber of Patterns, slowly ascending the stairs. At the top he looked around for remaining lizard priests, but the area seemed abandoned. Finding an acolyte's cell nearby, he laid down on the pallet, feeling exhausted physically and emotionally. In scarcely a few breaths he fell asleep.

He saw them standing together—Burdalane and Tritavia, the Star Goddess. They stood holding each other in the boat beneath the stars. The commander's face was filled with joy, and stars shone in his eyes. Tritavia, also, seemed joyful, and the wavelets danced at her every gesture.

Abderian felt happy for his cousin, happy for them both. He waved at them, to greet them and wish them well. They did not see him, did not even look toward him. Abderian felt distant. So very distant. And so alone.

• • •

Abderian awoke slowly, feeling mournful. Deep within him, the prince knew the world around him mourned also. *What new catastrophes, plagues, famines, deaths am I causing just because I feel sorrow at the loss of my friend?* It seemed terribly unfair that misery should cause more misery, that pain should cause more pain. His only consolation was that it would soon be over.

Just then Hirci poked her head in the door. "Ah-ha! There you are. Here is some food for you, and some wine. And here is the robe you must wear for the ceremony." She placed a bundle of white cloth, a tray, and a flask on a low shelf on the wall. "We begin at sunset, so you have about half an hour." Without waiting for a reply, Hirci turned and left.

"Good evening to you too," Abderian muttered. He got up and went to the shelf. On the tray were a couple of hard rolls, some dried meat, and some sweaty cheese. The prince wondered if this was standard fare in Castle Mamelon these days, or if this was all the Star cult could smuggle into the temple. He tried the wine and found that it, at least, was of reasonable quality.

He ate only a little, emotional numbness damping his hunger as much as the unappetizing fare. Trying on the white robe, he found it to be a little large, but comfortable. A white sash came with it that he tied around his waist. Idly he wondered if this meant he was now officially a member of the Star cult, or if he was to wear it only for the ritual.

In a while Hirci returned, accompanied by four gray-robed women. As Abderian stepped out of the cell they took position, two ahead of him and two behind. Silently he was escorted back down the stairs to the Chamber of Patterns.

Abderian stopped at the bottom of the stairs, surprised. The entire room had been whitewashed, and smelled strongly of lime. Acolytes of the Star cult, in robes of shades of gray from charcoal to pearl, stood in a circle around the room. The floor was still covered with lines, but there seemed to be fewer than before. In the center of the room a small platform had been placed directly beneath the hole in the dome. Through the hole Abderian could see a piece of sunset-purple sky.

The prince felt a tugging on his right arm and turned his head. Entheali was standing beside him, holding his arm and pushing up his loose sleeve. Taking a cloth from a basin in an acolyte's hands, he rubbed his arm with a substance that felt like alcohol. She was saying something, but Abderian could not catch the meaning of the sounds. Her speech seemed muddy, wavering, indistinct.

He felt someone take his other arm and lead him toward the platform. He was glad for the support, as the floor seemed suddenly unstable and the room spun a little as he walked. By the time he reached the platform, he was grateful for the instruction to lie down. Even standing had become a problem, with the room wobbling as it was. Staring up at the ceiling, he saw the piece of sky, now indigo blue, doing lazy circles over his head. He closed his eyes to keep from feeling sick. *Something about this isn't normal*, the prince thought. But, for the life of him, he could not figure out what was wrong.

He felt someone lay down beside him on his right side. Opening his eyes, he saw Maja's face inches away from his. "Hullo, Maja!" he said, grinning. She closed her eyes and, with a sigh, turned her head away. The prince wondered what he could possibly have said to make her so sad.

Entheali and Onym appeared at his feet. "The sun has set," the Star Mother said. "Let us begin."

Entheali raised his right arm and Maja's left and crossed their wrists. Then she bound them together with silver wire—wrapping some high on Abderian's forearm, over the cursemark, to a similar point on Maja's left arm.

How pretty, thought the prince, *but it seems a bit impractical for us both to wear the same bracelet.*

In Abderian's right hand the Star Mother placed the Nightsword. In Maja's left she placed the sword of Sagamore.

Oh, now I get it. We're going to be like those figures in heraldry who stand with crossed swords . . . but weren't they supposed to be doing something about my cursemark?

Onym opened a huge book in his hands and intoned, "As it has been so ordered by King Thalion that a kin of Sagamore must wear the enchantment, cementing the joy of the soul to the joy of Euthymia, and as the Lady Maja has been judged sufficiently near of blood—"

Is Maja related to Me? Let's see, if she's related to Horaphthia, who is my cousin's aunt . . . Abderian fuzzily realized there was a connection somewhere, but he didn't have enough fingers to figure it out.

"—Let the power of She of the Stars now aid us in our endeavor," Onym finished. Abderian had the feeling he had missed something important, but it did not bother him much.

Entheali raised her arms to the open sky above, and Onym began to chant. Abderian looked overhead and saw one point of light grow brighter and brighter, as if a comet were falling out of the sky down to where he stood. Suddenly the blade of the Nightsword was bathed in brilliant white light, and Abderian had to squeeze his eyes shut or be blinded. He could almost feel the light as it reached the hilt and then his hand. When the light touched the silver wire, it was as if lightning had wrapped itself around his arm, tingling sharply on his skin and aching numbingly down to his bones. His cursemark blazed with a searing pain, as if a hot coal had been applied to it.

Then came the pulling—something was reaching into his very being and tearing part of him away. With an ache of loss he felt a part of him pass up through his arm, along the silver wire, and into the Nightsword. Abderian heard a distant cry of anguish and realized it was his own.

A bolt of white light shot out from the tip of the Nightsword to Sagamore's blade, igniting it with gold fire. This raced down the sword until it reached the silver wire on Maja's wrist. Maja began to gasp and her face contorted, tears welling up in her eyes. But she did not move or cry out as the golden fire wound around her arm and a patch of her skin melted and blazed as if fire were breaking out from inside her.

Onym's chanting reached a crescendo and then, with a clap of thunder, the light leaped off Maja's arm and fled to the sky, fading the farther it went.

Abderian heard himself gasping and he blinked, seeing large dark spots before his eyes. With a shuddering sob Maja sank back against the platform.

A feeling battered at the prince's mind. Something had gone terribly, terribly wrong. He was in pain, in tears, and Maja was hurt too. But what had happened?

The prince groaned as the Star Mother grasped his arm and unwrapped the wire. As Maja's left arm came free the girl held it tight against her body, crying softly. Entheali's cool hand covered the prince's brow, and she said, "Rest now. Your part is over."

Many arms lifted the prince off the platform. He took a last look at Maja as he was borne away. *How odd*, he thought, *she has a mark on her arm just like I do. I never noticed that.* Then the room spun violently, and Abderian saw nothing more.

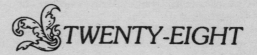

TWENTY-EIGHT

ABDERIAN FELT A fluttering on his chest and awoke with a mouthful of feathers.

"Awk! Leggo my wing!"

"Brownie?" Abderian sat up, rubbing his eyes.

"Take a while to wake up, don't you, fledgling? Say, you certainly gave me the slip this time. Took me a couple of days to find you, but I figured you'd be here."

"Is that so?" Abderian mumbled. He yawned, stretching his arms out in front of him. With a start he noticed the skin on his right arm was completely unblemished. "They did it! The cursemark is gone!" Fuzzy memories returned of the night before—the swords, the light, the pain, Maja's face . . . "Maja has it!" he whispered.

Abderian jumped out of bed, sending Brownie flapping onto the blanket. Flinging off the white robe he still wore, the prince yanked open the door and stormed out of the cell.

"Wait!" called Brownie. He flew after the prince and fluttered around his head. "I want to talk to you! I remember, almost, why I'm following you. It has something to do with this place too!"

"Shut up."

"Is that any way to treat an old friend?"

"I don't care."

Abderian found a priestess in dove-gray robes and grabbed her by the shoulders. "Where's Entheali?"

The priestess, looking offended, said, "She's in her office. You must—"

"I must speak to her. Now!"

"Very well. This way."

Abderian was led to the same room where he was interviewed by Tingalut so many days before.

"I'll just wait out here," said Brownie.

"Fine," Abderian snarled as he stomped into the office.

Entheali sat at a table, manuscripts bearing the seal of the royal scribes spread out before her. Onym stood behind her, looking over her shoulder. Both looked up, annoyed, at Abderian as he walked in.

"The cursemark," the prince began. "Maja has it now, doesn't she? You were supposed to remove it for good, but instead you just transferred to *her!* And you drugged me so I couldn't complain! Why?"

Entheali eyed the prince coldly. "You asked that we remove the curse *from you* and that is what we have done. We have fulfilled our part of the bargain."

"Indeed, Abderian, this ingratitude is unseemly," said Onym, wagging a finger. "The result you say you truly wanted would be impossible in any case. For me to even consider permanent removal of the spell would be a severe offense to my late King Thalion."

"Even though the spell has become a curse and made a mess of Euthymia?"

"That, I would say, has been due to the hearts of those who have borne it," Onym sniffed.

"But why Maja? It will do no more good on her than it did on me!"

Entheali's eyes flashed in anger. "It will do a great deal of good on Maja. The Star Goddess has shown wisdom in Her plan. Your mother, Queen Pleonexia, is intending to abdicate the throne in favor of Prince Cyprian, on the condition that he marries. We will see that he marries Maja."

"What!"

"Think of it, boy," said Onym, quite pleased with himself. "With their union will come the uniting of the two families, Thalion's and Sagamore's. Political opposition will be circumvented. The throne of Euthymia again will be a symbol of peace and unity. And since Maja bears the cursemark, which the people believe indicates the 'true ruler,' they will readily accept her as queen."

Abderian let out his breath and sagged against the wall behind him. "And you are going to use her. Just as Lord Javel and Tingalut would have used me. You're no better than they were!"

"We will train Maja to handle the responsibilities of the curse well."

"Yes, to put you in power!"

"For the good of the kingdom!"

"For the good of yourselves!" Abderian felt enraged. For the way they had used him. For the way they were going to use Maja. For the death of Burdalane. "If you have any sense of honor left, you will take the curse off Maja. In the name of the crown of Sagamore, I demand that you do so!"

"You are no longer in a position to demand anything," Entheali said icily. "I suggest you depart to meditate on the sins of ungratefulness. We have much other work to be done, and will not appreciate your interference."

"May I at least see Maja?"

"No. There is no reason for her to have anything more to do with you."

Abderian strode out of the office, slamming the door shut behind him. He let his feet take him where they would, not caring anymore. Now he wished he had the power to cause earthquakes, to shatter buildings to rubble. He'd eagerly bring the temple down on the heads of everyone. But, of course, he no longer bore the cursemark. The world would no longer act according to his will.

By the time his feet had carried him to the Chamber of Patterns, his anger was largely spent. The hall was empty, and no one prevented his entry. Morning sunlight slanted in through the hole in the dome, illuminating dancing dust motes in its path.

He sat on the floor, feeling helpless and alone. *Just when I think I've finally gotten what I want, I lose everything.* Though Abderian recognized the irony in this, he was unable to appreciate it. *You will lose that which you do not value,* the Star Goddess had said. He had lost the cursemark, which he certainly had not valued . . . though now, in a way he would never have previously believed, he wished he still bore it.

He had lost Maja. *Even if she weren't going to marry Cyprian, I doubt she would have forgiven me for Khanda.*

Most painful of all, the prince felt the loss of control over events around him. Although, he reminded himself, that was not something he ever had. For all his early life he had been dominated by his parents and elder brothers. And the past year, he now knew, he had been manipulated by the whims of goddesses and priests. Feeling hopeless, Abderian's thoughts turned again to writing a suicide note. This time, however, it would be genuine.

A fluttering sound disturbed his planning, and Abderian felt Brownie land on his shoulder.

"Go away."

"Hey, what's the problem, fledgling? What have I done to you?"

"You haven't done anything. Look, just shut up and let me think, all right?"

"Whatever you say. But don't you want to know why I'm here?"

"No. Just be quiet." Abderian got up and began to pace the floor. The problem was, he reflected, that he wouldn't feel right about taking his own life until he had exacted some sort of revenge. Too much had been done to him to let it go unpunished. *But what could I do that would not seem too petty? What would have impact?* Immolating himself at the wedding was a possibility, but Abderian did not want to distress Maja further. And if he killed himself in the temple, Entheali would probably view it as a useful sacrifice rather than as a desecration. *What, then?*

Abderian wished he had been able to convince Dolus to teach him some magic. What would be most appropriate now would be some grand spell that would bollix up all of Entheali's plans. Or even a little spell, so long as it had the same result. The prince tried to remember every magic spell he had seen Dolus do, racking his brain to see if there was something... some little bit of Dolus's magic he could use as his own.

Abderian paced and paced, not noticing what direction his feet were taking. Not noticing that his path was tracing out a particular pattern of lines through the dust on the floor. As Abderian came near the point where he had begun, he felt a curious weariness, as if he had expended more effort than mere walking. He slowed to a stop, not knowing why.

Suddenly his whole body stood rigid as an enormous surge of energy pulsed through him. He felt as though he stood in the midst of a lightning bolt. He felt no pain, but his very bones vibrated and hummed and his skin tingled unbearably. He felt as though he might explode.

With a shock something hit him, and he realized it was the floor. The prince rolled back and forth, feeling as though he were wrestling with a demon that had crawled inside his skin. He gritted his teeth and wished fervently that this would stop.

To his surprise, the jangling of his nerves eased, and he found he could sit up. He still felt charged with energy, but it seemed, for the moment, under control. "What was that?" he said, holding his head.

"I—I don't know!" said Brownie, flopping unsteadily in the dust on the floor. "Am I still here? What am I—no, wait a minute, that's not right."

"What are you babbling about? Gods, I feel strange." Abderian squeezed his upper arms, hugging them to his chest as if something might burst from within.

"Abderian! Have they got you in here too? Oh, no, then all is lost!"

"What are you talking about, Brownie?" the prince murmured. He noticed that something in the quality of the bird's voice had changed.

"What do you mean, Brownie? What kind of a nickname is that?"

"It's what I've always called you. You didn't complain before."

"But . . . you never called me that! I'm Paralian, your brother. Don't you recognize me? No, I guess you wouldn't. I'm sorry, little brother, but I have put us both in grave danger."

"Paralian? Don't be silly. You're a bird. Besides, Paralian's probably miles away, or dead, by now."

"I am not! And I'm only a bird because I changed myself into one to escape Tingalut's plotting. I sneaked into your tower two nights ago and transferred my cursemark onto your arm. I didn't want to encumber you with it, but it can be transferred only to a family relation, and you were the only one I trusted."

"You *are* Paralian!" Abderian wanted to reach out and hug the little bird tightly.

"Augh!" Paralian squawked. "I'm being suffocated! Tingalut has begun his torments. Help me!"

"What? What can I do?" Abderian gasped. Something inside him relaxed, and he saw the bird relax also.

"Phew!" sighed Paralian. "That was close"

"What is going on?" Abderian asked, bewildered.

"Tingalut, no doubt, has discovered what I've done and is

punishing me. I felt strong sorcery surround me. Most likely I survived only because the power of your cursemark protected me. I am grateful to you, brother. With your help we might yet escape him."

"None of this is making sense. For one thing, you gave me the cursemark a year ago, not two nights ago. For another, Tingalut is gone—his goddess was defeated by the cult of the Star Goddess, who have taken back this temple. And for a third, I no longer wear the cursemark, because the high priestess of the Star cult took it from me and put it on her daughter."

"Now you're the one not making sense. Unless..."

"Unless what?"

"After I did the transformation to a bird, I had ... visions. Dreams, I thought. You were in them, and I seemed to be chasing after you for some unknown reason."

"They weren't dreams, Paralian. You were a bird who had lost its memory, and you did follow me around."

"By all the ... and it's been a year, you say?"

"Yes. But how did you get trapped by Tingalut?"

"He simply told me he wanted to reveal to me the secrets of the cursemark. Goddess knows how he learned of it. But what he really wanted was to transfer the power of the cursemark to the temple itself, giving him and his priests control of the kingdom."

"Is that possible?"

"Apparently he thought so. If you look over on that part of the floor, you'll see where they are starting to carve the curse pattern into the temple itself. Fortunately their work is slow. I had the time to use one of their patterns to transform myself and escape. But you say Tingalut has fled? Then good fortune has come to us at last."

"Not really. In my stupid haste to get rid of the curse I allowed a different cult, that of the Star Goddess, to take it from me and put it on one of their own. And their leader turns out to be as power-hungry as Tingalut."

The bird sucked in air through its beak. "Then my efforts were for nought. I am sorry, Abderian. I gave the mark to you precisely because you had little love of politics and power. Now Euthymia will have a sorcerous despot. We must stop them, Abderian."

"My thoughts exactly."

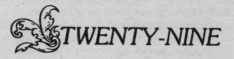# TWENTY-NINE

"I'VE ARRANGED FOR an audience with Mother," Abderian said, staring out the window of Paralian's tower, "though I don't think that will be of much help." He looked at the sea of female faces lit by the late afternoon sun that filled the castle courtyard.

Over by the guardhouse two guardswomen were teasing the crowd by singing:

> Now Cyprian's sword is quite busy, we hear,
> It's been in and out of the forges all year,
> He's made such a name with his sword that it seems
> 'Twill be worn away by the time he's nineteen.

Abderian shut his eyes and shook his head.

"Well, you have to start somewhere," said Paralian, hopping onto the windowsill.

"But if she cares more for the temple than for Euthymia, she may not help me."

"Then you must present it to her as being in the temple's interest. Besides, we have other friends in the castle. Lady Chevaline, for example. Great-aunt Chevy has helped me out of more scrapes than I care to remember."

"Hmm. Do you think my plan has any chance of working, Paralian?"

"Well, given that apparently Maja is, however distantly, related to Cyprian and you, and given the little magic I know, and the fact that I've done this spell before, it *should* work."

"But will it?"

"Anyone ever tell you that you worry too much?"

"I can't help it. I still feel strange from what happened in the temple this morning. I wish I knew what it was."

"No doubt you triggered some old spell set by the Lizard cult. That floor was so covered in patterns, you could walk in any direction and set something off."

"That is what frightens me. What spell did I set off?"

"Perhaps it is only a spell to make people feel strange."

"Oh, come now, Paralian. The scaly ones never did anything that simple."

"How do you know? Did they tell you all their secrets?"

Abderian made a face at the bird and sighed with frustration. He reached up and grabbed his hair with both hands, pulling on it as if to pull thoughts from his mind. "Oh, Paralian, how am I going to do this?"

As the bird was about to reply a shimmering appeared at the other end of the room, as if the air were turning to water. Out of the shimmering stepped Dolus and Horaphthia, both scowling.

"It's about time!" said the sorceress. "What, by all the demons, has been going on here? And who's responsible for the sleep drug in my wine?"

"I think, dear brother," said the bird with a smile in his voice, "your answer may have just arrived."

Abderian waited restlessly in one of the smaller audience chambers off the throne room. It had been annoying to press through all the petitioners and the favor-seekers just to get in. It was more annoying that those same people would be delaying the queen on her way to speak to him. He wanted to get this over with, and he dearly longed to be somewhere, anywhere, else.

At last the intricately carved door opened. Her Supreme Majesty, Queen Pleonexia, stepped through, waving away hands that reached to clutch her sleeve or thrust something into her hands. Closing the door on the noisy rabble, she leaned against it and sighed a moment before looking up to see the prince.

"Abderian! My son, my dear son, I'm so proud of you!"

"Proud of me, Mother?"

"For what you have done! I am told that you nearly single-handedly drove those nasty lizard worshippers out of the temple so that the Star Goddess can have it back. I am so pleased that

Her plans have given you an important role. I had, I must confess, worried that you would not amount to much. I am pleased that She has proved me wrong."

"Er, thank you. Mother, has Enth—the Star Mother, told you of her further intentions?"

"I have not had the chance to meet with her yet, but I understand she has a bride in mind for Cyprian. This, of course, will take higher priority than the offerings of the other noble families, and I expect I shall find her choice suitable."

"And if Cyprian likes her," Abderian said, barely breathing in anticipation.

"What? Oh, yes, if Cyprian likes the girl. I did promise him that much when he agreed to the arrangement."

Now or never. "In that case, dear Mother, may I ask that you allow me the honor of handling the introduction of Entheali's choice to Cyprian myself. Although he and I may have fought in the past, we have also been close at times. I believe I know how to present this girl to Cyprian such that he will accept her, and want her for his own. I know you are busy with the concerns of the kingdom, and I would be happy to take this small load from you." Abderian tried to keep his voice as casual as possible, but his hands made awkward gestures as he spoke.

"Yes," she said almost to herself, "so many burdens. I shall be quite relieved when Cyprian takes over the crown. Well, I had looked forward to making the arrangements myself"—she turned and beamed at the prince—"but I am proud that you again choose to serve on Her behalf. How could I deny you this additional chance to honor yourself. Ah, my youngest one, I am indeed pleased with you. If Cyprian were not the elder . . . well, that is fruitless. Go and do this for me, then, and I shall be ever grateful."

"Will you send word to Entheali that it is your wish that I do this?"

"If you like. Yes, I suppose that shall make things less confusing. I will see to it."

The prince was so overwhelmed with relief that he had to cover his expression with a low bow.

"You will have to hurry, you know. Cyprian is supposed to make his choice by tomorrow evening."

"Tomorrow!"

"The sooner this affair is settled, the better off Euthymia will be. I'm sure, if I let him, Cyprian would dilly-dally over a choice for years. Now, off you go on your sacred mission. You'll find your brother down in the Hall of Ministers, I think."

Abderian rushed from the audience room, nearly bowling over several velvet-robed petitioners. *Tomorrow! So little time.* He hoped, by whatever remaining gods who smiled on him, that it would be enough.

Abderian found Cyprian sitting alone in the scrivener's office, poring over sheets of parchment. Petition scrolls and painted portraits covered the desks and the floor around him. Cyprian rested his fair-haired head in his hands and sighed.

"Look at this mess, will you? I—Abderian! It's you!"

To the younger prince's surprise, Cyprian seemed very pleased to see him again. Then, after a firm embrace and some affectionate back-pounding, Cyprian boxed Abderian's ear.

"Hey! What was that for?"

"That was for that little trick two weeks ago where you chased the stable girl, telling her you were me. Do you know how long I had my eye on her? Now she'll have nothing to do with me!"

Abderian stifled a surprised chuckle. So few of his jests went right. "I'm so sorry, Cyprian."

"Sure you are. Now, when did you get back? Where have you been? What was that bit I heard about you and the lizard priests? Sit down and tell me all about it."

"Well, I can't talk for long, Cyprian. Besides, I see you are busy—"

"Busy! I'd appreciate anything right now to distract me from this chore. Look at this!" He flung his arms out to indicate the clutter. "And have you *seen* the courtyard? I doubt any man has ever had so much attention from so many women."

"Just what you always wanted."

"Very amusing. Except that I have to pick one that my mother will agree to by tomorrow evening."

"So I heard."

"Well, how would you do it?"

"Have you considered drawing lots?"

"Naw. With my luck, the winner would be a wrinkled old bag with warts and missing teeth."

"I doubt that Mother would wish such a bride on you."

"Oh, I don't know. I almost think she gets a secret pleasure out of seeing me go through this torment."

"I don't think she sees it like that. But not to worry. Your problems may be over."

"How's that? Has Mother decided I don't have to marry after all?"

"No. But I've a candidate for a bride that I think you ought to meet."

Cyprian groaned. "Not you too! Do you know how many noble families have tried to interest me in their daughters, sisters, nieces, or maiden aunts? There must be at least a hundred right here." With a wave of his arm Cyprian swept a small mountain of papers off one desk. "'She's the perfect bride for you' they all say. And they are all wrong."

"Just give this one a chance."

"They all say that too."

"Look, you don't have to promise me or her anything. Just agree to meet with her for, say, two minutes tomorrow morning. You and I can have some tea together, and then I'll introduce you. If you don't like her, say so right away and it's over."

"I shouldn't show favoritism, you know. There are many petitions ahead of you."

"Not even for me, your own brother?"

"Don't push your luck."

"Sorry. Won't you please consider it?"

"Oh . . . very well. Two minutes tomorrow morning and that's it. No promises."

"No promises," Abderian agreed, grinning. "My thanks. You won't regret it."

"Ha."

"Meet you tomorrow at ten o'clock, say?"

"Fine."

"Excellent. Now I really must be going. I have to, uh, go make sure my candidate can be ready then."

"As you wish. But I'll expect to hear more of your news later."

"Of course."

"Say, could you possibly leave by the side door there? The servants are scrubbing the main hallway for the betrothal ceremony, and I wouldn't want you to slip."

"Certainly," Abderian said, heading for the side door. Suddenly he stopped and looked back at Cyprian. "I didn't see any servants in the hallway when I came in. You wouldn't, by any chance, be playing a jest on me?"

Cyprian raised his eyebrows in mock innocence.

"Well, if you don't mind, then, I think I'll take my chances
with the main hall door."

Cyprian smiled and shrugged expansively. Abderian, keeping one eye on his brother, marched to the main door and
opened it. And tripped over the servant who was scrubbing the
floor just outside.

Home, sweet home, Abderian thought darkly as he floun-
dered on the soapy stone. With Cyprian's laughter and the
servant's quiet swearing in his ears, the young prince got up
and hurried on.

"I'm going to get him. I swear I'm going to get him!"

"Easy, now, Abderian, one bit of revenge at a time," said
Dolus as they reached the bottom of the stairs leading to the
wizard's quarters. "A pity, though, that this must be done by
tomorrow. It gives us no time to prepare contingency plans."

"What?"

"In case something goes wrong."

"Oh. Well, it will help if the book we need is here."

"Yes, I—oh, dear, dear, dear."

As they entered Dolus's cellar chambers they saw that all
the crockery and glassware lay shattered on the floor. Tomes
and scrolls had been pushed about in disarray on the shelves.
The larger items of furniture had been smashed or stood atilt
against the walls.

"This is going to be harder than I thought," sighed the
wizard.

"Do you think the demons of Castle Doom did this?"

"Only if the 'demons' wore the armor of the castle guard.
I smell Maduro's work in this. No doubt he was rather miffed
at my escape."

They stepped into the main room, kicking shards and splinters aside.

"I wonder how long that's been there?" Abderian said, in-
dicating a huge plank of wood that covered the door to Castle
Doom. Carved on the plank were designs similar to those on
the floor of the temple.

"I wonder how long it will last." Dolus chuckled sardonically. "Ah, well. We'd best start searching for the transfer spell. I fear this may take a while."

As Abderian began to poke through one of the shelves he asked, "What if we don't find it here?"

"Then we search Paralian's tower. A pity he does not remember where he left the book. It would simplify things greatly. One moment . . . hmm."

"What is it?"

"Something's wrong," Dolus said, staring through the doorway into the darkness of his storage room.

"Oh, I wouldn't say that," said Captain Maduro, stepping out of the darkness with two of his men. "In fact, I'd say things are going smashingly well."

"So I would gather," said Dolus, looking around the room.

Abderian felt as though his heart had stopped. "What do you want, Captain Maduro? Why are you here?"

"Well, now, ain't that a coincidence, Your Highness. I was about to ask you the same question. Come to see the wages of your sins, have you?"

"I don't understand."

"Oh, come now, Your Highness. Surely you've heard about the death of His Late Majesty."

"Of course."

"'Of course,'" mocked the captain. "Is that all you can say for your poor dead father? No tears? No sighs of lost affection?"

"I . . . grieved for him a while ago. When I first learned of his death."

"Ah, but you only just arrived, didn't you?"

"I heard about it shortly after it happened! What are you getting at? I was told my father's death was an accident!"

"An accident, you say?" the captain purred with menace. "No intelligent person in the castle believes that. And I doubt that you would either, were you honest."

"Here, now—" Dolus protested.

"And none of your tricks, wizard! Don't you think it's just a little suspect that His Majesty should die just a day after you leave? And now that things are about to be settled again, you two reappear . . . to continue your scheming."

"Wait a minute, Maduro," said the prince, "we had nothing to do with my father's death. If you doubt me, just speak to my mother." Abderian didn't dare directly accuse her before the captain. He'd be thrown in the dungeons for certain.

"Her Majesty is quite busy these days, as I'm sure you know. We wouldn't want to disturb her with so trivial a case as yours. If you are blameless, as you say, I'm sure you won't mind spending a couple of days in a nice cozy cell until things blow over. Then your case may be examined by King Cyprian at his leisure. You see, I am not an unreasonable man, am I?"

Abderian's breathing came quick and shallow with fear. *No, not now! I mustn't be stopped now, not when I'm so close ...* Trying to keep his voice strong and even, the prince said, "Maduro, listen: We had nothing to do with my father's death. We have no designs on the throne. We are innocent. You must believe me." But despite the testimony of his voice, Abderian's hands betrayed his fear, fluttering in foolish, helpless gestures.

"I must believe you," Maduro said softly.

Abderian blinked, not certain he had heard right. "We are working to help Her Majesty and Prince Cyprian. If you want to question us later, that's fine. But please leave us for now."

"Leave you for now," repeated the captain. He straightened up suddenly, and turned to his men. "Well? You heard His Royal Highness! What are you still mucking about here for? They have work to do. Get going!"

With puzzled expressions the guardsmen nodded to the captain and headed out. Captain Maduro turned back to the prince and gave him an energetic salute. "Always happy to serve you, Your Highness," he said. Then, smartly spinning on his heel, he strode out the door.

Abderian stared after him, as bewildered as the captain's men. He looked at Dolus, who was staring back at him, aghast.

"You . . ." the wizard breathed.

"Me what? What just happened?"

"My power!" Dolus exclaimed. "You have my power!" He grabbed the prince's shoulders and shook him firmly. "What are you doing with it? How did you get it?"

"Wait! Stop! I don't have your power!"

Dolus seemed to gain control of himself and released the prince. "Tell me, then, how did you do that complex and highly unethical spell?"

"I did that?" A sudden realization struck the prince. "The weird feeling at the temple . . . that must be it. I got it from the temple!"

"How?"

"I walked a pattern on the floor without knowing it. Paralian said I must have released one of their spells."

Dolus's eyes widened. "When my magic powers were stripped from me, they were being stored in a pattern on the temple floor, no doubt for the priests to call upon. Your walking the pattern must have re-released it. Though I am surprised a non-sorcerer such as yourself could absorb it without damage. Perhaps because you once carried the Curse of Sagamore, your body was used to accepting great magical potential."

"Perhaps. You can have your power back if you want. I don't want to steal it from you."

Dolus smiled ruefully. "It is not that simple, lad. But don't worry. I do not begrudge it in you. In fact, I think it may make your whole crazy scheme possible. Come, let us continue to search for that spell. Then it is time I teach you a few things."

THIRTY

IT WAS NEAR midnight when Abderian and Lady Chevaline gained admittance to what was now the Temple of the Star Goddess.

"You are rather late, don't you think?" asked Entheali.

"My apologies, Star Mother. There were things I had to do."

"Hm. Good evening, Lady Chevaline."

The elderly lady nodded silently, but her eyes shone with interest.

"I trust my mother has told you that I am arranging the meeting between Maja and my brother Cyprian."

"Yes," Entheali replied cautiously. "And I must say it surprised me somewhat."

"I assure you, Star Mother, that my selfish anger of this afternoon has abated and my attitude has changed. I am now ready to do what we know to be best for the kingdom."

"Hmf." Entheali seemed to study the prince intently.

"I have spoken to Cyprian and he has agreed to the meeting." Abderian hoped that the priestess did not know the "meeting" was arranged for tomorrow.

"And you think, thanks to your efforts, that your brother will react favorably to her?"

"I am certain, Star Mother, that she will leave a lasting impression upon him." The prince wished he could use Dolus's magical powers to influence her, but he did not dare. If she were to perceive it, the plan would be ruined.

At last Entheali sighed, saying, "Very well. Your mother has a high opinion of your attitude. And though that is typical of mothers, due to her good service I am inclined to believe her. I shall go fetch Maja."

As Entheali stepped out of the room Abderian let out his breath in relief.

"So far, so good, eh?" Lady Chevaline said softly.

Entheali returned with Maja in tow. Maja was dressed in a lovely white robe edged with gold. But her eyes seemed cold with anger and she would not look directly at the prince.

"Go with Abderian now, Maja. He will introduce you to your future husband. And do try to put on a smile! He's not likely to want you for his queen if you scowl like that. Lady Chevaline, I am grateful that you offered to chaperon them on their way. Queen Pleonexia has spoken highly of you, and I am pleased to have another in Castle Mamelon whom I can trust."

"I am pleased at your approval of me, Entheali. Now we really should be on our way, before it gets much later."

As they recrossed the courtyard Maja still radiated hostility, though she said nothing.

"I must tell you, Abderian," said Lady Chevaline, "that I think what you are doing is simply delightful. It will give me no end of pleasure to see Entheali get what she deserves."

"Hmp," snorted Maja.

Lady Chevaline led them to the base of her tower, where she moved her hands over a section of wall. With a low rumble that portion receded into the rest of the wall, revealing another one of Castle Mamelon's secret passages.

"This will lead you to your destination faster, and unseen."

"Thank you, Aunt Chevy." Abderian let Maja step in ahead of him.

"Good luck to both of you. If I can be of any more help, you need only ask." She shut the door after them, and Abderian had to pull out a candle and light it to see their way.

Their shoes made loud reports in the tiny corridor, and Abderian wondered if someone outside might hear them go by. After a couple of wrong turns they finally came out from behind an arras in a waiting room in the southern wing, where Abderian had arranged to meet the others.

At this point it seemed Maja could contain her anger no longer, and burst out, "Look, I don't know what you're getting out of this, or what Mother offered you, but I won't go through with it! I am tired of being pushed around and told what to do!

I never wanted your horrid cursemark! I don't want to be queen, and I'm not going to marry your stupid brother!"

"Good."

"And I'm . . . what?"

"I said, 'Good.' You won't have to. In fact, I'm glad to hear your dissatisfaction."

"You are? What about your brother?"

"I am taking you to meet him, but not in the way your mother or mine thinks. You see, I have this plan. . . ."

And as Maja listened with growing astonishment, Abderian told her what he intended to do.

Some minutes later Dolus entered the room with a large book bound in green leather under his arm and Paralian perched on his left shoulder.

"Ah, you found the spellbook, I see," said the prince.

"Yes," Dolus patted the book binding. "It was in Paralian's tower. Just where the birdbrain here left it."

Paralian shrugged. "My apologies. Blame it on King Sagamore and his ridiculous forest."

"Brownie!" said Maja. "What are you doing here?"

"His real name is Paralian, Maja. And it turns out he's my brother. He transformed himself into a bird to escape Tingalut."

"That bird is your *brother?*"

"Paralian, allow me to introduce the Lady Maja, daughter of Lord Javel of King Thalion's line. Maja, allow me to present His Royal Highness, Prince Paralian."

The bird bowed. "Honored to meet you, My Lady."

After a curtsy Maja said, "Abderian, you have a strange family."

"You're telling me?"

"I presume, Lady Maja," said Dolus, "that Abderian has explained to you his scheme."

"Yes. I think you're all crazy. And I'm grateful."

"You're quite welcome," Abderian said. "Dolus, how is Horaphthia adjusting to her role in this?"

"Surprisingly well. I think she will do an excellent job. And she feels it is an extremely fitting revenge upon Lord Javel, wherever his spirit may wander."

"That's true; she missed out on her chance at the temple. Paralian, is our 'host' prepared to receive visitors?"

"I flew through his window and scattered the sleep dust, if that's what you mean."

"Are you sure you want to go through with this, Abderian," Dolus asked, "after all you've been through?"

"Paralian and I talked about this. We decided it was best for everybody."

"Even yourself?"

"Well." Abderian shrugged. "I always did want to learn magic."

"Then if everything is ready, we'd best be on our way."

Silent as winter, the conspirators went out into the night and headed for Cyprian's tower.

At nearly ten o'clock the following morning Abderian left the castle kitchens carrying a teapot and two mugs. In the courtyard, just outside the windows of the throne room, he saw a little brown bird dipping its beak into a bag of seeds, spilling them on the ground in the process.

"Good morning, little brother," said Paralian, seed husks falling from his beak.

"I hope it is," said Abderian. "How are you doing?"

"Fine. These seeds taste much better than that ink did last night."

"Hey, you're supposed to be scattering those seeds, not eating them!"

"Say, a hard-working bird's entitled to a snack now and then, isn't he? Off with you. Cyprian awaits."

"Right. Now to see if our efforts last night accomplished anything."

It was awkward for the prince to knock on Cyprian's door while holding a teapot and two mugs, but somehow he managed it. There came a groan from within that sounded like "Come in," so he entered. Cyprian, still in dressing robe, sat at a table, holding his head in his hands.

"Did you have to knock so loud?" the elder prince moaned.

"My apologies. Did you have a hard night of it?" Abderian asked innocently. He was rewarded with an evil red-eyed glare from his brother.

"I don't know the cause, but if it has anything to do with the wine served at dinner, I shall have the wine steward executed once I am king. I had nightmares all night, and this morning I felt as though a boulder has been dropped on my back. My head's like an overstuffed sausage, and I've got this huge bruise on my right arm. You'd better hope you had nothing to do with this, or I'll send you to the block with the wine steward."

"Oh, you poor fellow. How about some tea to bring you around?" Abderian set the mugs on the table and filled them with aromatic liquid from the pot.

"That does smell good," Cyprian sighed. Then his eyes narrowed. "And why have you chosen to be kind to me all of a sudden?"

"There's that girl I want you to meet, remember?"

"Oh. Right. Well, I'm in no shape to meet anyone this morning."

"She won't mind. She thinks you're—" Abderian abruptly stared out the window. "What the—those women are taking their clothes off!"

"What? Where?" Cyprian rushed to the window and Abderian shuffled the mugs around. "I don't see any—ah, now I understand." The elder prince turned and looked at the mugs with disgust. "I may be a mess right now, but I'm not that far gone. Which one has the poison?"

"Poison?"

"Or potion, or whatever it is you are trying to slip into me."

"I wouldn't try to poison you, Cyprian. I swear on Sagamore's pointed cap, there's no poison in the tea."

"I heard you move those mugs around."

"I just wanted to set one by your chair. There is nothing harmful in the tea, honest!"

"Indeed? Then you drink from one."

"As you wish." Abderian picked up the mug by Cyprian's chair and began to drink.

"Wait! I'll take that one."

"As you like." Abderian cheerfully handed the mug to him.

Cyprian stared at the steaming mug in his hand, then at the mug on the table, torn with uncertainty. "Very well, what are you trying to pull?"

"Look, I can drink from both of them if you wish. There is nothing harmful in the tea! Behold!" The younger prince took a big gulp from one mug and then from the other, swallowing the tea with relish. Wiping his lips on his sleeve, he said, "See? No poison."

Cyprian relented with a sigh. "I am sorry. It must be my mood this morning." He took a long drink from the mug in his hand and sat down again. "Now, about this girl you've brought me . . . is she pretty?"

"Well, *I* think so."

"Now I am truly worried. Anything else special about her?"

"Among other things, she is directly related to King Thalion, so she would earn the favor of those supporting the old royal line. She also has access to magical powers that could be of assistance in restoring the kingdom to stability."

"But is she pretty?"

"Look, why don't I let you decide for yourself. She's waiting just outside."

"What, now? Oh, very well. Two minutes, mind."

"Two minutes is all she'll need." Abderian smiled and set down his mug. He strolled to the door and stepped out, saying, "His Highness, Prince Cyprian, will see you now," as his veiled co-conspirator passed him on the threshold.

Feeling anxious and elated, the prince trotted down the tower stairs, reflecting on the elegance of two-stage love spells. The potion both he and Cyprian had imbibed with the tea was, indeed, harmless . . . by itself. Nothing would happen without the second part of the enchantment. *And Cyprian*, Abderian thought, *should be experiencing that—right about now.*

THIRTY-ONE

EVENING CAME AT a snail's pace. Abderian paced his tower room at a considerably faster rate. Hours to go, hoping that all the planning and furtive action had been enough—that it would all work. Of all the things he had done in the past few days, the waiting was the hardest task of all.

Occasionally Paralian would appear on the windowsill with reports of minor details. But otherwise, Abderian spent the afternoon alone.

From his window, which the glaziers had not yet repaired, he watched the courtyard being cleared of its female inhabitants and filled again with finely dressed nobles attending the ceremony. He dearly wished he could go to the Throne Room, where preparations were being made for the betrothal announcement. He knew, however, that he did not dare show his face anywhere near that room until the ceremony began. The last thing he needed was for Entheali or Captain Maduro to become suspicious of his skulking around. It was far safer to seem inoffensive and harmless, just sitting in his tower, waiting.

Finally he heard the blare of trumpets from the top of the guards' tower, and the heralds calling out, "Oye! Oye! The hour has come for Prince Cyprian to make his betrothal announcement. Come ye and welcome his bride and queen-to-be!"

This is it! Abderian ran the entire distance between his tower and the Throne Room, arriving quite out of breath. Even so, at the doorway to the huge chamber he gasped. Never in all his life had the prince seen such splendor. Any noble with any

224

sense of self-worth, and quite a few without, was there, dressed
in the finest of velvets, satins, silk brocade, and pressed linen.
Rings flashing rubies and emeralds seemed to adorn every
finger. Brooches, pectorals, and necklaces were everywhere,
as large and gaudy as possible. The air was heavy with the
aroma of pomades, perfume, and indelicate sweat—and a hint
of garlic from those who had eaten early. Even in his best blue
velvet tunic and finest silk hose, Abderian felt dowdy.

He squeezed through the throng of finery, looking for faces
he recognized. He saw no sign of Maja or Horaphthia. *Good.
Things may be going as planned.*

It took him a while to notice Dolus, who had strategically
located himself across the room, next to one of the windows
looking out on the courtyard. The wizard had altered his appearance, having cut his hair short and dressed in the style of
a lesser noble of the western provinces. He nodded at the prince
when their eyes met, showing he was ready.

Hearing familiar voices behind him, Abderian turned to see
Entheali and Onym enter the room arm-in-arm behind him.
They gave the prince only the barest of nods and smiles as
they passed.

"The restoration of the temple is going quite well, thank
you, Onym." Entheali was saying. "And with the favor of the
old and new queens, we should be able to give it the rich
furnishing it deserves."

"Excellent," said Onym. "I hope this ceremony does not
take long. Did I tell you I've already applied for the position
of court wizard?"

"Clever dear. You are the natural candidate for that position
after all. And with myself as spiritual advisor, there should be
no trouble—"

At this point the two stepped out of Abderian's range of
hearing. He wondered if he was glad he could not hear more.
If the plan fails and Onym does become court wizard . . . The
prince shuddered.

A flourish of trumpets heralded the arrival of Queen
Pleonexia. Immediately everyone in the room kneeled as she
entered, accompanied by Prince Cyprian. Both were resplend-
ent in garments of gold brocade with white silk linings. The
queen's crown was scarcely more than a small tiara, but it was
set with brilliant diamonds that sparkled like stars. Despite its

beauty, Abderian did not like the way the crown reminded him of those whom his mother served.

A path was cleared for the royal pair through the assemblage, and the queen and the prince threaded their way to the throne dais. Cyprian sat on the smaller throne that was the queen's when Valgus lived. Queen Pleonexia stood before the assemblage and motioned for them to rise. When all were once again standing, she spoke.

"My Lords, Ladies, and dear friends, it is with great pleasure that I inform you that tonight we are to be graced with the knowledge of the choice of bride-to-be of my eldest living son, Prince Cyprian."

As spontaneous cheers went up, Abderian wondered if Paralian was nearby, and had heard "eldest living son" applied to his younger brother. The queen continued to speak, but Abderian paid little attention. Instead, noting that Entheali and Onym stood near the dais, he moved into a good position from which to watch their faces. Should all go well, he did not want to miss seeing their expressions. Then again, should things go sour, he also wished to be conveniently close to an exit.

The queen finished speaking, and Cyprian stood as she sat on the larger throne. Facing the assembly, he raised his arms for silence. "Good subjects of Euthymia, it has been my task these past few days to make a momentous decision. I have had to select the woman to whom I would devote my love for the rest of my life. The choice I have had to make must be made for the sake of the kingdom as well as my own heart, for the woman I choose must rule beside me and earn my subjects' love as well as my own. She must help unite our people and give inspiration and wise counsel to all who see her. It should please you to know that I have found such a woman. And I have my dear brother, Abderian, to thank for the introduction that has led to my choice."

A few faces, among them Entheali's and Onym's, turned toward the younger prince and smiled. Abderian made a slight bow, then turned his attention back to his brother.

"This woman is of the blood of Thalion's line, and therefore shall unite the kingdom in peace. She has mystic powers at her command, that she may rule with wisdom. She has character and poise that shall inspire anyone who views her. I now present to you all she who has captured my heart."

Sweet, high-toned bells chimed in the distance, and the large double doors to the rear of the hall opened. Again the assembled nobles moved aside to form a path as the betrothal procession entered. First came a group of solemn-faced children, scattering mint leaves and flower petals in their wake. This filled the hall with a gentle perfume and provoked occasional sneezes from some in the audience. After the first group came six young girls dressed in blue silk, singing a traditional love song, "This Is the Hour I Am Yours." *At least,* thought Abderian, *it's not that song that's so popular among the fighting women.*

At last the palanquin of the betrothed entered the room. It was borne by four men from the castle guard, each dressed in his finest red livery. Four blond girls, identically dressed in green silk gowns and veils, supported a corner of a gauze canopy that billowed above the palanquin. The figure seated under the canopy was completely veiled in silver cloth.

Abderian strained on his tiptoes to see the seated figure— looking for some confirmation that this portion of his scheme was successful. He had no clue until the palanquin passed near him and one of the canopy bearers, a blond girl, winked at him. He relaxed with a smile. Everything was going to be all right.

The palanquin reached the dais and the veiled figure was helped out of her seat and up the two velvet-carpeted steps to stand beside Prince Cyprian.

"Behold my beloved!" said Cyprian as he flung the veils off the figure beside him. And there, looking stunning in a purple silk gown, stood the sorceress Horaphthia.

A murmur of wonder arose in the room. Entheali and Onym were aghast.

"What treachery is this!" cried the Star Mother. "Where is Maja?"

"I'm right here, Mother." said the blond girl with the canopy pole. With a deft flick of her hand she removed the blond wig and smiled.

"Why is that not you standing up there?" Entheali demanded. "Did you not speak to Cyprian yourself?"

"Oh, I saw him all right, but he must have liked Horaphthia better."

Entheali rounded on Abderian. "This is your doing!"

Cyprian and Queen Pleonexia looked at the priestess, perplexed.

"What is your trouble, woman?" asked Cyprian.

The queen stood and stepped closer to Entheali. "Is this not the one you had intended for Cyprian's bride?"

"It is not, Your Majesty!"

Onym stared at the sorceress and said, "Horaphthia, stop this nonsense and get down from there! Your Majesty, that woman is my daughter. She is old enough to be your son's great-grandmother!"

"Then I am certainly beyond an age when you have a say over my behavior, Father," Horaphthia said wryly.

"You must forbid this betrothal!" Entheali cried at the queen.

Pleonexia wrung her hands in confusion and looked anxiously at Cyprian. Dolus called out from the floor, "Who is this woman who speaks to our queen in this manner?"

"Aye," said a lady beside him, "this outburst is most unseemly."

"You dare not forbid me my choice, Mother," said Cyprian, "for I shall have none other than Horaphthia as my bride."

"You fool!" Entheali said to the prince. "You have been ensorcelled by that witch, and—"

"Hold your tongue, priestess!" Cyprian roared. "You and your minions are allowed here upon royal sufferance. Should you annoy me further, I shall see that your cult is disbanded and your temple razed when I am king!"

Entheali staggered back, shocked. Onym raised his hands in a sinister manner, saying, "How dare you speak to the Star Mother that way! She whose efforts have led to your ascending to the throne. I should cause your ungracious tongue to tie in knots for that!"

"Are you threatening me, mage?"

Quickly Entheali seemed to gather her wits and she pulled Onym aside, whispering fiercely in his ear. Turning back to Pleonexia, she stated in a calmer tone, "Your Majesty, the reason for my objection to this woman is that the candidate I had intended, my daughter Maja, is most obviously suitable for the throne. You see, it is she who now wears the Mark of Sagamore."

A collective gasp came from the crowd and all turned to face Maja.

She smiled and said, "No, I don't, Mother . . . look!" She bared both of her arms and waved them in the air for all to see.

Entheali strode over and roughly examined the girl's forearms. "What foolishness is this? How could you have lost it? Who has it now?" Entheali again turned angry eyes on Abderian.

"The item you are seeking," Horaphthia said loftily, "is precisely where it should be. On the arm of the one intended to rule Euthymia. Behold!" She pulled back Cyprian's left sleeve to reveal a familiar-looking cinnamon-colored patch of intricate lines.

Entheali's eyes grew wide, and her breathing became rapid and shallow. "I see. But is there proof that his mark is genuine?"

Uh-oh, thought Abderian. He had prepared for this contingency, but he had no idea if it would work. He signaled to Maja, who said, "There is a simple proof, Mother, as you know. The bearer of the cursemark has his heart tied to the fortunes of the kingdom. No doubt, with concentration, he can demonstrate that this is so."

"Yes," said Horaphthia, "think, dear Cyprian, of your love for the kingdom and its people."

Cyprian smiled and closed his eyes. Abderian did likewise and began to move his hands subtly in the patterns Dolus had taught him.

Dolus, meanwhile, stared out the window and exclaimed, "By Valgus's crown, look at that!"

"I don't see anything," another voice said. Abderian concentrated harder. From the sudden explosion of exclamations that followed, he then knew he had succeeded.

"I've never seen the like! The courtyard is alive with wildflowers!"

"They're beautiful! This Mark of Sagamore is indeed powerful!"

When Abderian opened his eyes again, even Entheali seemed uncertain.

"You must admit, Star Mother," said Pleonexia, "that the presence of the cursemark changes things."

"Yes," said Cyprian, "if you take from me my beloved Horaphthia, not only shall I suffer, but the entire kingdom shall suffer as well."

"Well, if she's the one you truly want—"

"But she's bewitched him!" Entheali protested.

"I know not who this strange priestess is," said Dolus, disguising his voice, "but I for one heartily approve of Prince Cyprian and his intended bride. Long live the king-to-be, and his bride!"

Other lords and ladies in the hall took up the cheer, until the throne room resounded with their clamor. Entheali's further comments were drowned in the sea of sound.

Queen Pleonexia gave the Star Mother an apologetic look. "It is the will of the people," she mouthed, and turned to look approvingly on the royal couple. Cyprian and Horaphthia bowed to the assembly, acknowledging their praise and support.

Abderian, unable to contain himself any longer, ran from the throne room, nearly jumping with joy. *It worked! It actually worked!* Not only had Horaphthia been accepted as queen, he thought gleefully, but they all believed the tattoo on Cyprian's arm was the cursemark.

Rounding a corner, Abderian found himself in a deserted portion of the castle grounds, and he leaned back against a wall, gasping. Checking to make sure no one was watching, he pulled back his right sleeve and regarded the mark—the genuine Mark of Sagamore—and laughed, and laughed, and laughed.

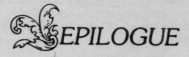# EPILOGUE

THE WEDDING WAS beautiful, as all royal weddings are when there is enough gold in the royal coffers. And the coronation afterward was spectacular. The festivities lasted long into the night, with much joyful revelry of a sort that Euthymia had not seen in many years. Even the mannikins on the ceiling of the dining hall were dressed, it was said, finer than they had ever been. And what few demons chose to make an appearance conducted themselves with a minimum of mischief, and even joined the mortals in their merrymaking.

"I'm still surprised," Maja said late the following afternoon in Abderian's tower.

"Hmm?" said Abderian, bent over one of Dolus's huge books of magic.

"That it worked. That Cyprian didn't wake up while Paralian tattooed the copy of your mark on your brother's arm. That it was so easy to transfer the real mark back to you—what did Dolus say? . . . It had an affinity for you or something. I guess my family was never meant to bear it anyway. But you know, now that you got it back, in a way you have proven that you are the rightful king after all."

"What?" Abderian looked up from the book at her. "What do you mean?"

"Well, not only have you regained the Mark of Sagamore—which some people think is a sign of the 'true king'—but you've earned it by your own family's rules too."

"What are you talking about?"

"Didn't you tell me that it used to be that the person who played the best jest in the family was the one given the throne? I'd say you certainly pulled off the best jest of all."

Abderian grinned and blushed a little. "That's dangerous talk, Maja. I don't want anyone else to know what we did—and I still have no wish to be king. Gods know I have enough to do now. Such as figuring out how to give Dolus his power back, then working on restoring Paralian to his original shape."

"I suppose you're right. Still, it's a pity you can't at least tell Cyprian. What good is a jest unless the victim knows he's been made a fool of?"

"Don't you think I'd like to? But I've no reason to think Cyprian will keep his mouth shut. If he were to tell anyone else, especially your mother, I'd have the same problems all over again. I'd much rather have Entheali's and Onym's attention on Cyprian than on me. I'll just have to appreciate my jest privately. Now, where was I?" He stuck his nose back into the book of magic.

Maja sighed and walked to a window, singing softly to herself:

> Abderian's sword is more than it might seem,
> He's used it to conquer the new Demon Queen—

"Maja—"

"Don't worry, Abderian. I can't finish the verse anyway."

"Oh? Why not?"

"Because," she replied, looking at the prince coyly, "I don't have enough firsthand experience to base it on."

"Oh. Would you like some, uh, experience? I'm willing to provide it if you want."

She did, so he did, and that's all you need to know.